Her Restless Heart

HER RESTLESS HEART

Stitches in Time Series

Barbara Cameron

Abingdon Press fiction
a novel approach to faith

Nashville, Tennessee

Her Restless Heart

Copyright © 2012 Barbara Cameron

ISBN 978-1-4267-1427-6

Published by Abingdon Press, P.O. Box 801, Nashville, TN 37202

www.abingdonpress.com

Library of Congress Cataloging-in-Publication Data

Cameron, Barbara, 1949-
Her restless heart / Barbara Cameron.
  p. cm.
  ISBN 978-1-4267-1427-6 (trade pbk. : alk. paper) 1. Amish—Fiction. I.
Title.
  PS3603.A4473R47 2012
  813'.6--dc23

                                                                    2011033310

Scripture quotations are taken from the King James or
Authorized Version of the Bible.

Printed in the United States of America

1 2 3 4 5 6 7 8 9 10 / 17 16 15 14 13 12

for Judy Rehm

Acknowledgments

I grew up with a mother who drilled manners into me. I don't think she thought you could say "thank you" enough. So I don't, either.

Thank you to Ramona Richards, my editor, for her enthusiasm, suggestions, and most of all, her patience. I couldn't get through this process without you, Ramona. I hope we'll work together for a very long time to come.

Writers need a lot of solitude to do what they do. . . . I so appreciate that friends and family give me that when I need it and always understand. You are important to me and I miss you when I have to stay at the computer to write.

I can always count on Judy Rehm, friend and Bible scholar, for her support and for helping me express a biblical truth better.

And thank you, Tera Moore, for helping me proof the manuscript. Your help was invaluable.

I have met so many wonderful friends through my writing Christian fiction. Nearly every day I get an email or Facebook message from someone who thanks me for writing one of my books. I'm always thrilled and humbled. In these days of tight money, I thank YOU for buying the book or getting it from your library and spending your precious time to read it.

I'm always awed when I look back on my life and see God's hand on it, which led me to this time in my life. . . .

I don't think I've ever been as happy as I am now except for that time when HE handed me two little creations we call children.

So thank You, God, and—since You can't be thanked enough—thank You, again!

1

A year ago, Mary Katherine wouldn't have imagined she'd be here. Back then, she'd been helping her parents on the family farm and hating every minute of it.

Now, she stood at the front window of Stitches in Time, her grandmother's shop, watching the *Englischers* moving about on the sidewalks outside the shop in Paradise. Even on vacation, they rushed about with purpose. She imagined them checking off the places they'd visited: Drive by an Amish farmhouse. Check. Buy a quilt and maybe some knitting supplies to try making a sweater when I get back home. Check.

She liked the last item. The shop had been busy all morning, but now, as people started getting hungry, they were patronizing the restaurants that advertised authentic Amish food and ticking off another item on their vacation checklist. Shoofly pie. Amish pretzels. Chow-chow. Check.

"Don't you worry, they'll be back," Leah, her grandmother, called out.

Smiling, Mary Katherine turned. "I know."

She wandered back to the center of the shop, set up like the comfortable parlor of an Amish farmhouse. Chairs were arranged in a circle around a quilting frame. Bolts of fabric of every color and print imaginable were stacked on shelves on several walls, spools of matching threads on another.

And yarn. There were skeins and skeins of the stuff. Mary Katherine loved running her hands over the fluffy fibers, feeling the textures of cotton and wool and silk. Some of the new yarns made from things like soybeans and corn just didn't feel the same when you knitted them or wove them into patterns—but some people made a fuss over them because they were made of something natural, plant-based, or more sustainable.

Mary Katherine thought it was a little strange to be using vegetables you ate to make clothes but once she got her hands on the yarns, she was impressed. Tourists were, too. They used terms like "green" and "ecological" and didn't mind spending a lot of money to buy them. And was it so much different to use vegetables when people had been taking oily, smelly wool from sheep and turning it into garments for people—silk from silkworms—that sort of thing?

"You have that look on your face again," her grandmother said.

"What look?"

"That serious, thoughtful look of yours. Tell me what you're thinking of."

"Working on my loom this afternoon."

"I figured you had itchy fingers." Her grandmother smiled.

She sighed. "I'm so glad you rescued me from working at the farm. And *Dat* not understanding about my weaving."

Leah nodded. "Some people need time to adjust."

Taking one of the chairs that was arranged in a circle around the quilt her grandmother and Naomi worked on, Mary Katherine propped her chin in her hand, her elbow on the arm of the chair. "It'd be a lot easier if I knitted or quilted."

Leah looked at her, obviously suppressing a smile. "You have never liked 'easy,' Mary Katherine."

Laughing, she nodded. "You're right."

Looking at Naomi and Anna, her cousins aged twenty and twenty-three, was like looking into a mirror, thought Mary Katherine. The three of them could have been sisters, not cousins. They had a similar appearance—oval faces, their hair center-parted and tucked back under snowy white *kapps*, and slim figures. Naomi and Anna had even chosen dresses of a similar color, one that reminded Mary Katherine of morning glories. In her rush out the door, Mary Katherine had grabbed the first available dress and now felt drab and dowdy in the brown dress she'd chosen.

Yes, they looked much alike, the three of them.

Until Mary Katherine stood. She'd continued growing after it seemed that everyone else had stopped. Now, at 5'8", she felt like a skinny beanpole next to her cousins. She felt awkward next to the young men she'd gone to school with. Although she knew it was wrong, there had been times when she'd secretly wished that God had made her petite and pretty like her cousins. And why had he chosen to give her red hair and freckles? Didn't she have enough she didn't like about her looks without that?

Like their looks, their personalities seemed similar on the surface. The three of them appeared calm and serene— especially Naomi. Anna tried to be, but it didn't last long. She was too mischievous.

And herself? Serenity seemed hard these days. In the past several years, Mary Katherine had been a little moody but lately it seemed her moods were going up and down like a road through rolling hills.

"Feeling restless?" Naomi asked, looking at her with concern. Nimbly, she tied a knot, snipped the thread with a scissors, then slid her needle into a pincushion.

Anna looked up from her knitting needles. "Mary Katherine was born restless."

"I think I'll take a short walk."

"No," Leah said quickly, holding up a hand. "Let's eat first, then you can take a walk. Otherwise you'll come back and customers will be here for the afternoon rush and you'll start helping and go hungry."

Mary Katherine was already mentally out the door, but she nodded her agreement. "You're right, of course."

Leah was a tall, spare woman who didn't appear old enough to be anyone's grandmother. Her face was smooth and unlined, and there wasn't a trace of gray in her hair, which she wore like her granddaughters.

"I made your favorite," Leah told Mary Katherine.

"Fried chicken? You made fried chicken? When did you have time to do that?"

Nodding, Leah tucked away her sewing supplies, and stood. "Before we came to work this morning. It didn't take long." She turned to Naomi. "And I made your favorite."

Naomi had been picking up stray strands of yarn from the wood floor. She looked up, her eyes bright. "Macaroni and cheese?"

"Oatmeal and raisin cookies?" Anna wanted to know. When her grandmother nodded, Anna set down her knitting needles and stood. "Just how early did you get up? Are you having trouble sleeping?"

"No earlier than usual," Leah replied cheerfully. "I made the macaroni and cheese and the cookies last night. But I don't need as much sleep as some other people I know."

"Can you blame me for sleeping in a little later?" Mary Katherine asked. "After all of those years of helping with farm chores? Besides, I was working on a design last night."

"Tell us all about it while we eat," Naomi said, glancing at the clock. "We won't have long before customers start coming in again."

"I worry about Grandmother," Anna whispered to Mary Katherine as they walked to the back room. "She does too much."

"She's always been like this."

"Yes, but she's getting older."

"Shh, don't be saying that around her!"

Leah turned. "Did somebody say something?"

"Anna said she's hungry," Mary Katherine said quickly. "And wondering how you picked a favorite when everything you make is her favorite."

Anna poked Mary Katherine in the ribs but everyone laughed because it was true. What was amazing was that no matter how much Anna ate, she never gained weight.

Nodding, Leah continued toward the back room. "We'll have it on the table in no time."

Anna grabbed Mary Katherine's arm, stopping her. "Shame on you," she hissed. "You know it's wrong to lie." Then she shook her head. "What am I saying? You've done so much worse!"

"Me? I have not! I can't imagine what you're talking about."

Turning so that her grandmother wouldn't see, Anna lifted her fingers to her lips and mimed smoking a cigarette.

Mary Katherine blushed. "You've been spying on me."

"Food's ready!" Leah called.

"Don't you dare tell her!" Mary Katherine whispered.

Anna's eyes danced. "What will you give me if I don't?"

She stared at her cousin. "I don't have anything—"

"Your afternoon off," Anna said suddenly. "That's what I'll take in trade."

Before she could respond, Anna hurried into the back room. Exasperated, Mary Katherine could do nothing but follow her.

The minute they finished eating, Mary Katherine jumped up and hurried over to wash her dishes. "I'll be right back," she promised, tying her bonnet on the run as she left the store.

Winter's chill was in the air. She shivered a little but didn't want to go back for her shawl. She shrugged. Once she got moving, she'd be warm enough.

She felt the curious stares as if she were being touched.

But that was okay. Mary Katherine was doing a lot of staring of her own. She had a great deal of curiosity about the *Englisch* and didn't mind admitting it.

She just hoped that her grandmother didn't know how much she'd thought about becoming one of them, of not being baptized into the Amish church.

As one of the tourists walked past, a pretty woman about her own age, Mary Katherine wondered what it felt like being covered in so little clothing. She suspected she'd feel half-naked in that dress she'd heard called a sundress. Although some of the tourists looked surprised when she and her cousins wore bright colors, the fact was that the *Ordnung* certainly didn't mandate black dresses.

Color had always been part of Mary Katherine's world. She'd loved all the shades of blue because they reminded her of the big blue bowl of the sky. Her father had complained that she didn't get her chores done in a timely manner because she was always walking around . . . noticing. She noticed everything around her, absorbed the colors and textures, and spent hours using them in her designs that didn't look like the quilts and crafts other Amish women created.

She paused at the display window of Stitches in Time. A wedding ring quilt that Naomi had sewn was draped over a quilt rack. Anna had knitted several darling little cupcake hats for babies to protect their heads and ears from the cold. And there was her own woven throw made of many different fibers and textures and colors of burnt orange, gold, brown, and green. All echoed the theme of the colder seasons, of the weddings that would come after summer harvests.

And all were silent testament to Leah's belief in the creativity of her granddaughters, thought Mary Katherine with a smile. The shop featured the traditional crafts tourists might expect but also the new directions the cousins came up with.

It was the best of both worlds Mary Katherine said to herself as she ventured out into the throng of tourists lining the sidewalks.

๛

Jacob saw Mary Katherine exit her grandmother's shop. His timing was perfect because he'd heard from a secret source what time they took a break to eat at the shop during the day.

He watched her stop to gaze at the display window and she smiled—the smile that had attracted him to her. Oh, she was pretty with those big blue eyes and soft skin with a blush of rose over her cheekbones. But her smile.

She hadn't always smiled like that. He started noticing it just a few months ago, after the shop had opened. It was as if she'd come to life. He'd passed by the shop one day a couple of weeks ago and stopped to glance inside, and he'd seen her working at her loom, a look of absorption on her face, a quiet smile on her lips.

Something had moved in his chest then, a feeling he hadn't had before. He'd resolved to figure this out.

He hadn't been in a rush to marry. It had been enough to take over the family farm, to make sure he didn't undo all the hard work that his *daed* had done to make it thrive. He didn't feel pride that he'd continued its success. After all, Plain people felt *hochmut* was wrong. In school, they had often practiced writing the proverb, "*Der Hochmut kummt vor dem Fall.*" Pride goeth before the fall.

But the farm, its continuity, its legacy for the family he wanted one day . . . that was important to him. To have that family, he knew he'd have to find a *fraa.* It was important to find the right one. After all, Plain people married for life. So he'd looked around but he had taken his time. He likened the process to a crop—you prepared the ground, planted the right seed, nurtured it, asked God's blessing, and then harvested at the right moment.

Such things took time.

Sometimes they even took perseverance. She had turned him down when he'd approached her and asked her out.

He decided not to let that discourage him.

She turned from the window and began walking down the sidewalk toward him. Look at her, he thought, walking with that bounce to her step. Look at the way she glanced around, taking in everything with such animation, such curiosity.

He waited for some sign of recognition, but she hadn't seen him yet. When they'd attended school, their teacher had often gently chided her for staring out the classroom window or doodling designs on a scrap of paper for the weaving she loved.

Mary Katherine moved through the sea of *Englisch* tourists on the sidewalk that parted for her when she walked as the waters had for Moses. He watched how they glanced at her the way she did them.

It was a mutual curiosity at its best.

He walked toward her, and when she stopped and blinked, he grinned.

"Jacob! What are you doing here?"

"You make it sound like I never come to town."

"I don't remember ever seeing you do it."

"I needed some supplies, and things are slower now with the harvest in. Have you eaten?" He'd found out from Anna when they took their noontime break, but he figured it was a good conversational device.

"Yes. We ate a little early at the shop."

He thought about that. Maybe he should have planned better. "I see. Well, how about having supper with me tonight?"

"Did you come all the way into town to ask me out?"

Jacob drew himself up. "Yes."

"But I've told you before—"

"That you're not interested in going out."

"Yes."

"But I haven't heard of you going out with anyone else."

She stared at him, oblivious of the people who streamed around them on the sidewalk. "Who did you ask?"

Her direct stare was unnerving. His collar felt tight, but he knew if he pulled it away from his neck he'd just appear guilty. "I'd have heard."

"I'm not interested in dating, Jacob."

When she started past him, he put out his hand to stop her. She looked down at his hand on her arm and then met his gaze. "Is it you're not interested in dating or you're not interested in dating me?"

Her lips quirked. "I'm not interested in dating. It's not you."

"I see."

She began walking again.

"Do you mind if I walk with you?"

"*Schur.*" She glanced at him. "Can you keep up?"

He found himself grinning. She was different from other young women he knew, more spirited and independent.

"Where are we going?"

She shrugged. "Nowhere in particular. I just needed to get out and get some fresh air."

Stopping at a shop window, she studied its display of tourist souvenirs. "Did you ever think about not staying here? In Paradise?"

"Not stay here? Where would you go?"

She turned to look at him and shrugged. "I don't know. It's a big world out there."

Jacob felt a chill race up his spine. "You can't mean it," he said slowly. "You belong here."

"Do I?" she asked. Pensive, she stared at the people passing. "Sometimes I'm not sure where I belong."

He took her shoulders and turned her to face the shop window. "This is where you belong," he told her.

She looked at the image of herself reflected in the glass as he directed. He liked the way they looked together in the reflection. She was a fine Amish woman, with a quiet beauty he'd admired for some time. He'd known her in school and, of course, they'd attended Sunday services and singings and such through the years. He hadn't been in a rush to get married, and he'd noticed she hadn't been, either. Both of them had been working hard, he at his farm, she in the shop she and her grandmother and cousins owned.

He began noticing her shortly after the shop opened for business. There was a different air about her. She seemed more confident, happier than she'd been before.

He reminded himself that she'd said she didn't date.

So why, he asked himself, was he trying again? Taking a deep breath, he turned to her. "Mary Katherine—"

"Jacob!" a man called.

He turned and saw a man striding toward him, a newcomer to the Plain community.

Though the man hailed him, his attention was clearly on Mary Katherine. He held out his hand. "Daniel Kurtz," he said. "Remember me?"

Out of the corner of his eye, Jacob saw Mary Katherine turn to the man and eye him with interest.

"You live in Florida now."

"I do." He studied the shop. "So, this is yours?"

"My grandmother's. My cousins and I help her."

Daniel nodded. "Very enterprising." He glanced around. "Is this the size of crowd you get this time of year?"

Mary Katherine nodded. "After-Christmas sales bring them out. But business slows down while people eat lunch."

"I came into town to pick up a few things and I'm hungry. Have you two eaten?"

"I asked Mary Katherine but—"

"We'll join you," she said quickly.

Jacob stared at her. But the two of them were already walking away. With an unexplained feeling of dread washing over him, he followed them.

2

*I*t wasn't often that Mary Katherine had not one but two handsome men sitting at a table talking to her.

Actually, it had never happened before, unless you counted the times she and Jacob and his brother Amos had sat at a table and done their studies when they'd been scholars. It hadn't been pleasant. Amos had pulled her braids and dabbed paste on her papers.

These two men were as different as night and day. Jacob's hair shone the blue-black of a raven's wing when he took off his hat. He had a square jaw and intense brown eyes that seemed to bore into you when he looked at you. And his hands. Well, they were big and strong, with blunt fingers, but he'd picked a delicate flower once when they were on a picnic with other youth and surprised her with it.

Daniel was as fair-haired as Jacob was dark, the strands of his hair streaked a lighter blond from the Florida sunlight. Both men were tanned from working in the fields but Daniel's was darker from more exposure. His features were finer, his hands smaller, and there was a glint in his blue eyes that spoke of charm and mischief, contrasting with Jacob's more serious manner.

Their clothing was similar, the Plain attire of black felt winter hats, black pants and jackets, and colored shirts. Both were tall and strong and muscular.

They had grown from schoolboys to fine, strapping Amish men. Both caught the eye of Plain folk and *Englischers* alike as they walked to the restaurant, and now as they sat at the table.

A waitress brought menus, took drink orders, and left.

"Florida," Mary Katherine mused as she glanced out the window. "Palm trees, warm sea breezes . . ." She watched as people hurried by dressed in jackets, coats, and hats. "Sounds wonderful."

Daniel grinned. "Well, we *work* in Florida, you know. My parents took a vacation there one winter and never wanted to come back to the weather here. So I stayed, too."

He looked at Mary Katherine over the top of the menu. "You've certainly changed from the gawky girl I remembered."

She felt a blush creeping over her face. "I—thank you."

"What brings you back to Paradise?" Jacob asked.

Her eyes flew to his. He didn't sound very friendly. Matter of fact, he didn't look it, either, his dark eyebrows drawn in a frown, his jaw set. Strange, she thought. Jacob was usually one of the friendliest people she knew.

"I'm here to finalize the sale of the family farm." Daniel opened his menu and scanned the choices.

"So you're breaking all ties here then?"

"I wouldn't say that," Daniel told him, closing his menu. "We still have family here. But we don't need the property and it's a good time to sell since there's less land available now in Lancaster County."

The waitress came to take food orders.

"Just the tea for me, thanks," Mary Katherine told her.

"You're not doing one of the *Englisch* diets, are you?" Daniel asked her. "You look great."

Blushing, she shook her head. "We ate at the shop. Grandmother brought fried chicken in today."

"I remember her fried chicken." He looked at the waitress as she walked toward the kitchen to hand in their order. "Should I have ordered the fried chicken here?"

"The pot roast is better," Mary Katherine and Jacob said at the same time. They looked at each other and grinned.

She caught Daniel looking questioningly at Jacob, then at her. "Tell us about where you live now," she said quickly.

"We vacationed in a town called Pinecraft, near Sarasota, for a couple of years. That's on the west coast of Florida," he explained. "You'd see some familiar names on the mailboxes if you went there, names like Stoltzfus, Yoder, Beiler. There are Mennonites there as well as Plain people. My family and I are members of the Beachy Amish Mennonite church there."

"Oh, that looks good," he exclaimed when their food arrived. "Not very many *Englischers* know we're there so we haven't become a tourist attraction like other Plain communities."

The men dug into the pot roast special. "You're right, it is good," he told Jacob.

The restaurant was filled with locals and tourists enjoying the "authentic Amish" food. Anything labeled "Amish" was popular with the tourists.

Daniel asked about mutual friends. Mary Katherine filled in the blanks for him, telling him who'd gotten married, who had children, who was engaged, who'd moved away to other Amish communities. He wanted to know about her grandmother, Leah, and cousins Naomi and Anna, too, and he seemed very interested in the shop.

"You were always sketching designs in school," he said as he buttered a roll. "Jacob, you remember how often our teacher chided Mary Katherine for doing that instead of schoolwork?" He chuckled. "But look how it paid off. Is the shop doing well?"

She nodded. "We had a very prosperous holiday season."

"But that's not what it's all about, is it?" he asked quietly.

Startled, her eyes met his. "No," she said at last. "I love what I do."

There was a slight sound to her left. Turning, she saw Jacob staring at her .

"Is something wrong?"

"No," he said quickly. "Could you—would you pass me the salt, please?"

"Sure." She handed him the shaker and watched him sprinkle it over his pot roast. "Just like my *dat.* He salts everything before he eats, too. *Mamm* keeps threatening to over-salt his food one day so he'll stop."

She frowned. *Dat* was so critical. There wasn't a family that loved their father more or worked harder for his approval. Yet he seldom thanked them or seemed to appreciate them.

"How is he?"

She looked up and smiled at Daniel. "Same *Dat* you remember. He hasn't changed."

"I had an *onkel* like that. He pointed at a chair one day and said he was just like that—he couldn't change. I decided right then and there I couldn't be like him." He fell silent as he ate his food.

Perhaps that was why he'd made the move to Florida with his parents. She started to ask him that, but something made her glance over at Jacob. He was staring at his plate and hadn't eaten much.

"Is something the matter with your food?"

He blinked. "What? Oh, no. I just was thinking about something."

"I don't remember you as being this quiet," Daniel teased him.

"I remember you as being this talkative," Jacob shot back.

"Boys, boys!" Mary Katherine said, laughing. "And I remember the two of you being good friends when we were scholars."

Daniel's grin faded. "Yes, I do as well. I'm sorry, Jacob. I should have kept in contact."

Jacob shrugged. "I understood. I figured you were busy or that maybe you decided that since you weren't coming back there was no point in staying friends."

"We *were* busy. Still am. But that's no excuse for not staying in contact with good friends."

"Well, we're here now," Mary Katherine said.

Daniel nodded. "I was on my way to take a look at Mary Katherine's shop. I thought I'd pick up a present to take back to my *mamm*."

He looked at Jacob. "Guess now that the harvest is finished you have a little more time?"

"*Ya*. While I was in town picking up supplies, I thought I'd see if Mary Katherine wanted to have lunch."

"Are the two of you dating?"

Mary Katherine choked on her tea. She looked at Jacob, but it was Daniel who rushed to pat her on the back.

"Why do you ask that?" she asked him when she got her breath back.

"He was coming to take you to lunch."

"He was coming to ask," she corrected. "That's different."

"I see," Daniel said slowly. He looked at Jacob. "So, are the two of you dating?"

Jacob watched Mary Katherine's gaze drop to the cup before her.

"We're friends," Jacob told him. "Just friends."

"*Ya?* I thought the two of you might be seeing each other."

He watched Daniel go back to eating and studied him for a long moment. As a rule, he tried to accept people at face value and not be looking for ulterior motives. But he couldn't help wondering if Daniel was interested in Mary Katherine.

If only Mary Katherine had agreed to have lunch with him. Then they wouldn't have run into Daniel. He wouldn't have had to sit here and watch another man look interested in her. He wouldn't have felt unaccustomed feelings of jealousy washing over him.

There was no way he could compete with Daniel. The man had known how to charm girls since he attended school, and he'd gotten even better at it since then. Mary Katherine had been smiling at him more than he ever remembered seeing her do since he'd known her. And every time the subject of Florida came up . . . well, it was obvious that it sounded romantic to her because she looked so dreamy when Daniel mentioned it.

What did he have to compete with that? A farm in Pennsylvania. That was hardly romantic to her. After all, she'd grown up here, worked on her family's farm, and always acted like she hated it. Florida with its mystery and warm weather was obviously appealing.

As was Daniel. Both of them were tanned from working in the fields, but his hair had been streaked by the sun, too. Women liked blond men, didn't they?

No, Mary Katherine wasn't so shallow that looks were that important to her.

And she was happy here. He knew that. Her work at the shop was obviously the fulfillment of everything she'd ever wanted. That dreamy girl who sketched in school instead of doing her lessons now worked at her loom all day at the shop and sold her work. She and her cousins were like sisters, and there were no closer sisters than Amish *schweschders*.

She attended Sunday services but hadn't yet been baptized into the church. However, that wasn't unusual. Sometimes people waited to be sure. Once they'd joined, if they changed their minds it meant they couldn't stay, that they'd be shunned. So such serious decisions merited serious consideration. Marriage, too. Once entered into, a marriage was for life, so most didn't rush to marry in their teens.

Mary Katherine wasn't even dating.

Maybe there was no need to worry that Daniel or some other man would be stepping in ahead of him to try to date her. And why had he even worried about Daniel? He'd be leaving soon, after he took care of selling the family farm.

Relieved, Jacob resumed eating and even found himself nodding when the waitress returned to ask if anyone wanted dessert. He ordered a slice of pumpkin pie and sat back with a second cup of coffee to listen while Mary Katherine talked animatedly about her weaving.

"How is your mother?" Daniel asked.

Jacob realized that he was talking to him. "They're fine." As the only son, he'd taken over caring for the farm after his *daed* died. His mother had moved out of the house later when she remarried.

"What about your parents? I guess they like it in Florida if they're selling the property?"

"They love it. *Mamm* was so tired of the snow here."

He set down his fork and wiped his mouth with his napkin. "If you'll excuse me, I should check the weather back home."

From his pocket he drew out a cell phone, one Mary Katherine recognized as the latest fancy kind she often saw the

Englisch tourists carrying. Flipping it open, he tapped his forefinger on the screen and a dizzying series of images flashed past. Pausing on one, he studied the screen.

"You use AgWired.com?" Jacob asked, leaning forward for a closer look. He pulled out his own cell phone and copied Daniel's steps. "I do, too."

"You men with the cell phones," Mary Katherine said. "You don't see us women using them."

"That's because we're the ones in business," Daniel murmured and then his head jerked up when he apparently realized what he'd said. "I mean, we're just usually the ones who have to conduct business and—"

Mary Katherine just raised her eyebrows. Jacob chuckled as he watched Daniel redden.

"It's all right," she told him. "I'm sure you've noticed that even with us Plain folk there have been some changes. Women have taken care of the business of the home for years so it's only natural that they are sometimes in business outside the home."

She leaned closer to see what the two men were so interested in on the cell phone. "What's that?"

"Weather website."

"It's for farmers?" Mary Katherine asked slowly.

Daniel looked up. "*Ya.*"

"But you're selling your farm here."

"I farm in Florida."

"I thought people just raised oranges there."

Daniel laughed. "Some people do. We grow celery, among other things." He tapped the screen again, and a photo of a farmhouse popped up. "That's the house. And here's one of the fields."

Jacob watched Mary Katherine. She'd seemed interested when Daniel talked about Florida earlier but now, as she gazed at the phone, a stillness came over her face.

"Very nice." She stood. "I have to go. I've been away from the shop longer than I should have been."

She pulled some money from her pocket and put it on the table. "I'll see you both later."

Jacob got to his feet, but she was already hurrying toward the door. When Daniel looked at him, his eyebrows raised in a question, Jacob shook his head and shrugged.

❧

The little bell over the door tinkled as Mary Katherine entered the shop. She hurried to hang up her bonnet and coat. "I'm sorry I was gone so long."

"You weren't," her grandmother assured her. "And it's been slow."

"Did you have a good time with Jacob?" Anna asked, her eyes sparkling with mischief.

Mary Katherine stopped. "How do you know I bumped into Jacob?" She narrowed her eyes. "Or wasn't it an accident that I bumped into him?"

Shrugging, Anna pushed a needle through the quilt she was working on.

"Anna?"

She looked up, the picture of innocence. "Yes, *Grossmudder*?"

"Are you matchmaking?"

Anna blinked. "No, *Grossmudder*."

Mary Katherine moved to stand near Anna. She put her hands on her hips and gave her a stern look. "So our running into each other was a coincidence?"

"No." She knotted the thread and resumed sewing. "He asked what time we ate dinner each day, and I told him we ate at the shop but you liked to take a walk about noon each day."

"I see."

Anna's lips twitched, and then she started giggling. "I'm sorry. But I saw the two of you talking last Sunday and you seemed interested in him."

"Mary Katherine's interested in someone?" Naomi asked as she walked out of the supply room. "Here, can you help me with these bolts of fabric?"

Taking several of the bolts that were threatening to slip from Naomi's grasp, Mary Katherine carried them to the cutting table. Naomi began unfolding a bolt and pulled a pair of scissors from a drawer.

"I'm not interested in Jacob," Mary Katherine told Naomi. "I was polite. Nothing more."

"You were gone a long time." Anna glanced up and batted her eyelashes. "That must have been some walk."

Mary Katherine walked over to the window and looked out. "We ran into Daniel—" she stopped and looked at Anna.

"I haven't talked to Daniel," Anna said quickly.

Nodding, Mary Katherine glanced out the window again. "Daniel and Jacob hadn't eaten, so I sat with them and had some tea."

Frowning, she walked over to her loom, sat down, and placed her feet on the treadle. Picking up the shuttle, she ran her fingers over the smooth wood. She touched the fibers that were the color of the ocean and began weaving the shuttle in and out, back and forth, and felt peace settling over her as she sat in her favorite place in the world.

"You were with *two* handsome men?"

"Anna, enough teasing!" Leah said sternly.

"Yes, *Grossmudder*."

Mary Katherine felt a hand on her shoulder and looked up.

"Are you *allrecht, liebschen*?" her grandmother asked, her blue eyes filled with concern.

"I'm fine." She looked over her design for a moment.

"Did Jacob say something to upset you?"

She shook her head.

"Daniel?"

She shook her head again.

"Then—?"

"I'm sure they'll be very happy together," Mary Katherine muttered.

Naomi's scissors clattered to the table. "Are you saying that Jacob and Daniel uh—um, don't like women?" she stammered, and her face went as scarlet as a *rotrieb*.

Mary Katherine laughed, and then she sighed. "*Nee*. I doubt they think about women much. *Farming* holds too much of their hearts."

The bell over the door jingled merrily as someone opened it. Mary Katherine glanced over and was surprised to see Daniel and Jacob entering the shop.

Anna greeted Daniel with a smile and after speaking with him a moment, led him to a display of yarns. Mary Katherine remembered that he'd said he wanted to get a gift for his mother.

Jacob stood by the front counter and looked over at Mary Katherine with that intense look of his.

"He seems very interested in you," Leah murmured.

"It doesn't matter," Mary Katherine said, pulling her gaze from him and returning to her weaving. "I told you. He's in love with farming."

Leah stared at her, perplexed. "There's something wrong with farming? Your father is a farmer."

Then she paused. "Oh, I see the problem," she said slowly.

"Do you?" asked Mary Katherine. She stopped and stared at the multi-colored pattern on the loom before her, wishing she could find one for her own life. Lifting her gaze, she looked into her grandmother's eyes. "Do you?"

3

*T*he shop door swung open and shut so quickly the bell over it gave a funny clanging noise as a man stepped inside the shop.

Mary Katherine glanced up from her seat at her loom and her heart sank.

"Your *grossmudder* in the back?" he asked in a brusque tone.

She nodded and watched him walk toward the back of the store, then open the door and shut it firmly behind him. It took a couple of minutes before she could return to her work. Even then her hands shook, and she fumbled with the pattern and had to redo half an inch.

The store was so quiet she could hear the tick-tock of the clock. Or was it the beat of her heart?

The bell rang merrily again, and when Mary Katherine looked over, she saw Naomi and Anna stroll in, arm in arm, their faces lit with laughter.

They stopped when they saw Mary Katherine and rushed over.

"What is it? What's the matter?" Naomi asked, taking Mary Katherine's hand in hers.

"Did we get robbed?"

Naomi elbowed Anna. "Oh stop! You're such a drama queen!"

With her free hand, she pulled up a chair and sat beside Mary Katherine. "If we'd been robbed she wouldn't be sitting here at her loom. She'd be chasing the crook down the sidewalk."

"I wish I were as brave as you think I am," Mary Katherine said through stiff lips.

"Your hand is cold as ice. What's upsetting you?" Anna wanted to know as she drew a chair up on the other side of her cousin.

Before Mary Katherine could speak, the door leading to the rear of the store opened and the man strode out, giving them a stern glance as he walked to the door, and then, just as he was about to exit, he turned and looked back at Mary Katherine. He opened his mouth and then hesitated.

Scowling, he wrenched open the door, letting in a blast of cold air, then left, shutting the door behind him with a bang. The bell jangled from the wind and the movement.

Mary Katherine shivered and gathered her shawl closer around her shoulders.

"Well, and hello to you, too," Anna muttered.

"Don't be rude," Naomi told her.

"Me? He's the one who's rude. He didn't even stop to say a word to us!" Anna exclaimed, indignant. "Why does he have to act so unfriendly?"

Mary Katherine frowned. "How should I know? I think he's always been grumpy." She rubbed her cold hands and turned her attention to her loom.

"Didn't he come to talk to you?"

Swallowing at the lump in her throat, Mary Katherine shook her head.

Leah walked into the room, carrying a box. "Oh, good, you're back," she said to Naomi and Anna.

Then she glanced at Mary Katherine. "Did your *dat* leave already?"

"*Ya.*"

"He didn't even say hello to us," Anna told her. She glanced at Mary Katherine, then at her grandmother. "I don't think he said a word to her."

Setting the box down on the counter next to the cash register, Leah crossed the room. "Is that true?"

Nodding, Mary Katherine kept her eyes on the steadily growing length of material in front of her. Focus on the waves, she told herself. Blue, blue, blue waves rolling out, rolling in. Peace. Serenity. Breathe in, breathe out.

Naomi, always sensitive to the moods of others, touched her arm. "So he said nothing to you?"

She shook her head. "He came to see *Grossmudder.*" She couldn't look at her. If her grandmother wanted her to know why he'd come today—if her father had wanted her to know—one of them would have told her. So she stared at her weaving, determined not to let it hurt that he hadn't even acknowledged her.

"But you're his daughter," Anna declared. She put her hands on her hips. "Since when does a father walk by his daughter and not say a word?"

"He nodded," Mary Katherine said through stiff lips. She put down the shuttle and stood. "I'll be right back."

Her grandmother reached out to touch her arm, but Mary Katherine rushed past, slipped into the restroom, and shut the door.

She clutched at the cold porcelain sink and stared at her reflection in the mirror. "I am not going to cry. I am not going to cry." She didn't. But her lips quivered and she had to blink again and again.

"Mary Katherine?" her grandmother called through the door. "Are you *allrecht?*"

"I'm fine! I'll be right out!"

She tore off a section of paper towel, wet it with cool water, and pressed it to her cheeks. When she felt composed, she threw the towel in the wastepaper basket and opened the door.

Her grandmother stood there, her hands folded at her waist, and regarded her with sympathy. "I'm sorry that he hurt your heart."

Mary Katherine held up a hand. "I'm fine. Really. I know he's never going to change." She started to walk past her grandmother.

"And you?"

She stopped and turned. "Me? Why do I need to change?"

Leah tilted her head and studied her. "Just because he doesn't understand you doesn't mean you can't forgive him."

"You want me to forgive him." Her voice was flat.

"I want you to *want* to forgive him."

Mary Katherine laughed but the sound held no humor. "He turned his back on me when I wanted to come here and work at the shop."

"I know. But you can forgive someone who doesn't know better, can't you?"

"I tried," Mary Katherine whispered. "I tried."

"I know." Leah regarded her with kind eyes. "Sometimes it takes two people. Actually, most of the time it takes two."

"He'll never change," Mary Katherine blurted out.

"Never say never."

With that, she left the room, going out into the shop, leaving Mary Katherine to stand there staring after her.

⟨⟩

Mary Katherine heard her name just as she started back into the shop from the back room.

She knew eavesdroppers never heard good about themselves. But she couldn't help herself. She stopped at the door, peered around it, and listened.

"Naomi?"

"*Ya?*"

"You don't think . . ."

Naomi looked up from stitching on her latest quilt. "Think what?"

"You don't think *Onkel* Isaac ever hurt Mary Katherine, do you?"

Naomi pressed her hand to her mouth, her eyes wide with shock. "Oh, no, he wouldn't—"

"No, he wouldn't," Mary Katherine said, coming into the room. "He never raised a hand to me."

"No, he just uses his words. And his cold shoulders."

"Anna, don't be so judgmental," Naomi chided.

The bell jangled as the door opened.

Mary Katherine smiled as a little girl who looked to be about six came to stand by her and stare at her loom.

"Sally, don't bother the lady."

"It's no bother," Mary Katherine told the child's mother. She continued sending her shuttle in and out of the warp she'd set up on the loom.

The little girl watched, rapt. Mary Katherine smiled at her.

"Would you like to try it?"

Sally nodded. Mary Katherine lifted her to sit on her lap, gave her the shuttle, and helped guide it through the colored strands. She worked the treadle and enjoyed how excited the child became as she learned how to weave.

"That's a beautiful piece you're making," the other woman said. "How long does it take to make?"

They chatted until Sally complained that her hands were tired. Her mother lifted her from Mary Katherine's lap and set her on her feet.

"I'm not through shopping yet," she warned her daughter.

"I have just the thing," Mary Katherine said. She walked to a display, found the small wooden potholders one of her male cousins carved, and invited Sally to sit at a child-sized table so she could demonstrate how to use it.

"Have you ever made a potholder?" she asked Sally.

"I'm not sure she knows what one is," her mother confessed, looking embarrassed. "I don't cook much."

Mary Katherine didn't know how anyone managed to get by without cooking—or why they would want to—but she pulled out the plastic bag of fabric loops and strung them on the loom.

Sally looked at the box. "Aunt Betty has one of these things. She uses them to keep from getting burned when she gets something out of the oven."

"That's right," Mary Katherine agreed, and she smiled. "They're good whether you use a regular oven or a microwave."

Sally's forehead puckered. "You don't use microwaves, right? Because you don't have 'lectricity?"

"That's right. Here, now you try weaving one of these loops through this way."

Sally watched, and then she took a loop and performed the same action, biting her bottom lip as she concentrated on what she was doing.

The woman smiled when she looked up. "You're so good with her." She glanced at Mary Katherine's left hand. "Do you have children?"

"I'm not married."

"I thought the Amish married young."

Mary Katherine shook her head. "Many of us are getting married later. Just like I heard the *Englisch* are doing."

"*Englisch*. Sounds so strange being called that." She nodded. "I was thirty before I got married. I think you know yourself better when you get married later."

She looked around the shop. "I'd like to get some kind of craft to do but I'm not up to a quilt. I have a job outside the home, so I don't have much leisure time."

"Every woman should have something she enjoys doing every day," Mary Katherine told her. "Even if all you can find is just fifteen minutes to yourself."

The woman eyed a quilt that was displayed on a wall. "You can't do that in fifteen minutes a day."

"You don't get it done in a week, but you can get it done. Are you interested in quilting?"

"I'm not sure what I'd like to do. You have so much here it's almost overwhelming."

"If you have a few minutes, we can help you."

"That'd be great." She looked over at her daughter, who was absorbed in making a potholder, and once assured that she wasn't needed, she walked around the shop with Mary Katherine.

"I'm Ellen," she introduced herself, and Mary Katherine did the same. "I have a quilt my grandmother made for me before she died. I've always wanted to try it."

"Let me show you some of our kits for people who want to do that," Mary Katherine said with a smile.

Quilting was so many things here in Paradise, Mary Katherine reflected. Women sewed them in the evenings to make something to warm their families or to sell to add to the family income. Groups of women of all ages gathered for quilting circles to chat and work together on quilts for auction.

Local women came into the shop for their supplies, and some of them taught classes for Stitches in Time.

And the *Englisch* loved to visit and buy locally while they played tourist. Naomi especially loved to hear the stories about how someone wanted to try to make a quilt; usually a customer said it was because their grandmother had made one for them. It gave her hope, she said, that the tradition would be passed down in the *Englisch* world. Too many of these women came in appearing so stressed, looking for something that would slow them down and give them something creative to do—rather than spend all their time away from their work and family responsibilities doing even more work.

"*Quilt in a Day?*" Ellen said dubiously. "I could only do that if I actually had an entire day. At most, I have a spare half hour every evening while we watch television. And I'm such an over-doer as it is, I'm afraid I'd just stress and try to do it all in one session and end up making myself nuts."

"I wouldn't take that one," Mary Katherine said, taking the kit from her and putting it back. "You know, most of the women I know who make quilts here don't try to do it all in one session, however long. After all, so many women here hold jobs, or, even if they're staying at home to take care of their *kinner*, they have a number of young ones and don't have the time, either. I think this would be a better choice," she said, putting a different kit in Ellen's hands.

"This one has you doing a small section whenever you can. You just set the quilt blocks aside, and when you've done them all, you can put it together on a day when you have more time. And the material is all cut out for you."

Ellen studied the kit. "Looks a lot more manageable. I think the toughest part will be picking out which kit to buy . . ."

"Get this one, Mommy," Sally told her, holding out the kit that featured a picture of a pink-toned quilt. "You can make it for my bed."

"It's decided," Ellen said with a grin. She handed the kit to Mary Katherine. "I'll take that one. Maybe if it turns out well, I'll try something harder next time."

"Have fun with it," Mary Katherine urged. "Don't rush, don't try to be perfect."

She hesitated for a moment and then, seeing how friendly the woman was, added, "I think of quilting like I do raising a child. You know how everyone says enjoy your children while they're little because they grow up so fast? Well, don't rush the making of your quilt. It's meant to be something to enjoy, to relax and be creative with."

Ellen glanced over at Sally and looked thoughtful. "I never appreciated how true that is about kids. It seems like yesterday that she was born."

She walked over and glanced out the window. "My husband decided he didn't want to come inside. Bet he's sorry now that he's had to sit on a bench outside and wait in the cold for us."

Mary Katherine remembered how years ago Hannah, a friend of hers who taught classes for the shop, had brought in Chris, a man she'd just met, and he'd clearly looked uncomfortable in the female-oriented atmosphere. Now Chris was her husband and he stopped by every so often to pick up supplies for Hannah when she couldn't come to town because she was busy taking care of their two *kinner.*

"Look what I did!" Sally exclaimed, showing Mary Katherine how she'd woven the potholder.

"Almost done," Mary Katherine said with a smile. She showed Sally how to finish off the edges of the potholder and watched as the child did it with great absorption.

"I made it all by myself!" Sally exclaimed, then she looked at Mary Katherine. "Well, almost by myself. You helped."

"It turned out so pretty," Mary Katherine told her.

Sally looked up at her mother. "Can we buy it?"

"You don't have to," Mary Katherine rushed to tell the mother. "She's welcome to take the potholder home, but it wasn't my intention to try to make you buy the loom."

Sally's mother brushed aside Mary Katherine's concern as she took out her wallet. "I know that. But she's had such fun, and it's so nice to see that with all the high-tech things kids play with these days, she enjoyed herself."

"One of my male cousins enjoys making them." She slid the loom inside the box and reached under the counter for another bag of fabric loops to include. Such looms could be found in metal but Mary Katherine liked the homey touch of the wooden ones.

"It's so nice the way Amish families are so close," the woman told her as she handed over money for her purchases.

Mary Katherine tried not to wince. If only the woman had seen how one Amish father had behaved toward his daughter just minutes earlier, she thought.

She put the quilt kit in a brown paper shopping bag and tied a length of fabric on the handle, then bagged Sally's loom and did the same with a strip of fabric with a child's print.

"Thank you, lady, I had fun," Sally told her.

Her mother beamed at her daughter and nodded her approval. Then she turned to Mary Katherine. "We both had fun here. I'll be sure to tell my friends to look up your store when they visit. It's become a very popular vacation destination, you know. Visiting an Amish community."

Mary Katherine nodded. It was nice to hear. Farmland had become so expensive that many Amish had turned to other ways to make a living. The shop had been wonderful for her grandmother and her cousins.

Business slowed as the afternoon wore on. They shifted to straightening and cleaning up for the next day. Leah took the day's earnings to the back room to count and prepare a deposit.

"Don't forget, Nick's coming to pick us up a few minutes early tonight," she said, pausing at the back room door.

Mary Katherine noticed that Naomi walked over to the tiny bathroom and checked her appearance in the mirror over the sink. She raised her brows at her cousin when she returned, and Naomi blushed. Hmm, she thought. Nick was one of the *Englisch* drivers the Amish hired to take them to and from work and on errands. She'd caught him gazing at Naomi several times and wondered if he was interested in her.

Finally, it was time to turn the "Open" sign around and lock up for the day. Mary Katherine paused as she did, feeling a little melancholy as she watched couples and families clearing the sidewalks and heading home—whether that was local or to a motel if they were tourists.

A young woman rapped on the glass as Mary Katherine turned the "Open" sign around. She started to say they were closed, and then she recognized the person.

"Jamie, what are you doing here?"

"I thought I'd come by and see if you wanted to catch some dinner, maybe a movie with me tonight?"

Mary Katherine hesitated as she looked at her *Englisch* friend. They were the same age, but Jamie seemed so much older. Maybe it was because she'd been on her own for a while. Jamie wore her hair short and standing in little tufts around her gamine face, and was dressed in a thin denim jacket and short skirt even though it was chilly.

"I had kind of a down day, thought it'd be nice to have some company. You can choose the movie."

Her own day hadn't been down, in Jamie's words, but Mary Katherine wasn't in a hurry to head home.

"Sure. Come inside and I'll tell my grandmother."

༺ళ༻

Jacob surveyed the fields and felt a little let down.

It was a *gut* thing to be done with the harvesting, but he was a man who enjoyed working the land, planting seed and nurturing it and watching crops grow to be touched by the sun. Hard work, but honest work, work he'd learned walking beside his *dat* each day from the time he learned to toddle.

Some said that farming was becoming a dying business in these parts. But he'd never seen himself doing anything else. Generations had farmed this land, and even if he hadn't wanted to continue, he'd have felt the responsibility, the duty, to do so.

His father had died when Jacob was in his early twenties, and so he'd taken over the duties of the farm and of his family. His five sisters were grown and married, and five years ago, his mother had remarried and moved into her new husband's house. When his mother's husband died two years ago, Jacob had asked his mother if she wanted to move back in with him, but she liked her independence. Now it was just him in the big old farmhouse that stood behind him as he watched the sun set before heading inside.

After all, there was no hurry, no one calling him inside to supper. He headed to the barn to do a last check, enjoying the earthy scents of horse and hay and the warmth the building retained.

Feeling a little restless, he looked at the woodworking projects he planned for the winter. Most of his fellow farmers also planned such projects. He enjoyed carving toys for his many nieces and nephews. Maybe he'd work on one of them before going in to eat.

But his stomach growled, reminding him that it had been hours and hours since he'd stopped for dinner, and that had been a hurried affair because he'd had errands that afternoon. So he gave a last stroke to his horse and left the barn, securing the door, and headed inside.

He lit the kerosene lamps and the light dispelled the shadows in the kitchen. Supper preparations didn't take long. All he had to do was retrieve a casserole that waited in the refrigerator for him and slide it into the oven. He set the timer and took a quick shower, returning before the timer could buzz.

The casserole was simple, but hot and filling. Chicken and rice and broccoli. It couldn't get better than that. He poured coffee and considered a handful of peanut butter cookies for dessert.

He might be unmarried, but he surely never suffered for a lack of nourishment. His sisters and his widowed mother made sure of that. They seemed to have a system going of supplying him with meals, homemade breads, and rolls. And desserts. Oh my, the desserts.

Thank goodness he'd discovered Tupperware. Now he could store some of the leftovers for times when one of his female relatives didn't show up with food. Not that it had happened yet. Like the U. S. Postal Service, they arrived bearing meals despite weather conditions. Or, in their case, despite pregnancies and child sicknesses or whatever. Or they called each other and made arrangements to have someone else do it.

He'd thought it was because they loved him. Well, he knew it was because they did. But it was also because he'd once confessed that he didn't know what to say when a *maedel* had arrived on his doorstep with a casserole. As much as he loved having a ready-made meal after a long day in the fields, he didn't want to have to entertain someone—especially if they had marriage in mind.

Now that his female relatives had formed a daisy chain of food deliveries, there hadn't been any single ladies showing up with a casserole.

But now he felt like an old bachelor as he ate alone at his kitchen table.

The front door opened, and his mother called in a greeting.

She entered the kitchen, a sturdy woman in her late fifties, her face smooth and unlined. Her eyes were the same brown as Jacob's, her hair a rich mahogany with nary a silver hair beneath her bonnet. Smiling, she bent and kissed his cheek.

In her hands was a Dutch apple pie. She set it down on the table near him, and its scent of warm apples and cinnamon warmed his heart as much as the sight of her did.

"I see I timed it just right," she remarked, looking at his empty dinner plate.

"It's always the right time for a visit from you."

"And always the right time for dessert, *ya?*"

He laughed and nodded.

Getting to his feet, he helped her take off her coat and hung it on a peg near the door.

"Can I get you a cup of *kaffe?* Or tea?"

She pulled off her bonnet and hung it on the peg next to her coat. "You're having *kaffe?* I'll have that."

"It's no trouble to fix you tea."

She patted his cheek and sat down at the table. "You're such a sweet *sohn*. I meant to tell you. The firewood you ordered was delivered today."

"I'd cut it for you myself, but I haven't had time," he said, setting a mug in front of her. He went to the cupboard for two plates, but she shook her head when he placed one before her.

"I have another delivery," she said and took a sip of her coffee.

"Oh? Which of my sisters are you visiting?"

She shook her head. "I'm going to visit a friend. Speaking of which, I heard you visited a certain friend in town several days ago."

Jacob pulled the pie toward him, cut a big slice, and placed it on his plate. He considered it for a moment. Before he could get up his mother had moved to the refrigerator with her usual energy. She pulled open the freezer drawer, took out a half-gallon of ice cream, and brought it back to the table.

"As I was saying, I heard you visited a friend in town," she told him as she rummaged in a nearby drawer and found a utensil. Seating herself, she opened the container and scooped up a big serving of vanilla on his pie.

"Thanks," he said, digging in. "Mmm, just what I needed."

"You need something else," she said, sitting and folding her hands in front of her on the table. "Some*one*."

When he groaned, she slapped a hand on the table and looked at him sternly. "Don't roll your eyes at me."

"Sorry. But you didn't come over here to again talk me into finding a wife, did you?"

"I just want you to think about it."

"Why don't you think about moving into the *dawdi haus*?"

"*What?*"

"You must be rattling around in your house and besides, it's getting harder to take care of it, isn't it?"

She stared at him as if he were crazy.

"Are you saying I'm elderly?" she demanded.

"Of course not, I—"

"I'll let you know when I'm ready to move into a *dawdi haus!*" With that, she started out of the room with what could only be described as a flounce.

She paused at the door and looked back at him. "There are some who do not think of me as an old lady."

"*Mamm*, I don't think of you as—"

But she opened the door and rushed out, slamming it behind her.

He followed her, but she refused to speak to him. She climbed into her buggy, picked up the reins, and rode away.

Jacob ran a hand over his hair and shook his head. What had just happened? One minute he'd been about to taste a bite of pie, and the next she was acting like he had insulted her.

He knew she was a woman, but he'd never seen her behave like this.

But as he sat at the table with the pie uneaten in front of him, the ice cream melting all over it, the room so silent he could hear the clock ticking, he knew she'd just said what he'd been thinking.

He needed a wife.

4

$y$ou did a good job with that customer."

Mary Katherine glanced at her grandmother while she fixed a cup of tea. "*Danki*. I didn't expect her to buy so much."

Leah patted the chair next to her and Mary Katherine sat, cupping her mug of tea in her hands.

"I'm not talking about how much she spent."

When Mary Katherine's eyebrows went up, Leah laughed. "Oh, I love a prosperous business day as much as the next shopkeeper, but that's not what I'm talking about here."

Leah offered the cookie jar to Mary Katherine, and she smiled. "Snickerdoodles!"

"I watched you teach the little girl how to weave a potholder and saw how good you were with her and with her mother," Leah continued. "They both walked out of here feeling like they'd had a nice time. They have a kit to make a quilt together, make a memory together."

Mary Katherine shrugged. "It's my job."

"You have a real way with people, *kind*," Leah said, touching her cheek. "It's so good to see you looking happier. Coming here was good for you. I knew it would be."

"I wish my parents understood that."

Leah sighed. "I know." She folded her hands in her lap and studied Mary Katherine.

Uh-oh, here it comes, Mary Katherine thought. She's got that look on her face.

"Have you thought any more about getting baptized?" she asked after a long moment.

It was so hard to disappoint her grandmother. But she just wasn't ready to do it yet. She wasn't even sure she would ever be ready.

"You know this isn't about having a wild *rumschpringe*, trying out alcohol, or being wild, all that—"

"Of course not," Leah interrupted her quickly.

"I'm sorry," she began. "I'm just not ready—"

"No, I don't want you to be sorry," Leah rushed to say. "I don't mean to pressure you."

"It's a big decision," she said, struggling to find the words, feeling her way. "If I joined the church, you know what would happen if I changed my mind and left. I'd be shunned—"

Leah waved her hands. "No, don't even use that word. I don't want to hear it. You wouldn't leave once you'd joined!"

Mary Katherine rubbed her temple. "I just feel like I don't know where I belong yet."

Leah turned pale. "You're not seriously thinking of becoming *Englisch*." She made it a statement, not a question. "I know you chafed at the rules sometimes growing up, that your *dat* was stricter with you than I thought he should be. But you're not really drawn to the *Englisch* life, are you?"

She hesitated. "There are freedoms . . ." Emotions welled up inside her. "You know me better than anyone. Yes, I chafed at the rules growing up, and yes, oh yes, my father was stricter than you thought he should be. He was—he was—" she stopped, struggled for composure. "He was so, so much stricter than you'll ever know."

Than she would ever tell her grandmother, she thought.

"Mary Katherine—"

She shook her head. "No, I don't want to talk about it. It's done now. It's over. But I need some time."

"It's been a year since you left your parents and came to live with me and work here."

"Not enough. Not nearly enough." She sighed.

"Have you asked God for direction?" Leah asked gently.

"God doesn't listen to me." She heard the bitter disappointment in her voice.

"Sometimes He talks to us, and we hear Him instantly, loud and clear," her grandmother said. "Sometimes He's soft and He whispers, and we almost miss Him. And sometimes He speaks through other people."

She leaned back in her seat. "I remember the first time that God spoke loudly to me. Scared me half to death."

"What happened?"

"I was driving the buggy home one evening. The *kinner* were asleep in the back. Suddenly this voice said, 'Pull over! A drunk driver's coming!' Well, I thought one of the *kinner* was playing a joke, being a ventriloquist. You know, throwing his voice, making it sound deeper. I glanced into the backseat and everyone was asleep. Then I glanced up and there were headlights from a car coming straight into my side of the road. I pulled the buggy over onto the grassy shoulder just in time."

Mary Katherine stared at her, wide-eyed. "You never told me that before."

"Well, you never know if someone will believe you about that sort of thing if they haven't experienced it. Besides, if God never speaks that loudly to them, they might think there's something wrong with their faith."

Maybe there *was* something wrong with her faith, Mary Katherine thought. She couldn't remember a time when she felt God talked to her.

They looked up when Naomi opened the door. "John's here. Do you mind if I take a break with him?"

"No, you go ahead. Tell Anna we'll be right out."

"*Danki, Grossmudder.* I won't be gone long."

Naomi shut the door.

"What is it?"

Mary Katherine looked at her grandmother, then away. She stirred her tea, but when she set the spoon down she didn't pick up the mug to drink. "I don't like him."

"John? Why not?"

"I don't know. I can't really put my finger on it. He's just always getting her off to himself instead of sharing her, you know?"

"Young love," Leah said lightly.

"It isn't just Anna and me. I think he's pushing away her friends."

The door opened. It was Anna. "Can one of you come out and help? The minute Naomi walked out the door a busload of tourists pulled up outside. I'm swamped."

Leah brightened. "*Wunderbaar!*"

Remembering how her grandmother had been probing about whether she would be joining the church, Mary Katherine thought the interruption was heaven-sent.

She jumped up. "Wonderful news. Coming, *Grossmudder?*"

❧

"Mary Katherine? Mary Katherine?"

She turned. "Hmm?" Naomi was staring at her with concern.

"You seem restless."

Shrugging, she crossed the room to take a seat at the quilting frame. A fire crackled merrily in the fireplace. Such a cozy scene, she thought, picking up a needle and threading it.

"I just like to stay busy."

"You're restless a lot lately," Naomi said quietly. "Do you want to talk about it?"

Mary Katherine glanced toward the door to the back room and shook her head. "Not now."

Naomi reached over and squeezed her hand. "Whenever you're ready."

"Me, too," Anna said. She smiled and sighed. "We don't often get a break," she reminded Mary Katherine. "Enjoy it. Maybe this way we'll get out a little early."

They stitched quietly for a few minutes, each of them intent on the section of quilt in front of them. Their grandmother walked into the room, took some receipts from the drawer under the cash register, gave them a fond look, then returned to the back room.

Mary Katherine glanced up and caught Naomi smiling dreamily.

"What's that smile for?"

"John asked her to supper," Anna said, her lips curved in an impish grin.

"Anna!"

"What?" Anna tied off her thread and used a pair of tiny scissors to clip the thread. "It's not a secret, is it?"

"I'd never have told you if it were," Naomi said tartly. "You don't know how to keep a secret."

"I do, too!" She straightened and tried to look indignant.

But as Mary Katherine and Naomi stared at her, she wilted and rolled her eyes. "Oh, okay, so I *used* to have a hard time keeping a secret. But I've changed."

Mary Katherine and Naomi exchanged a look.

"Well, I haven't told anyone about that cigarette, Mary Katherine—" Anna stopped and clapped her hands over her mouth. Her eyes grew wide.

Mary Katherine couldn't help it. She burst out laughing. "You'll never change, will you? Just for that, I don't have to work for you like I said."

Anna's lip jutted out. "But—"

"No buts. The deal was you were supposed to stay quiet."

"A cigarette," Naomi said slowly. "You've been smoking?"

"I just tried one."

"I'll bet Jamie got you to do it," Anna said, frowning. "I don't think she's a good influence."

"Anna, I'm sure she's a nice girl," Naomi said, and her frown matched Anna's.

Mary Katherine raised her eyebrows. "Well, that could be taken a lot of ways, I'm sure." She looked from one to the other. "I'm *sure* she's a good girl. I'm sure she's a *good* girl."

Her emphasis on the "good" sounded anything but.

"I know she seems a little . . . different than the average *Englischer*, but she really *is* a nice person."

"I never saw someone who dresses the way she does."

Mary Katherine remembered what Jamie wore the first time she saw her. She smiled. "She's creative. Artistic. She enjoys being that way with her appearance. I think that makes her kind of interesting."

She looked down at her own dress. Jamie probably thought she was the most boring person ever based on the way she dressed.

Well, she just might be surprised tonight.

"So, what do you think, Mary Katherine?"

She blinked and came back to the present. "About what?"

"Daydreaming again?"

"Anna, stop teasing her," Naomi said.

Mary Katherine grinned and shook her head. For as far back as she could remember, Anna was the mischievous one, always teasing, and Naomi was the serene one, always mothering, always in control. They were cousins, but you'd have thought they were sisters the way they were so close, the three of them, she thought.

The only thing that bothered her was how Anna wouldn't talk to them—or to her grandmother—about Gideon, the man she'd married when she was so young. And he'd been the most important man in her life . . . anytime they tried, she clammed up and walked away.

"Just thinking about my plans for tonight," she said casually, and smiled to herself when Anna dropped her needle and leaned.

"Where are you going? You never said anything before this. Who asked you out? Where are you going?"

"Anna, Anna, Anna," Naomi said, clucking her tongue.

Mary Katherine just laughed.

❧

The pizza place was nice and warm from the ovens, the air spicy and delicious with the scents of garlic, sausage, onions, and pepperoni.

The restaurant was located on the outskirts of town. Mary Katherine had visited it once before on the way home from being out of town. She didn't get to eat out much, so it was a treat. But Jamie looked bored.

"Want to share a pepperoni pizza?"

Jamie tossed her menu down on the table. "Sure. Guess you don't get to places like this often, huh?"

"Sometimes my cousins and I go someplace like this for lunch break from the shop. It's not too far of a walk. But not often, no. We bring lunch from home." She looked around and then smiled at Jamie. "Looks like it's date night."

"Yeah. Robert and I come here sometimes on Friday." She frowned. "He had to work tonight."

The waitress came to take their drink orders and grinned at Jamie. "Hey, girl, haven't seen you in ages."

"Yeah, Robert's been working a lot of extra hours. How's things?"

"Busy." The waitress whose nametag read Janie shrugged. "Always busy. You working? I think the owner'd take you back."

Jamie shook her head. "I'm taking classes and working in the school cafeteria. But thanks."

"Sounds great. What are you girls having tonight?"

"A large pepperoni pizza," Jamie told her. "Pitcher of Diet Coke."

The waitress took their order and went to place it.

Jamie drummed her fingers on the table as she studied Mary Katherine. "You really look different dressed normal."

It was the reason they'd become friends. Although her community didn't encourage becoming friends with *Englischers*, they didn't interfere in such relationships because the two communities were so often helping each other, buying from each other.

"Normal?" Mary Katherine glanced down at her shirt and jeans.

"Maybe I shouldn't have said 'normal,'" Jamie said quickly. "I should have said *Englisch*. I mean, it's so different from your regular clothes."

Mary Katherine nodded. Wearing jeans felt a little strange, but a good strange. They were comfortable and certainly warmer than a dress on a cold night. She'd gotten them from an Amish friend who'd bought them during her *rumschpringe*. Her friend had decided to get baptized and had given them to Mary Katherine.

Who still didn't know if she was going to stay . . . or go.

"It feels so different to me."

The waitress brought a little plate of antipasto. "On the house," she said with a grin.

"Gee, thanks," Jamie said, and Mary Katherine thanked her, too.

Jamie watched her move to another table to take an order. She frowned. "I hated it here. My new job isn't much better, but at least I feel like I'm getting somewhere."

"College sounds like fun."

Jamie shrugged. "It's just community college. But even there it's like . . . I dunno, I don't feel like I fit in with many of the students when I'm in class. A lot of them don't have to work; they haven't gone through what I have."

She took a sip of her drink. "It's like so weird that you and I became friends. I mean, on the surface we couldn't be more different. You being Amish, and me being regular—well, I know you call us *Englisch*, and we're Americans, not British. But we have so much in common."

Mary Katherine nodded. Jamie had walked into Stitches in Time to browse and had stayed for hours. She'd said she was taking a fabrics arts class at the community college and just wanted to look around. When she stopped and stared at one of Mary Katherine's quilts hanging on a wall, they'd started talking about it. Since then they'd met for coffee, and Mary Katherine had looked at Jamie's art class textbooks, visited her apartment for long talks, and shared personal stories.

Jamie's father could have been related to Mary Katherine's father, he was so stern and unsupportive. Her mother was more assertive than Mary Katherine's, but still deferred to her husband whenever a conflict arose. So Jamie had moved out as soon as she graduated from high school and had found a job and an apartment.

Mary Katherine was just a little in awe of Jamie. There were very few Amish young women who did such a thing. And higher education? She didn't want to go to college like Jamie, but those art classes—the ones that had to do with fabric— Mary Katherine secretly harbored a desire to sit in on one and learn.

So far she'd kept it to herself, but she wondered if Jamie had figured it out. Last week she'd given her a tote bag of textbooks and magazines she said she was giving away.

Mary Katherine had stayed up late every night since then reading and reading and reading.

They were so engrossed in talking, Mary Katherine didn't realize that somebody was standing by the table until he said her name.

She looked up, and there stood Jacob.

⊷⊷

Jacob couldn't believe his eyes.

He'd walked into the popular restaurant with his friend Ben to have a pizza, and as they looked for an empty booth, he thought he heard a familiar voice.

Then he saw Mary Katherine.

He came to a screeching halt, and Ben bumped into him from behind when he couldn't stop in time.

She wore *Englisch* clothes—a soft gray sweater and jeans. Jeans!

And her hair. He couldn't take his eyes off her hair. It flowed around her shoulders, full and soft and shiny. He'd known it was a sort of auburn color, but with it uncovered and brushed out, there were glints of gold and bronze.

Her mouth was moving. Ben elbowed him, and Jacob forced himself to pay attention. Mary Katherine was saying hello and introducing him to her friend. James. No, Jamie. Then she looked at Ben and introduced him to Jamie.

"You guys want to join us?" Jamie asked.

Mary Katherine looked shocked and cast a wary glance at her friend.

Jacob hesitated.

"Really, it's okay."

"Heads up, it's hot," said the waitress, moving between the men to put the pizza down on the table.

"That looks good," Ben said.

"If you like pepperoni, you could start eating now and order another one," Jamie said.

"Sounds great," Ben said, and he slid into the booth next to Jamie. "C'mon, Jacob, I'm starving and the place is busy. This is a perfect solution."

Then he turned red. "Well, I mean, it's not every day that I get invited to eat with two pretty girls."

Jacob took a seat next to Mary Katherine. "You don't get that kind of offer anytime," he said, and he saw Mary Katherine smile for the first time since they'd walked up to the table.

The pizza was quickly transferred to plates, and drinks for Jacob and Ben were brought to the table by the waitress.

"We're having a girl's night out," Jamie said as she served Jacob another slice of pizza.

"Guess we kind of spoiled that. I'm not sorry, though." Ben was grinning at Jamie, completely ignoring his pizza.

Jacob wondered what was going on. Mary Katherine was sitting here looking like an *Englischer,* and Ben was . . . flirting with this Jamie? He wondered if he was seeing things. "So, guess you're not going to a singing dressed like that," Ben said suddenly, looking directly at Mary Katherine.

"Uh, no." She blushed.

"I don't get the whole thing about clothing," Jamie said. "Why do the Amish dress different than us *Englisch*?"

Ben shrugged. "Just part of us being Plain. The *Ordnung*—the rules—in each community decide how we dress, all sorts of things."

The locals were used to seeing the Amish mix with the *Englisch* in the community, but there were still stares from some people—probably tourists.

It didn't bother Mary Katherine. She was used to it. The men were too busy eating to notice. And Jamie? Hmm. She was too busy taking surreptitious glances at Ben.

Interesting, thought Mary Katherine.

5

*M*ary Katherine just didn't understand.

Jamie had invited her for pizza and a movie. But after the pizza, she'd asked if they could just go to her apartment and watch a movie there. Mary Katherine was fine with that. She was more interested in the company than the movie, anyway. But Jamie's mood had changed, and she didn't quite understand what had happened.

"You can pick one from the movie rental store on the way home," Jamie said.

"I don't know much about movies. I've only seen a few."

"Pick what looks interesting to you. If I've seen something and it's not good, I'll tell you."

The store was like a candy store to Mary Katherine. She'd never seen so many videos of so many types. There were rows marked with signs that said "Action Movies" and "Romantic Comedies" and "Mysteries" and "Horror"—the pizza she'd eaten nearly came up at the sight of some of the pictures on the video covers. She decided she liked the aisle marked "Romantic Comedies" the best.

And there was candy, too, big boxes like the kind Mary Katherine had bought when she went to a real movie theater sometime back. She bought a box each of the kind she liked—she remembered Jamie liked Raisinets—and picked up a box of microwave popcorn. It didn't taste as good to her as the kind her family popped in the fireplace, but Jamie didn't have a fireplace in her little apartment.

They settled in on the sofa to watch the movie, but Jamie seemed bored. She kept texting on her phone and seemed to get more and more tense. Mary Katherine tried to ask her what was wrong, but Jamie waved at her for quiet.

Actually, the reason Mary Katherine hadn't minded watching a movie at home was because she was hoping to talk to Jamie, something that wasn't allowed in theaters. In one, she'd heard people shushing others who were talking during the commercials for the new movies coming out.

"What a jerk," Jamie muttered and threw her cell phone on the coffee table.

"Something wrong?"

"Yeah, my boyfriend says someone texted him that he saw me out with another guy at the pizza joint."

"He was spying on you?"

Jamie glared at the movie. "I dunno about that. He could have just gotten lucky seeing me there. My boyfriend's friend, I mean. But Robert made it sound like you and I were out double-dating."

Mary Katherine stared at her, shocked. "We weren't double-dating!"

"I know that and you know that, but my boyfriend doesn't."

"Then I'll tell him."

Jamie stared at her. "Yeah, he might believe you. The Amish are known for being honest, aren't they?"

She shrugged. "We're not perfect. But I know that I don't lie."

Well, she always claimed she didn't care about dating. She wanted to get married one day. Far into the distance. Maybe a couple decades from now. When she felt like she'd know for sure not to marry someone as autocratic as her father—a man who wouldn't try to crush the creativity out of her. After all, her *grossmudder* had found one. Surely there had to be one that God had set aside for her. Someday. Somewhere.

Schur, said a cynical little inner voice.

Schur.

Double-dating. Jamie's boyfriend had thought they were double-dating. Mary Katherine found her attention wandering. She'd seen the way Jacob had been staring at her, and even while she seldom got those looks from the men she knew, she could tell he was interested in her in a way he'd never been before.

He hadn't been able to take his eyes off her hair. Or her body. Her face flamed as she remembered. She glanced at Jamie, afraid that she might have noticed the color in her cheeks. But Jamie was staring at the movie.

Her thoughts wandered again, down the path that led to Jacob. She wondered why he'd never married even though he was popular with the girls at their school. One of them was always hanging around him at singings or trying to get him to give her a ride home after the gathering.

He'd always been nice to her—quite a contrast to Daniel back in *schul*—but had never paid her any special attention. But she had to admit she didn't have the confidence to do what some of the other girls did, either. Oh, the Amish girls weren't as forward as *Englisch* ones, but the Amish girls knew how to get attention in their own way.

One of them was to do the usual things like flirt and put themselves in a position of needing a ride and things like that.

And one of them was to use that old wile of getting a man through his stomach.

She frowned. That hadn't worked with Jacob. His mother and sisters were always taking him food. She'd observed their buggies parked in his drive and seen them carrying in baking dishes and pie carriers and baskets covered with checked cloths.

Jamie glanced over. "You watching this?"

"Yes. Why?"

She shrugged. "You just seemed to be someplace else."

"You, too."

"Yeah, well, I've seen it about a dozen times."

Mary Katherine sat up straighter. "Why did you let me pick it if you'd seen it?"

"It's good, and besides, you hadn't gotten to see it. Might never get to." She picked up the remote and paused the movie. "We don't have to watch it if you're bored."

"I'm hardly ever bored," Mary Katherine told her. "Is there something else you'd rather do?"

The cell phone vibrated on the coffee table. "Yeah, get Robert off my back."

But instead of ignoring the call, she picked it up. "Yeah? Listen, I texted you about this. Enough already."

She glanced at Mary Katherine and then got up. "Wait a minute. No, not for me to tell a guy to be quiet," she snapped. "I want to turn the movie back on for Mary Katherine, who is not, and I repeat, not sitting here with me and any guys, for your information. Not that it's any of your business." She picked up the remote, pressed the button to resume the movie, then stalked off to the kitchen, where Mary Katherine could hear her arguing with him.

Boyfriend. Mary Katherine could admit some envy when girls she knew had boyfriends, but lately she felt a little uneasy

at how the man who was seeing her cousin Naomi seemed
. . . possessive. And Jamie's boyfriend. She didn't know him—
hadn't met him—but all she'd seen was that he had upset her
tonight with his texts and now the phone call that was obviously not pleasant.

She glanced back into the kitchen and saw Jamie pacing,
angrily punctuating the air with a cigarette in her hand. And
her words . . . well, Mary Katherine had never heard some of
them before. When the noise level increased, she studied the
remote in her hands and wished she knew how to make the
movie louder.

Jamie came out of the kitchen and threw herself on the sofa.
"Jerks. Guys are jerks." She looked at Mary Katherine.

She lifted her shoulders and let them fall. "I wouldn't
know."

"You don't have a boyfriend?"

Mary Katherine shook her head.

"Have you ever had a boyfriend?"

"No."

"Well, that guy who joined us tonight? Jacob? He sure
couldn't take his eyes off you."

"He's just a friend."

"You sure he doesn't want to be more than a friend? He just
about jumped into the booth when we asked if he and Ben
wanted to join us."

"Do you want to watch the movie?" Mary Katherine asked
her, uncomfortable with where Jamie's questions were going.

"Nah." Jamie slid down on the sofa, put her legs on the back,
and stared at the ceiling. "Guys are so hard to understand." She
twirled a lock of hair around her finger.

"Is your father a jerk?" she asked suddenly, looking over
at Mary Katherine. "Mine is. I'm repeating the pattern of my
parents."

"Pattern?"

"Mom said she liked the way Dad was this take-charge guy. Trouble was, later all he wanted to do was tell her what to do."

"My father is like that," Mary Katherine said slowly. "I think his favorite thing to do is tell other people what to do. And my mother always does what he wants."

Jamie studied the ceiling. "My mom's always saying, 'Can't live with 'em, can't live without 'em.' D'you know they say one in two marriages ends in divorce in this country?"

"No, really?"

"No. It's actually not true. It's like one in eight. I found out in one of my classes."

"We don't believe in divorce."

Jamie stared at her, shocked. "No way. No divorce?"

She shook her head.

"What about murder?"

"Murder?"

"No one ever kills their spouse when they can't stand it anymore?"

Mary Katherine burst out laughing. "No," she said. "We're peaceful people." Right on the heels of her words she remembered the rumor that had gone around the Amish grapevine about how Lavinia Stoltzfus had chased her husband out of their house and not let him come back for days when she thought her husband looked a little too friendly with the woman who lived next door to them.

"I dunno," Jamie said, leaning over to grab her Raisinets and pop a few in her mouth. "Those Amish men always look so stern," she said around the mouthful of chocolate and raisins.

A key rattled in the lock, and the door opened.

A tall, lanky man walked in, dressed in a chain restaurant uniform. He had shaggy blond hair, and bright blue eyes that were scanning the room. When he spotted Mary Katherine, he gave her a sheepish grin.

Jamie sat up and glared at him. "Thought you had to work late."

"Things got slow. You know how that is."

She gave him a disparaging look. "You asked your boss if you could go home early."

"Well, you know how it is, baby."

"Yeah, I do, *baby*." She glanced at Mary Katherine. "This is Robert. Robert, Mary Katherine."

"Hi."

Jamie got up. "Admit it. You came over because you thought the guy from the pizza place was here."

"Well, you know how it is."

"Yeah." She turned to Mary Katherine. "Excuse us for a minute."

She grabbed Robert by the shirt, pulled him into her bedroom, and shut the door.

Mary Katherine blushed and started the movie up again.

When the voices that came from the bedroom came loud and angry, she fiddled with the remote until she figured out how to increase the volume button and tried to focus on the movie. Long minutes later, the voices quieted and she glanced at the door, wondering when the two of them would come out.

The movie ended. Mary Katherine had spent the night here several times, so she tried to remember what to do to get the television to show regular stuff. The news came on. Mary Katherine wasn't naïve—she knew that bad things happened out in the world. Sometimes they even happened in her community. But she had no idea of all the bad things that had happened today while she'd enjoyed herself: murders and rapes and robberies and bad car accidents. Oh, most of them outside of Lancaster County. But the television was like a window into a world she didn't know much about, since all she saw of the *Englisch* world was when she worked at the shop and walked around the town.

After the news, a comedian came on that Mary Katherine didn't think was so funny because he kept bringing up headlines from the news and she didn't know what he was talking about. She changed the channel and found a nature show. When she realized she was drifting off watching it, she made up the sofa with the sheets and blankets Jamie had put on the coffee table for her. Tired from her day, she slept.

⁓❧

Mary Katherine woke before dawn and lay there on the lumpy sofa, remembering the events of the previous night.

Her back hurt, so she shifted and tried to find a more comfortable position. Jamie had shrugged when she first told her that she had a nice apartment and said most of the furniture had come from thrift shops and stuff that friends were getting rid of. Jamie had used her artistic talents with color and fabric and made it a charming space, Mary Katherine thought. She wondered what it was like to have a space of your own that was totally yours, not part of a relative's home . . .

Her back hurt. Jamie had said the sofa was a bargain. Mary Katherine wondered if Jamie had ever slept on it. One night, and Mary Katherine's back was killing her.

Jamie's door was still closed. She didn't know if Robert had stayed, but it wasn't any of her business, anyway. After dressing in her regular clothes, she brushed and did up her hair, then put on her *kapp,* bonnet, and coat. She headed for the door, only remembering her overnight bag at the last minute after making sure her jeans were safely inside.

The walk to the shop wasn't short, but along the way there was a bakery where she bought cinnamon rolls and hot chocolate, and numerous stores where she could window-shop on her way to work.

She used her key to open the shop, keeping the sign turned to "Closed" and went into the back room to enjoy her breakfast. When she looked at the clock, she decided to fill the percolator with coffee and water and get it started on the stove. Her grandmother always liked to have a cup when she arrived.

When she heard the bell jangle a little while later, she called out to let whoever it was coming in know that she was there.

Her grandmother walked in. "Well, this is a surprise. What are you doing here so early?"

"It didn't take long to walk over from Jamie's apartment."

Leah nodded. "But I told you that you could come in late if you wanted."

Mary Katherine shrugged and pushed the plate of cinnamon rolls across the table. "Have one. I stopped at the bakery on the way here. I didn't want to wake Jamie by fixing breakfast."

Truth was, when she went to store the leftover pizza the night before, she'd found Jamie's refrigerator contained several cups of yogurt and a paper container of food from a Chinese restaurant. There hadn't been anything to fix the kind of breakfast she was used to eating.

"Did you have a good evening?" her grandmother asked as she poured herself a cup of coffee and took a seat.

Mary Katherine nodded. "We had pizza and then watched a movie at Jamie's apartment."

"She doesn't live with her parents?"

"No. She's had her own place for about a year—since she moved out of her mom's house. She's putting herself through the community college."

Her grandmother broke off a piece of a cinnamon roll and tasted it. "Not bad."

"Not as good as Naomi's."

Leah smiled. "No."

Mary Katherine stirred her hot chocolate. "I'm spoiled. You won't let me cook at your house."

"I thought you got enough of that at your house. I wanted you to have a break from it so you could work on your weaving. Besides, I enjoy it." She frowned. "Maybe I'm not doing you a service. If you forget everything you know, you'll have to learn how to cook all over again when you get married."

"Hah! Like that's going to happen!"

Leah tilted her head and studied her. "You don't think God has a *mann* set aside for you?"

"If He has, He's taking a long time to show him to me."

"*Liebschen*, you're just twenty-two. Don't talk like you're an old *maedel*."

Mary Katherine thought about seeing Jacob last night. He'd certainly grown to be a handsome man since they'd left school.

And he'd obviously found something attractive about her last night. Well, she could tell he'd been surprised at seeing how she was dressed . . . and wore her hair. Amish women wore their hair in a bun and covered by a *kapp*. Maybe he'd just been intrigued by seeing her hair. Most Amish men didn't see a woman's unbound hair unless she was his wife or girlfriend.

She brought herself back to the present. Her grandmother was regarding her, a puzzled frown creasing her forehead.

"What?" she asked.

"You seem a little troubled. Didn't you have fun last night? Did something happen?"

Mary Katherine shrugged. "Jamie's boyfriend was upset with her. He thought she was out on a double date."

"Why would he think that? Were the two of you out with men?" Then she shook her head and held up a hand. "Never mind. It's your business."

Mary Katherine appreciated her grandmother respecting her right to privacy during this time of getting to go out into the world and explore for herself before committing to baptism. She'd just had dinner with a friend, and Jacob and Ben had shown up and joined them. So she told her grandmother that.

"Jacob, eh? I remember him hanging around your house a lot," Leah said. "He even came over to see you at my house a couple of times."

"He was just a friend."

"I haven't seen him much lately."

"He's been busy taking care of the farm. He bought it from his parents."

Leah nodded. "I heard. I've also heard he hasn't married."

"No."

"He's a nice-looking man."

Mary Katherine nodded and tried to think of some way to change the direction her grandmother was headed in.

"Want some more coffee?"

"*Nee, danki.* So, if you two had supper together, does that mean you're interested in him?"

"You had dinner with a man? I thought you were going out with Jamie?"

Mary Katherine turned to see Anna standing in the doorway.

"I didn't hear you come in."

"You had dinner with a man? Who?" Anna asked. She put her purse in a cupboard and started taking off her coat and bonnet.

"Anna," her grandmother warned.

"It's okay," Mary Katherine said. "Jacob happened upon Jamie and me eating pizza, and she asked him if he wanted to join us and that was it." She finished her hot chocolate and got up to wash her mug.

"What was it?" Naomi asked as she walked in.

"Jacob and Mary Katherine had dinner last night," Anna told her as she helped herself to a cinnamon roll.

"I thought you were having supper with Jamie." Naomi put her purse away and hung her coat next to Anna's.

Mary Katherine rolled her eyes. "Did. Jacob came in the same restaurant. She asked him to join us. That was it." She paused. "Now if we're finished with the inquisition, I'm going out to work."

Leah chuckled. "Me, too."

∽❧

Jacob walked his fields, his shoulders hunched against the chill wind.

Being outside, walking the land that had been tended by generations before him, always helped him think. The land didn't change.

But people surely did.

He'd never expected to come upon Mary Katherine dressed in *Englisch* clothes, sitting with a woman he'd never met, an *Englisch* woman whose clothes bordered on the strange.

Oh, he knew that Mary Katherine wasn't like most other Amish girls. She had daydreamed a lot when they were in *schul*, and often scribbled on a pad of paper when the teacher wasn't looking. But he'd seen that pad and it didn't have the kind of girlish ramblings on it like "I love Jacob" or spell out their name with one of the boy's last names attached.

No, she drew patterns for quilts and weaving projects and sketched woven caps and scarves and shawls and lengths that she pictured being worn over a woman's shoulders. Her scribbles were of names for these things—a stole?—and colors like emerald morning and cobalt sky and misty purple.

He frowned. Daniel had been the one to mention her work when they had eaten that day at the restaurant. That was something he had forgotten. Several months ago he'd noticed that she seemed happier, but he hadn't connected that to her working at her grandmother's shop. Well, of course she would, given her girlish interest in such things years ago.

Why hadn't he been the one who had mentioned it to her? he asked himself. Why had he let some other man look like he was sensitive and interested in her? Women loved that in a man. Even he, who hadn't had much to do with women—he certainly hadn't courted one yet.

While he didn't think anyone should pretend to be something other than he was—a sure way to disaster—he was interested in Mary Katherine and could have found a way to know more about her, to approach her, before this. Now Daniel was in town and he was clearly interested in Mary Katherine.

And she had seemed interested in him and where he lived.

He kicked at a clod of dirt. He'd probably blown it. At this moment, Daniel and Mary Katherine could be sitting together somewhere talking about Florida.

"Jacob!"

He jerked his head up and saw his sister Rebecca waving from the edge of the field. She held up a casserole in her hands, and he nodded his understanding. Supper was here! He started walking toward her.

Leaning down to give her cheek a quick kiss, he took the heavy casserole dish from her hands.

"*Gut-n-owed.*"

"*Gut-n-owed.*"

He sniffed at the contents. "Stuffed peppers?"

"*Ya.*"

"It's the best dish you make."

"You think so? You don't think my meatloaf is better?"

"Your meatloaf is wonderful. But to me, this is the best thing you make."

They climbed the stairs to the house, and she held the door open for him since his hands were occupied.

"So, what's your favorite dish that Linda makes?" she asked.

She tried to look casual, but Jacob knew better. The two of them had always been a little competitive in spirit. But as twins, they were the first to defend each other whenever necessary.

Jacob put the casserole in the oven, set the temperature on low, and turned around. He stroked his chin and thought about it. "Well, I think Linda's best dish is chicken and noodles."

Rebecca smirked. "I taught her how to make that."

"*Mamm* taught you how to make that."

"But I improved on it and taught it to Linda."

"Better not let her hear you say that."

"Linda?"

"No. *Mamm.*"

"But it's true. I make it better than her."

Jacob noticed that she looked over her shoulder as she said it. Laughing, he shook his head. "Yeah, better not let her hear you saying that."

Mamm was sweet but firm and more than once had quietly walked up on them saying or doing something they shouldn't have.

He pulled a mug from the cupboard. "Do you have time for a cup of coffee?"

She glanced at the clock. "A quick one."

He poured it for her and gestured at a chair but she stood instead.

"So, have you been to town lately?" he asked, hoping he sounded casual.

"Haven't had time. Why?"

He shrugged and poured himself a cup of coffee. "I thought I'd make a run there next day or two. Pick up *Mamm's* birthday present."

Rebecca's eyes narrowed. "It's not for two weeks."

"Don't want to wait until the last minute."

She laughed and set her coffee down. "You always wait until the last minute for that sort of thing. A couple of times you'd have even forgotten if one of us hadn't reminded you."

Remembering how his timing with Mary Katherine hadn't gone so well, he set down his coffee. Suddenly it tasted bitter.

"Yes, well, maybe it's time to admit that my timing's been a little off in some things." He knew just where he was going to go for that present.

Maybe he'd get a second chance with Mary Katherine.

She put the back of her hand to his forehead. "Are you feeling *allrecht?*"

He pulled her hand away. "I'm not one of your *kinner.* I'm fine." He kissed her hand to take away any possible sting from his words.

"I worry about you, baby brother. You're living alone here with no one to take care of you."

"I'm a man. I can take care of myself."

"*Schur.* That's why I just brought you supper. If I didn't, you wouldn't eat."

Stung, he stared at her. "I appreciate the meals but I'm not totally helpless in the kitchen, you know. I can cook."

"You've never cooked."

"Well, how hard can it be?"

Rebecca drew herself up. Her eyes flashed. "Maybe you should find out."

With that, she stomped toward the front door.

"Rebecca! Come back! I'm sorry! I just put my foot in my mouth!"

"Try some salt and pepper with it!" She shut the front door with a snap.

Jacob ran a hand through his hair. "What a *dumbkoff*," he muttered.

First his mother. Now his sister.

What was he doing wrong with the women in his family lately?

Maybe if he was this inept, he should stay away from Mary Katherine so he didn't offend her when he approached her again. A guy had only so many chances with a woman. A single man, that is. At least, that's what he'd heard.

6

"That makes five," Mary Katherine said as the door to the shop closed.

"Hmm?" Leah looked up from her study of the day's receipts. "Five? Five what?"

"Every one of the Miller girls has stopped in to the shop this week."

"Really?"

"I don't think they've all visited in one month, let alone one week before, do you? Not even in the weeks before Christmas when we get a lot of women who like to make gifts for friends and family."

Setting her reading glasses aside, Leah tilted her head and regarded Mary Katherine. "So what are you saying?"

"I don't know. I just—well, it seems strange, that's all." She straightened the display table where Anna's adorable cupcake hats for babies were displayed. They were one of the most popular items in the shop.

"Jacob's mother came in, too."

Mary Katherine's hands stilled on the hats. "Really? When? I didn't see her."

"Yesterday, when you went to lunch with Anna. I didn't think anything of it at the time, but now that you mention it, she asked about you."

"Me? Why? What did she say?"

Leah gathered up her receipts. "She asked how you were doing." She paused and looked thoughtful.

"What?"

"Well, I didn't think anything of it at the time."

"What?" Mary Katherine put her hands on her hips and waited impatiently.

Smiling, Leah walked around the counter. "Well, she didn't ask about Naomi or Anna."

Mary Katherine stared at her grandmother as she walked to the back room. What was she supposed to think about that?

A customer walked in, an *Englisch* one, and smiled at her. Mary Katherine returned her smile.

"Can I help you with anything?"

"I'd like to browse a little if you don't mind."

"Of course. Let me know if I can be of any help," Mary Katherine told her.

A glance through the shop window showed few shoppers out. No wonder. It had been drizzling since early morning. Her grandmother and her cousins were doing inventory, leaving Mary Katherine in charge.

The woman walked around the shop, studying the quilts displayed on the walls, especially the collage quilt Mary Katherine had made.

Mary Katherine walked over to her loom and studied her pattern.

"Are you Mary Katherine?"

She looked up at the customer. "Yes."

"Jamie told me about you. Jamie Patterson. She said I should stop by your shop. I'm Allie Prentice, one of Jamie's college instructors."

She studied Mary Katherine's work on the loom. "This is lovely. Quite a creative use of pattern and color. Where did you learn to do this?"

"An aunt of mine taught me years ago."

"Could I get you to come in and talk to my class about your weaving?"

Shocked, Mary Katherine stared at her. "I—I wouldn't know what to say. I just . . . weave."

"And quilt," the woman said, gesturing at the collage quilt. "I love the images, the unusual quality to it. I haven't seen many examples of collage quilts. I'd like you to talk about both to my Fabric Arts class."

"Jamie let me see her textbook for that class," Mary Katherine said, excitement welling up in her. "It looks so interesting."

The woman smiled. "Why don't you come in and speak, and then you can observe the class a few times if you like?"

"Observe?"

"Sit in, see what we do. You don't have to pay. Or take the quizzes," she added with a smile.

Mary Katherine hesitated. "When is the class?"

"Ten to eleven a.m. on Tuesdays and Thursdays." She pulled a business card from her purse and handed it to her. "Think about it and let me know what day is best for you. Oh, and I can send a driver to pick you up and bring you back."

She looked at the card in her hand, then at the woman. "I'll think about it and let you know."

"Great." The woman glanced at the clock on the wall. "Well, much as I'd like to browse for hours in here, I need to get back to campus. I have a ton of work to do."

Her grandmother came out a little while later. "Still quiet out here?" She peered at Mary Katherine. "You look a little flushed. Are you feeling *allrecht?*"

She still didn't know what to think of the visitor who'd walked out the door just a few minutes ago. "Wait until you hear who came in."

"Not another Miller."

Mary Katherine laughed. "No." She told her grandmother about the professor and how she wanted her to speak to the class.

"I don't know why she thinks I have anything important to tell the students," Mary Katherine said.

"Will you hide your light beneath a bushel?" Leah asked her quietly. "Child, I know that we teach—we live—working at not being filled with *hochmut*, with pride. But it's not prideful to share yourself and what you know with others, *liebschen*. You're not bragging about yourself, about your God-given gift, are you?"

Mary Katherine shook her head. "Never."

"And I've never known you to be self-important. As a matter of fact—"

"What?"

Leah sighed and reached out to touch Mary Katherine's cheek. "I love my *bruder*, but he is not an easy man to be around. You've blossomed here."

Unbearably touched, Mary Katherine hugged her. "*Danki*," she whispered. "I was miserable on the farm."

"It wasn't the farm, it was—"

Conversation ceased as Naomi and Anna entered. They stopped when they saw their grandmother embracing Mary Katherine.

"Is everything all right?" Naomi asked, looking concerned.

"It's fine," Leah rushed to say. She stepped back from Mary Katherine. "Why don't you tell them your news while I make us some tea?"

"News?" Anna grabbed Mary Katherine's hand and began leading her to the back room. She held up the bag she clutched in her other hand. "We got some more of those cinnamon rolls from the bakery. You can have the first one if you tell me your news."

"It's hardly big news," Mary Katherine said.

Anna stopped. "Does it have anything to do with the Miller family?"

Mary Katherine and her grandmother exchanged a look. "No. Why would it?" She followed Anna into the kitchen, eager to find out what she knew about the Miller family coming into the shop this week.

"They were in here a lot this week," Anna said as she got a plate from the cabinet and arranged the rolls on it.

"So of course, Anna's imagination is running wild," Naomi remarked. But there was no censure in her tone. "*Grossmudder*, sit down, I'll get the tea."

"*Danki*," Leah said with a sigh as she sat. "It's been a long morning."

"You're sure there's no engagement in your future?" Anna persisted. She waved a roll under Mary Katherine's nose. "I can make you talk."

"That works on you, not Mary Katherine," Naomi said, frowning at Anna.

"True," said Anna, biting into the roll. Then, with a grin, she offered the plate of rolls to Mary Katherine.

"It would be kind of hard hiding an engagement from you, don't you think?" Mary Katherine pointed out as she chose a roll and passed the plate to her grandmother.

Naomi got mugs out, filled them with boiling water, and set one before each of them.

Mary Katherine chose a tea bag—peppermint tea, her winter favorite—and passed around a bowl filled with a selection of tea bags.

"So why do you think we all of a sudden had so many Millers in here, then?" Anna asked. "First Jacob and then all his sisters and his mother."

Naomi gave Mary Katherine a sympathetic look. "She's like a dog with a bone."

"I have no idea why they came. We did have a wonderful after-Christmas sale."

Anna stared at her for a long moment, and then she burst out laughing. "*Ya,* I'm sure that was it."

The shop door opened. Mary Katherine glanced out. "I'll take care of our customer."

"Did you see who it is?" Anna could be heard asking. "Maybe it's another Miller."

Mary Katherine shut the door behind her. "*Wie geht's,* Jacob," she said, smiling.

❧

"My mother loved her gift."

He was struck again by that smile of hers. It had been worth the cold ride into town for that smile.

"I thought the thimble was for her birthday."

"I—decided to give it to her early." He felt the color creep up his neck. "So I need to get her something else."

He started to look away, and then he realized that she was struggling to hide her smile. "What?"

"What did you do?" she asked, covering her mouth with her hand. "You look so guilty."

"I do not!" he protested. Then, as she continued to look at him, he shrugged. "It just seemed like a good time to give her a gift. And you can't do enough for your *mamm*, do you think?"

He watched her smile fade and could have kicked himself. She'd never said much about either of her parents, but he didn't think they were as loving as his parents were. The Amish loved children, considered them a gift from God, but he had never seen any outward sign they appreciated Mary Katherine. Her grandmother, though . . . why she just adored Mary Katherine and her cousins.

"What I mean is, most boys really make life interesting for their mothers, don't you think?"

"I wouldn't know about boys," she said, sounding subdued. "But I don't remember you being like your brother."

"I had my moments." Few, admittedly, compared to his brother. But he wasn't about to tell Mary Katherine how he'd managed to get his mother and one of his sisters upset with him this week.

"I don't know what you want to spend, but I think your mother would really love this laptop quilting frame," she said, moving quickly to its display table. "She's looked at it quite a few times when she's been in, but like with the fancy thimble, she doesn't seem able to buy it for herself."

It was a bit pricey. But as he thought about what he'd said—how you couldn't do enough for your *mamm*, especially when she had lost her *mann* and worked so hard to raise her brood without complaining. Had he been guilty of taking her for granted the way his sister had said he'd done with them? He'd had a good year with his crops. Why shouldn't his *mamm* have the quilting frame?

"I think you're right," he said. "I'll take it."

She smiled again. "Shall I gift wrap it for you? There's no charge."

He nodded. "*Danki*. I think I'll look around a little more while you do that."

"If you need any gift suggestions for your sisters, just let me know. I saw them looking at a few things this week."

"You—what? When were they in?"

"Well, I can't tell you the exact days each of them was here. But they were all in this week. Even your mother."

He couldn't have moved if his life depended on it. All of them? Even his mother?

"I had no idea. Do they all come in often?" He got his feet moving and followed her to the front counter.

"No. That's why I thought it was kind of strange."

Jacob remembered how he'd blurted out that he was thinking of someone when they were nagging him about finding a wife. As he'd left that day, he'd overheard his sister ask his mother about the thimble.

So she'd obviously put two and two together and come up with five. So all of them had waltzed in here to see what they could find out. Since Mary Katherine was acting so casual, he figured his mother and sisters hadn't said anything to let her know what he'd said. Most Amish couples—not that Mary Katherine and he were a couple—kept their relationship, their dating—quiet until they were engaged, so even if they *had* been thinking about more he doubted any of them would get anything from Mary Katherine, anyway.

He watched her tear a piece of wrapping paper from a big roll behind the counter. She put the box on top of it on the counter and began covering it with the paper.

"Here, give me your hand."

Jacob held it out, not sure what she was after. She placed it on top of the paper to hold it closed, pulled a length of tape from a dispenser, and sealed the seam, doing the same with each end. His fingers tingled at the contact. He shoved them inside his pocket and tried not to let her know that her touch had affected him.

"*Danki*," she said.

"*Wilkuum*."

She added a premade bow and set aside the package. When she looked at him, he realized she was waiting for payment. He counted out the bills and watched her write up his receipt.

Books displayed on a shelf nearby caught his eye. He wandered over to look at them when he realized that they were spiral-bound cookbooks by a local Amish author.

What could be better than a cookbook with authentic recipes for the kind of food he loved? As he flipped through the pages of the book, he saw recipes that didn't look so hard to make. He hoped.

"I'll take this, too," he said, pulling out his wallet. It was already feeling a good deal lighter.

"One of my grandmother's friends wrote that," she said, taking the money, making change, and then adding it to the receipt. "Who's the gift for?"

She glanced up when he didn't speak. "I won't tell," she said, smiling.

He watched the dimple that flashed in her cheek and wondered how he could find a way to spend more time with her as he tucked his wallet away.

But just as he opened his mouth to ask if she'd like to have supper with him, the door to the back room opened and Naomi, Anna, and Leah came walking out. With a sigh he quickly repressed when Mary Katherine glanced up at him, he gathered up his packages and prepared to leave.

"Do you want me to wrap the cookbook?"

"*Nee*," he said. "It's not for a gift. Thanks for the help." He touched the brim of his hat to the others. "*Gut-n-owed*."

Mary Katherine caught the almost avaricious look on Anna's face and knew for certain that an inquisition would ensue shortly.

"Let me help you out to your buggy with these," she said brightly, reaching behind her for a shawl hung near the door.

"I don't—" he started to say, but she slid her eyes toward the others, then gave him a beseeching look.

"*Danki*, I appreciate that," he said.

She quickly plucked up the cookbook she'd tucked into a shopping bag and marched toward the door.

"What was that about?" he asked the moment they were outside.

"Anna has been after me about why your sisters and mother were in this week," she said, taking a deep breath of the cold air.

Jacob knew why, but he couldn't tell her. "She was always relentless, even as a little girl."

"You remember Anna well," she said, laughing, and they shared a grin. "I won't escape the grilling she'll give me about why one more Miller came to the shop. I've merely postponed it. But at least I got away from her for a while."

He placed the big box in the buggy, then turned to take the bag containing the cookbook from her. Their hands touched.

"I know you said you don't date, but friends can have supper together, can't they?"

Her smile faded as she caught his seriousness. "Yes," she said slowly. "I suppose so."

"Maybe we can have supper some night?"

She nodded.

He grinned. "Great. Maybe Friday?"

"I'm probably going out with Jamie on Friday. It's a regular thing for us lately."

"For pizza?"

"I—I don't know."

"I wouldn't crash your supper."

"No?"

He shook his head, and his grin faded. "No. If you want to see me, you know where to find me."

"*Ya*," she said, nodding, not smiling herself now. Something had passed between them, something she hadn't felt before. "*Ya*, I do."

He climbed into his buggy and leaned back against the cushions. "*Gut-n-owed.*"

⁂

Mary Katherine sat at the table in the back room, glumly studying her notes.

What makes you think you can talk to a class? A college class?

She jerked her head up and glanced around. But she was alone in the room.

Think you're too good to work on a farm, do you?

No need to look up and around to see who spoke. She recognized the voice now. It was her father's. He'd chastised her for years for the way her teacher said she daydreamed in class, even though she'd overheard him saying he hadn't done well in *schul* himself.

But he *had* repeatedly criticized her for not liking work on the farm and seemed to dole out the most unpleasant chores to her, to the point where she'd stopped complaining.

Her grandmother had saved her by bringing her to work at Stitches in Time.

"What's all this?" Naomi asked as she entered the back room of the shop.

Mary Katherine moved some of her papers so that Naomi could join her at the table.

"I'm making notes for my talk."

"Ah, yes, the talk. I'm sure you'll do a fine talk."

"I'm not so sure," Mary Katherine muttered, frowning at what she'd scribbled on index cards. "I'm no speaker."

"No," Naomi agreed. She held up her hand and smiled when her cousin jerked to attention. "But you're a natural-born teacher. I saw how you taught that little girl how to make a potholder one day. And you're always explaining to people how to weave when they stop and ask questions. I think you love it."

"I love to talk to people about what I love to do," Mary Katherine pointed out, meeting her cousin's gaze. "I don't know how many of the students in the fabric arts class are that interested in weaving."

"I'd imagine the professor wouldn't have asked you if she thought you'd bore her class. And they're students interested in making clothes and such. Some of them might be very interested."

Mary Katherine nodded. "I hope you're right. But if I see the students dozing off, I'm going to stop."

Naomi laughed. "Okay, I don't see that happening, but if they do, *ya*, I guess it'd be a good idea to turn the class back to the professor. I'm sure she'll know how to deal with it."

Propping her elbow on the table, Mary Katherine rested her chin in her hand and glumly studied her notes.

What makes me think I can talk to a college class? she asked herself. *I'm no expert.*

"Stop worrying," Naomi said, and on her way out the door, she stopped to lean down and kiss the top of Mary Katherine's head. "You'll do fine."

"Do fine at what?"

Mary Katherine looked up. "Hannah!" She glanced at the clock. "Is it that time already?"

"Beginner's quilting at 2 p.m. and Advanced at 3." Hannah, who taught quilting at the shop, shed her coat and bonnet, hung them, then returned to the kitchen table.

"How is Chris?"

Hannah frowned. "He had to go to a funeral. Friend of his in the service. He'll be home this evening." She sighed as she eased down into a chair and rested her hand on her abdomen. "Phoebe is watching the *kinner*."

"You glow."

"I always feel like a whale at this stage, but thanks."

"You really enjoy teaching, don't you?"

She nodded. "It surprised me. I'd never thought about it, but then Leah needed someone when Fannie Mae couldn't do the classes anymore." She leaned forward to study the index cards spread over the surface of the table. "What's this?"

"I've been invited to talk to a fabric arts class at the community college."

Hannah's face lit up. "Oh, that's *wunderbaar*! You're going to talk to them about weaving?"

"If I don't die of anxiety first."

"You're a natural-born teacher. And a self-taught weaver."

"Naomi was in here cheering me on earlier. Now you. If I can just take the two of you with me on that day, maybe I'll do okay."

Hannah patted her hand. "You'll do fine." She hauled herself to her feet. "Time for class."

"Heard there was hot tea in here."

"Jenny!" Mary Katherine smiled at her cousin Matthew's wife.

"Am I interrupting?" Jenny gestured at the note cards.

"*Nee*, come on in." She gathered up the cards, bound them with a rubber band, and set them aside.

Jenny placed the folder she carried on the table, then walked to the stove. She held up a mug, asking Mary Katherine if she wanted more tea before pouring some for herself and coming over to sit down.

She'd been a ghost of the woman she was now when she came here to Paradise to live with her grandmother. The bombing that had ripped at her body had scarred her soul as well, Mary Katherine knew. But as she renewed her relationship with Matthew—they'd fallen in love as teenagers here but been yanked apart by her father—Jenny had healed emotionally as well as physically. She had married Matthew, and just a few years ago, had even experienced what many thought was one of God's miracles when she had a baby.

She carried a quiet contentment now, a serenity and inner spirit of joy that was more than physical beauty. Mary Katherine envied—just a little—that surety of purpose Jenny carried. Inside, Mary Katherine felt like a big jumble of questions and indecision.

"How's Gabriel?"

Jenny beamed, and her gray eyes sparkled. "Such a happy *kind*. It's hard to believe he's one year old already." She glanced at the folder she had placed on the table. "Thought I'd work while Hannah teaches her class. As long as I'm not bothering you?"

"No, I was just taking a break to work on something for a few minutes. Did you come here with her?" The two women lived next door to each other and had grown as close as sisters since Jenny married Hannah's brother.

She nodded. "I promised Chris I'd keep an eye on her while he's out of town. You remember how she started bleeding when she went into labor last time."

Mary Katherine nodded. Hannah might have lost her baby if a man hadn't come along and delivered the baby—a man who had caused her and her husband, Chris, a lot of trouble.

"Can I ask you something?" Mary Katherine blurted out.

"Sure."

"I heard you used to work on television when you were *Englisch*, before you joined the Amish church. You were a reporter?"

"Yes, I remember those days well." She glanced down at her Plain clothes and smiled ruefully. "I bet people would really be surprised at how I look now. On the other hand, so many people are fascinated by the Amish these days . . ." her voice trailed off, and she became lost in thought.

She shook her head. "I'm sorry, I got sidetracked there for a minute. I guess I really need some caffeine to stay awake today. I was up late last night—the book deadline looms. Anyway, you asked me about being on television?"

"Were you ever nervous?"

Jenny laughed. "Oh, my, yes! I didn't ever think of myself as a reporter. I just wanted to get the story out about how children were being affected by war overseas. Are you making notes for a talk?" she asked, glancing at the index cards.

Mary Katherine looked at them and shivered. "This professor wants me to talk about my weaving to her class. I can't imagine talking to a lot of people."

"I never thought about how many people might be listening to me," Jenny told her seriously. "That would have scared me to death. I just talked to one person—the cameraman."

"But you had an important message." Mary Katherine got up and paced around the room. "You were passionate about it, and for good reason. It's not like I have some great purpose here with my talk."

"You're passionate about weaving, and for good reason. You're good at it, you're creative, and the things you create help someone make their home a warmer, brighter place."

Jenny tilted her head. "Look, I don't want to talk badly about your father, but I hear things and I wonder if your self-esteem isn't suffering a little from all his criticism."

Self-esteem? That wasn't a term used often in the Plain community. Mary Katherine barely knew what it was. She knew she felt bad when he criticized her, and here, in the shop, she felt free and appreciated—and not just because the occasional customer admired her work or even bought it.

"The class probably won't be expecting you to be some practiced speaker," Jenny pointed out. "They'll appreciate hearing how you learned, how you work."

Mary Katherine acknowledged that with a nod and returned to sit at the table.

"And when it comes time to talk, do what I did when I had to talk to a group," Jenny suggested. "Focus at first on one person who has what I call 'kind' eyeballs."

"What are those?"

Jenny grinned. "You know. Someone who looks encouraging, who seems really interested in hearing what you have to say. Like this." She mimed interest by placing her arms on the table, leaning forward, and gazing at Mary Katherine with wide eyes, her mouth hanging open just a bit, her jaw slightly slack.

Mary Katherine stared at Jenny for a moment and then collapsed into giggles. "Kind eyeballs, eh?" she managed to say between giggles. "I'm not sure you look smart enough to be in the class."

Getting to her feet, she picked up Jenny's cup, warmed it up with more hot coffee, and set it before her. "Here, have some more caffeine. As Jamie, my *Englisch* friend, would say, you are losing it."

"I haven't met her. At least I don't remember meeting her."

Mary Katherine laughed. "You'd remember if you had. Jamie's rather colorful. This week she has a purple streak in her hair."

Her smile faded as she traced her finger on the wooden grain of the table. "Jenny?"

"Yes?"

She bit her lip and lifted her eyes to meet Jenny's. "May I ask you something?"

"Sure."

"I'm used to seeing Plain people leaving—"

"But not an *Englischer* like me—or Chris—coming to stay?" Jenny smiled and nodded.

"*Ya*. And you seem happy here. Even with all the rules. The lack of things like a computer to write with," she said, waving her hand at the notepad in front of Jenny.

"Well, I always liked writing by hand, but I know what you mean. It seems backward to you for me to leave what I had and move here. But you see, things weren't important to me. I met this man and his three children, and we became a family. And then along came another special little someone and, well . . . what more could I want?"

Jenny reached out and touched Mary Katherine's hand. "I'm not suggesting that all you have to do is meet the right man and everything will be fine. You have to know who you are and what you want first. I know you still don't know if joining the church and living here is right for you. Only you can decide that. Well, you and God."

Mary Katherine felt a stab of embarrassment. She hadn't talked to Him much lately. She'd felt He had left her, had abandoned her to live unhappily with her earthly father.

She glanced at the clock and rose. Unlike her father, her grandmother never watched the clock and treated her like a slave. "I'd better get back to work. It was so nice to talk to you."

Impulsively, she bent down to hug Jenny. "Thanks."

"I know you're struggling," Jenny told her quietly as she returned the hug. "I've been there. Once you trust Him, you'll have the answers to your questions about where you belong."

"I hope so."

"Mary Katherine?"

"Yes?"

"You seem so happy since you came to work here. I think God had such a good plan for you with living at your grandmother's and working here at the shop with her and your cousins, don't you? Can you have that somewhere else?"

Mary Katherine found herself thinking about what Jenny had said as she worked in the shop the rest of the afternoon. She was tired of being in limbo, of feeling she was living a temporary existence, caught between two worlds.

Was it possible she wasn't seeing this last year as a sign that God had indeed been thinking of her, making a plan, looking to help her create a happy future?

7

*J*acob studied the page in the cookbook spread open on the kitchen counter.

Maybe he shouldn't have told his sister cooking couldn't be that hard.

He'd made a quick survey of what he had on hand. There were always breakfast makings like oatmeal and toast and eggs. He managed those okay, although sometimes the eggs were a problem. For dinner, he often made a sandwich or ate leftovers from supper the night before, or vice versa, dinner leftovers for supper. His sisters were generous with portions, and he'd always been grateful for that.

Yesterday, he'd poked through the freezer and found the right cut of meat to make pot roast. Then he realized he couldn't use it until he defrosted it. Now he was ready to make it for supper. He wasn't going to have to make do with a sandwich and some soup he found in the freezer.

Except, according to the recipe in the cookbook, the pot roast needed several hours in the oven.

He sighed. Back it went into the refrigerator while he looked to see what else he could make in a shorter amount of time.

He thought about his favorite foods this time of year: meatloaf, baked chicken, chicken pot pie, macaroni and cheese.

But as he flipped through the cookbook, he realized how many dishes required supplies and planning ahead. One section explained how to use items from the pantry. He checked his and found it was stocked with some canned vegetables and fruit from the harvest. But he didn't have a lot of supplies like flour and stuff you used for baking.

Not that he was going to try anything as hard as baking. Just a glance at what it took to make bread or pie crust was enough to send a man screaming from the kitchen. His respect for the women in his family was growing.

He flipped through the main dish section. There was a recipe for meatloaf . . . but it needed hamburger—and not solidly frozen hamburger.

His stomach growled. Just for a moment, he envied *Englisch* men. If they couldn't cook—or didn't want to—they could just drive to a fast food place and fill up on a huge menu of items. *Schur*, he could hitch up the buggy and make a ride into town. But that would take longer than he wanted, and besides, buggy travel wasn't the safest with fast-driving *cars* on dark roads.

He thought of the last restaurant he'd visited. It had been that night when he'd eaten pizza with Mary Katherine, Jamie, and his friend, Ben. Pizza was a good idea. It might be Italian, but many Amish cooks made their own pizzas and other such food at home. He looked in the index to see if there was a recipe for pizza. Yes, there it was, in a section called "Quick and Easy Dinners." There were several recipes for pizza. One used something called a Boboli, a pizza crust you could buy at the grocery store. Jacob hadn't been in a grocery store in . . . well, a long time. He read on. A pizza could also be made with some dough you got in a tube like biscuits. Little individual pizzas could also be made with English muffins.

Hmm, interesting, he thought. Pulling a notepad and pencil from a kitchen drawer, he began making a grocery list. Even if the pizza he made wasn't as good as that he'd eaten at the restaurant, it would still be a good thing to make to eat, especially on a cold winter night. It was quick, simple, and, according to the cookbook, delicious. He jotted down the ingredients.

But that still didn't help with supper tonight. He flipped more pages and found a recipe for macaroni and cheese, one of his favorites. Macaroni, Velveeta cheese, milk. He brightened. He had those. Velveeta was a popular item in the Amish household. And from what he read, after boiling the macaroni, it just took about a half hour for the dish to bake and be ready to eat. He could handle that. It was likely there was something to snack on while he waited.

He filled a pot with water, set it on the stove, and turned on the flame beneath it. When the water boiled, he poured in the macaroni, stirred it, and nodded with satisfaction. Not so bad, so far.

Next, he had to cut up the cheese. He got out a knife and started cubing the cheese. A loud sizzle—water boiling over in the macaroni pot—made him jerk up his head, and as he did, the knife slipped and sliced his thumb. Blood welled up. He pressed down on his thumb to stop the bleeding as he rushed to the stove to move the pot off the heat.

His hand touched the metal handle, and he hollered and jerked it back, muffling an uncharacteristic curse. He stuck his burned fingers in his mouth, but that only made them hurt more. Grabbing a potholder from a hook near the stove, he moved the pan away from the heat for a moment while he turned the flame lower. He stirred the macaroni, tossed the potholder on the counter, and turned to run cold water over his burned fingers. As he did, he saw that the slice on his thumb wasn't as bad as he'd feared.

There was a funny noise—a whoosh!—and an orange color moved at the periphery of his vision. He turned and saw the potholder in flames. He must have set it down too close to the stove. Snatching up the thing, he threw it in the sink and ran water over it. When the flames died down, he plucked up the blackened, sodden mess and threw it into the kitchen garbage can.

Sighing, he searched for the first-aid kit in a nearby cabinet and tended to his wounds. A Band-Aid, some burn ointment, and he was good as new. Well, nearly every inch of his hand throbbed, but with a spirit of determination, he snapped the lid to the kit shut.

Backtracking to the stove, he turned off the flame. This time, when he touched the pot handle, he used another potholder and carried the pot to the sink. Draining the water was a bit tricky. He'd seen his sister use a thing he thought was called a colander but he wasn't sure he had one and besides, how hard could this be? A few macaroni slipped over the edge of the pan and slithered down the sink like fat white worms rushing to a watery grave.

He left the pot in the sink while he found a baking pan and dumped the macaroni into it, then the cheese. After checking the recipe, he added pats of butter and milk and stirred it all with a big wooden spoon he found in the silverware drawer. There, ready for the oven. He opened the oven door, put the pan on the rack inside, and set the oven to 375 degrees.

Collapsing into a kitchen chair, he sighed. Yup, an apology was definitely due Rebecca. He'd made one dish—one—and he felt exhausted.

Sitting in the warm kitchen, the scent of cheesy macaroni scenting the air, he drowsed.

Something was burning. He woke, coughing at the smoke that was coming from the oven. Jumping to his feet, he ran to fling the door open. The top of the macaroni was dark brown, almost black. He turned off the heat, gingerly removed the casserole with potholders, and set it on the kitchen table.

Sighing, he sat down again and regarded the dish. "Honey," he called out. "Supper's ready."

~❧~

Mary Katherine sat with the women and tried not to fidget as the worship service dragged on.

The thing was, she used to enjoy the service. She loved the singing, the way the lay ministers spoke about the Bible, visiting with friends she had little time for during the week because she—and they—worked so hard. Sometimes on the alternate Sundays, when there was no worship service, she visited with them, but mostly she enjoyed quiet time with a book or staying in her room sketching a new design to weave.

She became aware someone was staring at her from the men's side. He was here. She'd avoided him the last two Sunday services, but she had the feeling she wouldn't escape him today.

"Stop that!" Naomi whispered.

Startled, she glanced at her cousin. "Stop what?"

"You keep sighing. What's wrong?"

"He's here. No, don't look!" she hissed when Naomi looked over at the men.

"But I thought you liked him."

"You're looking at the wrong man."

"Oh."

"Help me avoid him."

"I'm not going to do that."

"What kind of cousin are you?"

Naomi opened her mouth, but when she received a quelling look from one of the older women, she shut it.

The second the service was over, Mary Katherine was up like a shot. Now all she had to do was grab her coat and sneak out.

"Mary Katherine, I'd like to talk to you."

She felt herself cringe at the voice behind her. A familiar voice. A voice—or rather, a person—she'd hoped to avoid.

Turning, she forced her stiff lips to smile. "Bishop Yoder. It's *gut* to see you."

He nodded but didn't return her smile. "You as well. Shall we step out onto the porch and talk?"

"I'll get my coat."

Worship services were being held in the Stoltzfus home. Suddenly cold, she slipped into the nearby bedroom, found her coat, and pulled it on. Grabbing her purse, she headed out to the porch. But her feet slowed as she approached the front door, and she stalled and stood in the doorway, trying to gather her nerve.

The bishop was standing there in a corner of the porch, his back to her. He wore a black felt hat with a wide brim, and his gaunt form was clad in a black overcoat. A cold wind sent the edges of his open coat flapping.

Mary Katherine hurried outside. He was old—it seemed to her that he had always looked old and wrinkled—and she had no wish for him to get chilled. And the sooner she got it over with, the better.

When he heard her footsteps, he turned and regarded her, looking at her over wire-rimmed glasses. His scraggly beard was almost completely white and flowed to the middle of his chest. He stroked it as the men in the community often did, looking thoughtful.

"I'm glad to see that you're still attending services," he said. "I know you've been reluctant to get baptized."

"As is my right until I am sure," she told him politely.

"*Ya.* When do you think you'll be ready?"

He was smiling, his mouth visible inside his crinkly long beard, but the smile didn't reach his cold blue eyes.

"I don't know."

"Child, I want to help you. I've known you since you were born. Tell me why you feel you can't commit to joining."

How could she explain to him what she didn't understand herself? Searching for words, she became aware that people were leaving the house now, heading home, walking just a few feet away.

Mary Katherine noticed that Hilda, a woman known as a gossip, didn't bother to hide her curiosity as she walked past.

She held onto her temper. "I'm not doing anything wrong."

"I've heard things in the community," he said in a disapproving tone. "You're not running around and being wild, but you are associating with an *Englischer* who looks . . . unusual."

"Jamie's a nice girl," Mary Katherine rushed to say in her defense. "Don't blame her for my hesitation. She's been a good friend to me."

"But instead of going to youth activities in our community, you're staying at her apartment in town."

"Are you listening to gossip, Bishop?"

He frowned. "I've never known you to be disrespectful, Mary Katherine."

"I'm not being disrespectful," she insisted. "I—"

"This is why I don't encourage friendship with some *Englischers*," he interrupted, overriding what she was saying. "The Bible says, 'Be ye not unequally yoked together with unbelievers: for what fellowship hath righteousness with unrighteousness? And what concord hath Christ with Belial?'"

She held on to her temper by the skin of her teeth. "Just because someone is *Englisch* and her hair and clothing is a little unusual—"

"Unusual? That's what you call it?"

"She's making a design statement."

He gave a snort of derision.

That riled her. "Well, she's creative, and she's just expressing it. She's a nice person, and I'm not ashamed to be seen with her."

His eyes hardened. "You're different than you used to be. Maybe it wasn't a *gut* thing that you moved out of your family's house."

Mary Katherine drew herself up and stared him down. "If my grandmother hadn't gotten me out of there when she did, I'd have left long ago and never come back. And the way I am now? I'm proud of the person I've become with her help."

Turning, she blinked away angry tears and ran down the steps. There was no way she wanted to go inside and upset her grandmother.

A hand touched her arm and she shoved it away and turned. "Leave me alone—" she stopped and stared not into the bishop's face but Jacob's.

"I called to you, but you didn't hear me. Are you all right? What did he say to upset you?"

She swiped at her tears with her hands. "Just the same old thing: When am I going to join the church?"

"Is that all?"

"That's not enough?" she demanded.

He shook his head. "No," he said. "I don't think that was all of it. That wouldn't make you cry."

Biting at her lip, she shrugged and began walking again.

"Where are you going?"

"I need to walk. I don't want to go into the house and get my grandmother upset."

"Mary Katherine, wait!"

She stopped and looked at him, impatient. "What?"

"Let me drive you home. I'll go tell your grandmother I'm taking you home."

Standing there, her feet in the snow, she realized how cold she was. She'd been so angry she hadn't noticed until now. There was no way she could walk all the way to her grandmother's house without freezing.

"Fine."

He turned but she reached out her hand to stop him. "I'm sorry, you're being kind, and that didn't sound very grateful of me."

"It's all right. You're upset."

"No, it's not all right," she said quietly. "I appreciate what you're trying to do."

"Let me go tell Leah, and then I'll be right back."

⸙

Leah was surprised when he told her that he was taking Mary Katherine home. But she simply nodded and thanked him and went back to talking to a friend as they enjoyed the light lunch served after the worship service.

He returned to Mary Katherine and found her standing in the same place and shivering hard. "Why didn't I tell you to wait in the barn out of the wind?" he said, shaking his head.

"I actually thought of it myself, but I decided not to. Some of the men are there. I didn't want to give them any more to talk about. Sometimes you men gossip more than women."

"We do not!"

She merely gave him a glance. "I'll wait here while you get the buggy, if you don't mind."

"I'll hurry."

When he returned, he could hear her teeth chattering, and he was glad he kept several blankets in the buggy. Reaching behind him, he grabbed a blanket and leaned over to flip it open to spread over her. But when he went to tuck it around her, he heard her indrawn breath and his gaze shot up to hers.

"I'll—I'll do that," she said, sounding a little breathless.

When she was finished tucking it around her feet and her lap, he handed her another blanket, and she wrapped it around her shoulders.

"Do you have to go straight home?" he asked her.

"No, why?"

"I thought maybe we could have lunch in town."

When she was silent, he glanced over at her. "What?"

"I'd think you arranged this but I know better."

He laughed. "You're right. The bishop isn't exactly a friend of mine." When she was silent, he looked over at her again. "Well?"

"I suppose we could."

"OW. Well, I can tell I've overwhelmed you with my offer."

She stared at him, and then she laughed. "I'm sorry. I guess I could have been more enthusiastic. But it's not a date. Right? It's just friends having a meal."

He clutched his chest. "Just wound me more."

Mary Katherine elbowed him. "Stop!"

"Story of my life lately."

Then he realized he'd said it aloud. He shot a glance at her, hoping she hadn't heard him. But of course she had.

"Has some other woman made you feel she was . . . underwhelmed by your invitation recently?"

He focused on the road. "Not a woman. That is, not a woman in the sense you mean. It wasn't someone I asked out."

"I see."

Grinning, he shook his head. "No, you don't."

Instead of pressing him—her cousin, Anna, always the inquisitor, would have had a great time at it—Mary Katherine said nothing. Instead, she huddled in the blankets and stared out at the passing scenery.

"Are you all right?" he asked finally. He'd never seen her so quiet. So troubled.

She turned to him. "I don't think I'm very good company today, Jacob. Maybe we should do this another time."

He checked to see if there were any cars following them and then pulled the buggy off to the side of the road. "I can take you home. But I'd like to be your friend, Mary Katherine."

"Why?" she asked him, her lips trembling, tears welling in her eyes.

"Because I care about you. I'm sorry now that I didn't walk out on that porch today and tell the bishop—"

"What did you hear him say?" she asked, straightening on the seat.

"I wasn't spying," he rushed to say. "I was about to walk out onto the porch when I saw the two of you, how unhappy he was making you. I wanted to do something to stop him, but I had no right—"

"No," she said slowly. Her eyes searched his. "No right. But I appreciate it. I appreciate it so much, Jacob." She bit her lip.

Without thinking, he reached out and stroked his forefinger across the fullness of her bottom lip. "Don't do that. Don't hurt yourself."

Her eyes went wide at his intimate touch, and he dropped his hand. "I'm sorry—"

"No, don't apologize. Jacob, I care about you, too. But don't you see that being friends is the only thing we can be right now? I'm so mixed up. I told you the bishop was asking me when I was joining the church—"

"I don't understand why you haven't," he interrupted. "You've seemed happier lately."

Mary Katherine nodded. "I have been. But it's a big decision, and he keeps trying to rush me."

"Well, he shouldn't. It has to be your decision." He grinned. "And doesn't he know that pushing won't do any good? It just makes you dig your heels in."

She smiled back. "You *do* know me, don't you?"

When he saw her shiver again, he called to his horse and started the buggy rolling again.

Once they were parked, he hurried them into the restaurant. It was warm inside, the air filled with the scents of the season: turkey, squash, pumpkin, apples, and cinnamon.

"Are you warmer?"

She wrapped her hands around the cup of hot coffee the waitress brought, breathed in the steam, and nodded.

Their meal came, they said a silent prayer of thanks, and she began eating. He had waited to ask her the question that had been nagging at him for the last half hour.

"I'm just curious," he said, trying to sound casual. She'd been upset enough today. "Tell me why you're hesitant to get baptized."

She closed her eyes as she shook her head, then she opened them again and stared at him, hurt.

"It must be nice to be so sure of things." She laid her fork down on her plate.

"What do you mean?"

"You belong here. You have a home. A family."

"Mary Katherine, you have those, too."

She shook her head sadly.

"I know your father isn't the easiest man to get along with."

There was a ghost of a smile on her face. "Really?"

"I've heard things."

"Folks, is there something wrong with the food?" their waitress interrupted to ask. "I notice you're not eating, miss," she said to Mary Katherine.

"It's fine," she told the woman. "I just—stopped for a minute."

It wasn't the Plain way to waste food, Jacob thought, or to possibly offend by not eating. But he wondered if perhaps he had just upset her again on top of what the bishop had done, and she just couldn't eat. Women were funny that way. A man could eat any time, any place—matter of fact, as he chewed a bite of meatloaf he found himself getting distracted by the idea of making it from the recipe in the cookbook after he went to the grocery store.

Mary Katherine put her forearms on the table and looked at him. "May I ask you a question?"

"*Schur.*"

"I remember you joined the church two years ago."

"That's right."

"Was it easy for you? The decision to join the church, I mean."

Surprised, he nodded.

"Tell me why."

He shrugged and spread his hands. "Why wouldn't it be? This is my place. My family's worked the farm for generations. My family and my friends are here. My church . . . I didn't need to look elsewhere when I found Him here."

She withdrew at that. He could see it, the drawing into herself, the blank look that came down over her face.

"You don't understand," she whispered. "You don't understand."

"Then help me," he said quietly. "Tell me what I don't understand."

8

Mary Katherine stared at him for a long time.

"Do I need to wipe my chin?" he asked, lifting his napkin.

She shook her head and smiled slightly. "I—" she began, and then she hesitated. "I don't know where I belong."

He looked surprised. "What do you mean?"

"You know I've always been a little different," she told him, feeling a little sheepish. "I was always daydreaming when we were in *schul*, drawing and not paying attention."

Frowning, she looked down at her plate, then lifted her eyes. "My father was always lecturing me about my grades."

"Well, it doesn't seem that how you did with your studies kept you from doing well with your weaving."

"*Dat* thinks it's just—"

"Just what?"

"Laziness," she said flatly. "Making products for the *Englisch* for them to have even more to decorate themselves and their homes."

"Ah, I see." He nodded thoughtfully.

"You, too?"

Jacob held up his hand. "I didn't mean I agree with your father. I meant I can understand some things about you."

Wary, she folded her arms across her chest. "Like what?"

"I'm sure it hurts that he said those things to you," he told her. "That he dismissed something so important to you. Even words that aren't meant to hurt can cut deeply."

She saw something happen then, some emotion that flitted across his face and was just as quickly gone.

"What is it?"

"Nothing," he said, too quickly for her to believe him. It wasn't that she thought he lied—he just didn't want to tell her.

"I'm proud of you."

Now it was her turn to be surprised. "Proud of me? Why?"

"You didn't let it stop you from doing what you clearly love."

"It wasn't all me. I mean, my grandmother probably wouldn't have let me. She doesn't just encourage us. She tells us everyone has a gift, and we're obligated to use it to thank God and to glorify Him."

Jacob nodded. "Leah is a very wise woman."

"I wish I was more like her," Mary Katherine blurted out. "She's so calm, and she just knows what to do, what to say. I—" she pressed her fingertips to her temples. "I just have all these questions inside my mind."

"You say you feel different than others here. But you grew up here. You went to *schul* here. Your friends and family are here."

She nodded.

"Do you think you belong in the *Englisch* world?"

Mary Katherine's eyes swept around the room filled with tourists. "I don't know. I just don't know."

Jacob reached out his hand and, without thinking, she put her hand out and he clasped it. "There's no rush," he told her. "There's no rush."

"Are you seeing him again?"

"Anna!"

She wrinkled her nose at Naomi. "It's just a simple question."

Naomi looked up from her stitching. "There's nothing simple about your question. You're prying again."

"You want to know, too."

She tried to look stern but ended up laughing. "She's right, Mary Katherine. I want to know, too, but I'm much too polite to ask."

Mary Katherine looked over from her seat at her loom. "Then I'll save you from yourself and not answer. Honestly, both of you. Jacob and I are just friends."

"You see him nearly every day," Anna pointed out as her knitting needles worked busily on one of the darling little cupcake hats that were selling like . . . cupcakes as she always liked to joke.

Her cousins were right, of course. Jacob seemed to find every excuse to see her since that day they'd gone to lunch. Several times he had come into town on business for his farm—he said—and had stopped by to see if he could take her to lunch or just to chat at the shop. They went for a lot of buggy rides and talked and talked. In fact, they'd gone for so many rides around the countryside that she'd teased him that he was giving her the tourist tour.

"You're smiling."

Naomi's eyes were warm when Mary Katherine looked at her. "I guess I am," she admitted. "He's a *friend*," she said. "A nice male *friend*. He was very understanding when I said I was just too unsure about whether I wanted to join the church."

"I don't understand—"

"Anna," Naomi warned, frowning at her.

"But—"

"We agreed to leave Mary Katherine alone about this."

Anna sniffed and her knitting needles clacked even faster. "We didn't agree. You told me to leave her alone. You're so bossy sometimes. Like you're the oldest or something. I'm the oldest. Why, I was even—" she stopped and looked away.

"Anyway," she said after a moment. "You're hardly a wise old woman."

"Did somebody call me?" Leah asked as she walked over to where the girls sat in front of the fireplace.

"Now, *Grossmudder*, you're wise—"

"But you're not old," Naomi finished for her.

"I'm a *grossmudder*," Leah told them. "Obviously that makes me old."

"No it doesn't," Mary Katherine said, glancing over from her work. "After all, a woman can be a grandmother in her late thirties."

"Well, I'm not in my late thirties, I'm in my early fifties," Leah said, sitting down in a chair and stretching out her feet. "I'm feeling very old and tired today. I find myself looking forward to closing and going home to my supper and my bed."

Mary Katherine exchanged looks with her cousins. She didn't remember ever hearing her grandmother talk like this.

Her grandmother noticed their looks. "It's just been a long winter," she said. "And we've been very busy all season. Not that I'm complaining. God's been very good to us."

The door opened, and Daniel strolled in.

"Daniel! This is a surprise."

He walked over to them, took a seat beside Leah, and handed her a package. "I'm playing mailman."

She glanced at the address and beamed. "It's from your *mamm*."

"Hurry up! Open it!" Anna said, putting her knitting needles in her lap.

"Patience, patience," Leah admonished. But she was tearing the brown wrapping paper off impatiently.

Inside the box were several big oranges and a conch shell. She lifted one of the oranges to her nose and inhaled deeply. "Oh, this smells *wunderbaar*. Here, girls, smell it!" She passed it to Naomi, who was nearest. Naomi sniffed at it and passed it to Anna, who passed it to Mary Katherine. She tossed it back to Daniel, who caught it neatly.

"I see you haven't lost your arm," Daniel said.

"I don't play baseball much these days," Mary Katherine told him, laughing. "But I used to trounce you at the game, that's for *schur!*"

"I let you slide into home that last game, as I remember."

"Ha! Your memory is aging faster than you are," she scoffed.

"Shh," Leah said, waving one hand as she used the other to hold the conch shell up to one ear. "I can hear the sea! Did your *mamm* find it on the beach in Sarasota?"

"No, she bought it in a local shop," he said, looking like he hated to admit it. "But there are others on the beach to pick up, and the weather is so warm there right now, compared to here."

"There's a letter in here, too," Leah said. She held it up for them to see, then unfolded it and gave it a quick scan. "She's inviting me to come for a little vacation."

"You should go. She misses you."

"Oh, I don't take vacations," she told him. "That's not the sort of thing I do."

"It would be good for you," Daniel said.

Leah got a faraway look in her eyes. Mary Katherine and her cousins exchanged another look.

"Why don't you?" Anna piped up as she picked up her knitting needles again. "You were just saying that you felt—"

"Like I need to go finish the deposit," she said, quickly getting to her feet.

As she moved quickly toward the back room, Naomi turned to Anna. "Why did you do that?"

Anna's needles stopped and she looked at Naomi with wide eyes. "Do what?"

Naomi rolled her eyes. "Sometimes I think you're still a little girl," she muttered. "You were about to say she felt old and tired."

"Well, she said it!"

"To us, not for us to say to her."

"Well! You just have to fuss at me for the least little thing," Anna said, getting to her feet as well. "I'll just take myself off into the other room so I don't say something else you don't like!"

With that she flounced out of the room and shut the door to the back room smartly behind her.

Daniel watched her, and then he looked back at Naomi and Mary Katherine.

"She hasn't changed a bit," he said, and they all laughed.

"I think I'll go turn the sign around and lock the door," Naomi said as she glanced at the nearby clock. "Daniel, you're welcome to stay and visit until we leave."

"*Nee, danki*," he said. "I have to be going. I'm having supper with some friends tonight."

"When do you leave for Florida?" Mary Katherine asked.

"The closing on the farm is in two weeks," he said. "Maybe we can have lunch sometime before then?"

"*Schur*, I'd like that," she told him.

He said goodbye to Naomi at the door, and, just as he was leaving, Jacob appeared at the door. They greeted each other, and Jacob walked over to Mary Katherine.

"He's still here?"

"He said the closing is in two weeks."

"Has he been visiting you much?"

Something about him caught her attention. He seemed casual, but she thought from the stiff way he held himself and the intense look in his eyes that he was waiting expectantly for her answer.

"I haven't seen him since the three of us had lunch that day," she told him. "Why?"

He shrugged but seemed to relax. "No reason." But he glanced at the door where Naomi was talking to Daniel. "Is he interested in Naomi?"

"It wouldn't matter," Mary Katherine told him as she got up from her seat before her loom. "She's been going to the singings with John Zook."

"I see."

"So what are you doing here?"

"I know this is last minute but I had to come in for my seed order, and I decided to stop by and ask if you want to have supper with me."

"You're celebrating your seed order?"

He stared at her for a long moment, and then he laughed. "Very funny. Just for that, I'm going to tell you my ideas for crop rotation as we eat."

Mary Katherine shuddered. "You're a cruel man, Jacob. I had no idea."

But over supper she was the one who talked, and she probably bored Jacob. But she had to admit he hid it well, asking her questions about the talk she was going to do at the college the next day and about how she was so nervous about it.

He listened, and then he said, "You'll do just fine. When you love what you do, it comes out."

"So you say."

Jacob grinned. "Yes, so I say. So it will be."

৵৶

Mary Katherine remembered his words the next day as she walked onto the campus. True to her word, the professor had sent her work-study student to give her a ride and help carry the things Mary Katherine wanted to show the students.

Everyone seemed to be in a hurry. Students rushed here and there, carrying their backpacks and chattering a mile a minute. The building looked huge, totally different from the little one-room schoolhouse she and Jacob had attended.

Students filed into the room as the professor helped her set up the fabric samples that she had brought. Mary Katherine placed her note cards on the podium and then sat down and waited for the professor to introduce her.

She was used to being stared at by *Englischers*, so it didn't bother her that they were staring and whispering to each other. Some of the girls were dressed like Jamie—with a flair for the creative with their colors and contrasting fabrics and styles. Secretly, Mary Katherine thought it might be interesting to dress like that. She wore Plain dresses and that was fine, but there was such a limitation on colors, and of course the fabrics were always solid, not patterned.

She looked for Jamie, but her friend didn't show. The professor took attendance and quietly asked Mary Katherine if she knew why Jamie wasn't there. Mary Katherine shook her head.

"I thought she'd be here." Mary Katherine's shoulders slumped. She'd hoped to see her friend at the class . . . well, she also had an ulterior motive: she wanted to use her for what Jenny had called "kind eyeballs" as she spoke. She'd just have to call Jamie later to find out why she was absent.

With an eye on the clock, the professor started the class and handed out an assignment sheet for that night's homework. It had something to do with little squares of fabric and a color wheel. Then the professor introduced her.

Mary Katherine did what Jenny had suggested: she focused on one or two of the students who gave her "kind eyeballs." That relieved her anxiety a little—she could then look around the room as she gave them a little background about herself. Then she told them about seeing a woman weaving one day at a county fair and how fascinated she'd been. An aunt did some weaving and gave her lessons. That led to her saving her money from a part-time job until she could afford a loom of her own.

She didn't tell them that her father had scoffed at her, that he'd proclaimed it a waste of money and a vanity. Instead, she described how she'd started making woven fabric and creating decorative pillows and throws and totes and all kinds of products at Stitches in Time.

A student raised her hand. "I know that shop. I got some material there for my class project."

"My grandmother buys her quilting supplies there," another said.

Another student raised her hand, but the professor asked the class to hold their questions until Mary Katherine was finished.

A bit embarrassed, thinking she should have known to do that, Mary Katherine dropped a couple of her note cards and had to bend to pick them up. Flustered, she found that they were out of order. She wished she had numbered them when she had trouble putting them back in order. Her palms got sweaty and she felt a moment's panic.

Then she remembered what Jacob had said. He was right, she did have a passion for what she did, and that was what she wanted to talk about. Taking a deep breath, she set the cards aside and began telling them how she got her inspiration from nature: how she went for walks in the nearby woods, where she got the idea for a fluffy throw with the delicate green of a fern frond, or a sofa pillow made from wool she twisted into strands of varying shades of brown.

It was a good thing she could see the clock because when she glanced at it her time was nearly up. She concluded by saying that the students were welcome to visit Stitches in Time to watch her weave.

The students applauded and then began pelting her with questions. Surprisingly, they were all on what she'd talked about, without any of them asking about her being Plain. Perhaps that was because so many of them had grown up in the community and saw Plain people so often they didn't regard them as an oddity to be questioned, as the tourists did. Or maybe they felt they'd be intruding.

With an eye on the clock, the professor thanked her, and the students applauded again. Exhilarated at what fun it had been, yet relieved it was over, Mary Katherine watched the students hurry out of the room, talking about their next class or their evening plans.

"Wonderful job," the professor told her, beaming. "I'm so glad you were able to come talk to my students."

"Thank you," Mary Katherine said. "I've never talked in front of a group before. I was so worried!"

"Well, you'd never know you hadn't done it before. I hope you'll consider talking to another class next semester."

"I'd be happy to," Mary Katherine said and meant it.

Students began filing into the room for another class. Mary Katherine quickly gathered up her materials as the professor waited, her briefcase in her hands.

"Susan's waiting downstairs to take you back to the shop."

"*Danki.* I mean, thank you."

"Thank *you.* I'll be seeing you, then." She sighed as she watched students enter a room down the hall. "I'd better go. If I'm late, the students start hoping that I'm not coming and that they can leave after fifteen minutes."

Mary Katherine watched her hurry down the hallway. Leave? These students had a chance to learn fabric arts, and they didn't appreciate it enough to want to sit and wait for their instructor? Why, what she wouldn't give for a chance to learn about creating . . . she stopped so suddenly a student ran into her from behind.

"Sorry," she stammered, but the student had already passed her, a cell phone pressed to her ear, and could be heard talking loudly.

The drive back to the shop was very different from the one to the college. It felt like a great load was lifted off her shoulders. She relaxed in the seat and chatted with Susan.

But when Susan turned down the road that led to Jacob's farmhouse, Mary Katherine couldn't help straightening and looking out her car window. Sure enough, she saw him standing in the fields, looking out at them. She remembered how what he'd said had helped her calm herself when she dropped her cards, how she'd used what he'd said about the passion she had for what she did and that the students would want to hear about that. The success she'd had today had happened because of those words.

She wanted to tell him. Thank him.

"Can you drop me off here?"

"Here?" Susan asked, glancing in her rearview mirror and pulling over to the side of the road. "Is this your house?"

"No, it's a friend's."

"You don't want me to drive you back to the shop?"

"He'll take me."

"He?" Susan grinned at her. "I see."

"Jacob's just a friend."

"Whatever you say."

Mary Katherine colored as she opened her car door.

"Need some help with your stuff?"

Her arms full, Mary Katherine shook her head. "I've got it. Thanks!"

"My pleasure. Take care." She checked for traffic, then pulled back onto the road.

Mary Katherine dumped her things on the porch and then went to find Jacob. He was still standing in his fields, just looking out, relaxed and easy, broad-shouldered and handsome. Carefully she picked her way across the frozen ground, avoiding the ice-crusted ruts and patches of snow.

She called his name. He turned and his face lit up. Her feet faltered, and it seemed for a moment that there must be an earthquake, for she swayed, unsure of her footing.

He was a friend, she'd insisted to Jamie, and to her grandmother and her cousins, too. But as she stood there, staring at him, struck speechless, she realized that everything had changed.

He was everything that she'd resisted—a farmer, tied to the land. And he was so sure of his place here in a way that was totally opposite her own uncertainty.

But she suddenly realized that he was beginning to be more to her—so much more.

Jacob knew the minute he set eyes on Mary Katherine that her talk had gone even better than she'd hoped. Her eyes were sparkling, her cheeks flushed with color. He heard it in her voice when she called his name, saw it in the way she fairly danced across the fields.

But then he saw her nearly trip, and she stood there, staring at him like she'd never done before. Concerned, he hurried toward her, but she shook her head and seemed to recover. He wondered if he'd been mistaken about something being wrong.

"What are you doing here?" he asked, peering around her for a vehicle.

"My ride dropped me off. I wanted to stop by and thank you."

"Thank me for what?"

Hugging herself with excitement, she told him about the talk, about dropping the note cards and panicking. Then she described how she remembered what he'd said and how it had helped her.

He listened, but more, he watched how animated she became as she talked. She was an attractive woman, but before his eyes, she seemed to transform into beautiful. Of course, he didn't prize physical beauty over inner beauty, but it was as if her heart shone in her eyes as she spoke.

"And they loved my designs."

"Who wouldn't?"

Her smile faded. "I'm probably boring you. It's not the kind of thing men are interested in. Matter of fact, most men avoid even walking into the shop."

"Well, you're wrong. I enjoyed hearing about your talk. I'm glad you had such a good time. And I think you should do it again if you're asked."

He saw her shiver. "We should go inside so you don't get chilled and catch a cold."

"You don't catch a cold just because you get cold."

"*Ach*, a few hours spent inside a college classroom and you're so smart, eh?"

She laughed. "*Ya.*"

"I made some coffee. Let's go inside and have a cup."

He watched her glance around. "We really shouldn't. It could cause talk."

"Then you go sit on the porch, and I'll bring it out."

"Sounds good." She climbed the stairs with him and sat in one of the rocking chairs on the porch.

When he brought out a tray with the coffee, he saw her eyes widen with pleasure.

"That looks good. Did one of your sisters make it?" she asked, pointing at the two squares of streusel-covered coffee cake. "Or your mother?"

"What makes you think I didn't?" he asked her as he handed her a plate.

He frowned when she laughed. "Oh *schur.* I've never known an Amish man to cook."

"Hannah's *mann* does." He set the tray down on the nearby table, took a seat, and picked up his own plate.

"Chris used to be *Englisch.* He learned how to cook before he went into the military and then came here."

She put a bite of coffee cake in her mouth and chewed. Then she raised her eyebrows. "Well, this is good."

"Try not to look so surprised."

"When did you start baking?"

"Well, this is my second attempt. The first one went into the trash. But I've been cooking for myself for a while now." He paused, then forged ahead, telling her what he'd said to his sister.

"I can't believe that," she said. "I've never known you to make an insensitive remark."

"Well, believe it. She invited me to use some salt and pepper on the foot I'd put in my mouth."

"And here I thought you were so wonderful for encouraging me about my talk today."

"*Ya*, well, I guess a guy is less sensitive with his sister than . . ." he hesitated—"his *friend*."

Jacob set his empty plate down and picked up his mug. He relaxed in his chair and with the heel of his boot set it rocking.

"What were you doing earlier? When I found you standing in the fields?"

He hesitated, wondering if she'd understand. "I remember my grandfather, then my father walking the fields nearly every day," he told her quietly. "He said the men in the family who took care of the land had always done it. It means a lot that I'm caring for the land that my ancestors settled so many years ago."

"It must be nice to know where you belong."

He glanced at her. "You belong here, too, Mary Katherine."

Jacob watched a shuttered expression come down over her face. He wasn't surprised when, a few minutes later, she asked if he'd give her a ride home.

He parked near the shop and helped Mary Katherine carry in the stuff she'd taken to the college. Naomi came to the door and opened it for them.

"Did you have a good time?"

"It was wonderful! I can't wait to tell you about it."

Naomi took a box from Mary Katherine's arms so she could shed her coat. "Jamie called right after you left. She asked if you were still coming over tonight." Naomi bit her lip. "Mary Katherine, she sounded really upset."

"I'll go give her a call."

"Pizza night?" Jacob asked.

She tilted her head. "Are you hoping you'll get an invitation to join us like last time?"

"Maybe."

"I'd have to ask Jamie."

"I could bring Ben. They seemed to enjoy talking."

Her eyes narrowed. "As long as you're not trying to make this into a date."

"Or a double date?" He held up his hands as she opened her mouth. "Friends. That's all. And good pizza."

"I need to get to work," she said quickly when several people walked past them and entered the shop. "I took time off today—"

"We'll be there at seven," he said. "So if you don't want us to join the two of you, that's fine." He grinned at her. "We won't pressure you to let us join you. Honest."

She laughed. "Okay. And you won't give us sulking looks from across the room?" she found herself teasing.

"I'll try not to. I make no promises for Ben."

9

The shop was busy, so there wasn't a spare moment for talk about what had happened at the college for some time after she returned.

It was obviously driving curious Anna crazy. Every time a customer left, she'd turn to Mary Katherine and start to ask a question.

And then another customer would walk in. It was an interesting time, thought Mary Katherine. There was nothing better than a busy spell at the store, but Anna dearly loved being able to talk and the two didn't mix.

So it was a real relief for her when the crowd thinned and they got a few minutes to sit down and chat.

"You look happy," Leah noted as she picked up one of the little cloth Amish dolls she was making.

"It was such fun."

"So it went well, did it?" Anna asked with a smug smile. "I knew you'd do a good job." She sat and began knitting.

"Pride isn't our way," Naomi reminded her. "Mary Katherine might not be baptized, but she knows that."

Mary Katherine glanced over from her loom. "That's right." Calmly, she set her shuttle down. Then she grinned at Annie. "But I have to say that the professor thought I did a good job."

Her smile faded when the bishop walked in. He was dressed in the same black hat and long coat that he'd worn the day they had talked at church. His expression was no less forbidding than it had been on that day.

He glanced over at Mary Katherine, and she started to get up but her grandmother shook her head.

"I'll talk to him," she said.

After exchanging a few words, she indicated with a gesture that said without words that he should look around the shop. She followed behind him as he walked around, pausing to peer over his glasses at each person's work, stopping to frown over Mary Katherine's display.

He turned and said something to Leah, and she straightened and turned to walk toward the door to the back room. He followed her inside, and she shut the door with a snap.

Naomi, Anna, and Mary Katherine exchanged glances.

"What do you suppose that's about?"

"Me," said Mary Katherine.

"You? Why do you say that?"

"He talked to me after church the other day. Wanted to know when I was going to get baptized."

Naomi came over to touch her shoulder. "Did you tell him that you need time to make your decision?"

"*Ya*, he shouldn't be pressuring you about a thing like that!" Anna told her, walking up to stand beside Naomi.

Mary Katherine nodded. "Of course. But he just wanted to pressure me." She glanced at the closed door. "Why is he in there talking to our grandmother? My decision has nothing to do with her."

"I didn't like the way he was walking around glaring at the things we've made," Anna said, frowning.

She stiffened when the back room door opened and the bishop walked out, gave them a sparing glance, then proceeded out the front shop door.

As one, they hurried to find out what had been spoken of behind closed doors.

They found their grandmother sitting at the table, her arms folded across her chest, a mutinous expression on her face.

"*Grossmudder*, I've never seen you look like that," Naomi ventured a bit carefully.

"You sound like Little Red Riding Hood," Anna said.

Mary Katherine ignored her. "Why did the bishop come here today?"

Leah got to her feet. "It was nothing important."

"If it was nothing important, you'd just tell us," Mary Katherine said slowly. "Why was he looking at the things in the shop?"

She watched her grandmother walk to the sink and fill the teakettle. "What makes you think that he wasn't asking when you were going to join the church?" Leah asked her.

"Because he did that after church last week."

Leah nodded. "I know."

"Then what was it?" Anna, always curious and impatient, demanded.

"It doesn't matter since he's not going to influence me."

"Influence you?" Naomi looked at her cousins. "He's trying to make you pressure Mary Katherine?"

"I'm not letting him do that," Mary Katherine began. "I'll go speak to him myself." She reached for her jacket hanging on the peg.

Leah sighed. "No, dear one. He didn't come here to talk about you. Not exactly."

The teakettle whistled. She turned and shut off the flame under it, then poured the hot water into mugs she set in front of them.

When Leah finally sat down, Mary Katherine tensed, and felt her cousins lean forward, waiting to hear their grandmother speak.

Leah took a sip of tea. "The bishop wanted to talk to me about the things we're making," she told them. "He feels we're straying from producing what is traditional for Amish handiwork."

"What?" Anna stared at her, looking incredulous.

Shrugging, Leah took another sip of her tea. "Apparently some of our work is too . . . different."

"He's talking about me. About my weaving," Mary Katherine said. "It's an old craft but I have very new ideas for my patterns."

"Tradition is good," said Leah. "Our lives are full of it. We create something traditional like an old standard quilt pattern or a knitted baby cap that's from the past—started at some point from a new idea by some woman."

"Is he saying he wants us to stop?" Naomi asked.

"I think he was . . . encouraging us to return to the type of goods that used to sell in shops like ours."

"Go back. We're supposed to go back?" Mary Katherine said flatly.

Leah nodded. "He feels we should. We're a symbol of our Plain community to the *Englischers*. His words, not mine," she added quickly when she saw Mary Katherine jump to her feet.

"We're a business, just like so many other businesses run by our community," Mary Katherine told her. "I bet he doesn't try that with some of the men. Does he tell them what to make and what to sell?"

She stopped and took a deep breath. "Okay, that was a dumb question. I know there are rules. But we have both the traditional Amish goods here and some wonderful things like some of Naomi's newer quilt designs and Anna's baby caps."

Picking up one of the caps, she shook her head. "How can you be against a cupcake cap, for goodness sake?"

Anna reached over to take Mary Katherine's hand. "Thanks for defending my cupcake hats."

"It's just like you to make a joke when something turns serious," Naomi said.

A strange expression flitted across Anna's face. She opened her mouth, but before she could say anything, Naomi touched Leah's arm.

"So what's going to happen? Are we going to stop doing what we do? The new things, I mean?"

"No." Leah looked at each of them in turn. "I don't believe we're doing anything wrong, so I don't think we should change anything."

The cousins looked at each other.

"What if he doesn't like that?"

"Then he can take it to the elders."

The bell jangled on the front door. Naomi stood, but Leah shook her head. "I'll get it. I need to do something to work off this—this urge I have to say something not so nice about the bishop!"

⋘≫

Mary Katherine chose to walk to Jamie's apartment. She felt like her grandmother—upset and needing some way to work off her churning emotions.

And she felt some guilt. The bishop had never come to the shop until she'd had that talk with him after church. Her conscience prodded her. Maybe she could have been more polite to him. *Allrecht*, she *should* have been more polite to him. She just hadn't been able to resist behaving the same way to him that she had with another over-bearing authority figure— her father.

Now maybe she'd just made trouble for all of them. She kicked at a stone in her path and watched it skitter ahead of her.

She climbed the stairs to Jamie's apartment and knocked on her door. Then again. When she knocked for the third time, she began to wonder if Jamie wasn't home—if she'd forgotten that they were going to spend the evening together.

Just as she started to knock once more, the door opened.

Jamie stood there dressed in sweats, her hair uncombed, her eyes reddened from crying. "You came."

"I said I would. What's the matter? Aren't you feeling well? Have you got the flu?"

Jamie wiped at her eyes. "No. I'm just upset about something. Listen, give me a minute, and I'll change."

"We don't have to go for pizza!" Mary Katherine called after her.

But Jamie had already entered her bedroom and closed the door. When she came out, she was dressed in jeans and a sweater, her hair was combed, and evidence of crying had been mostly hidden with cosmetics.

"We don't have to go anywhere," Mary Katherine repeated. "We can stay here and talk."

"No, it'll be good for me to get out. Besides, I haven't eaten all day, and now I'm starving."

Mary Katherine told her about how Jacob wanted to join them and hoped to bring Ben along. "I told Jacob I had to ask you, and he said they'd sit at another table if we didn't want company."

"No, it's okay. Jacob really seems to like you. And Ben is cool to talk to. It doesn't hurt that he's cute, too."

"But you have a boyfriend."

Jamie's mouth tightened, and she frowned. "Not anymore."

"Do you want to talk about it?"

"No, let's go."

They walked to the restaurant, their breath huffing white in the cold air. When they arrived at the restaurant, they saw Jacob and Ben standing outside.

Jamie smiled at them. "So, you two handsome guys want to have pizza with us?"

Mary Katherine's eyes widened. She didn't know any Amish girls who would talk like that.

Ben rushed to hold the door open for them.

"Such a gentleman," Jamie said as she looked at him, and Ben reddened.

Jacob motioned for her and Mary Katherine to precede them into the restaurant.

"You're a gentleman, too," Mary Katherine teased as she walked past them.

"*Ya*, that's me," he said with a grin.

They were seated in a booth, a small one that made Mary Katherine uncomfortably aware of Jacob sitting beside her. She pulled her skirts close to her body, but when her hand accidentally touched his thigh covered in wool fabric there was a crackle of static electricity.

Trying not to look at him, she picked up her menu and studied it. To her mortification, she heard her stomach growl.

Jacob quirked an eyebrow at her.

"I didn't have lunch," she said. "I got back to the shop and we were busy."

"I'd have made you a sandwich instead of coffee cake if I'd known."

"It was good coffee cake."

"*Danki*. I actually enjoyed making it."

She put her elbow on the table and set her chin in her hand. "Maybe you should tell your sister. Maybe she did you a favor." She paused for a moment. "Like that professor did for me by asking me to do something I'd never done before. And now you're cooking, something you never really did much before."

Their eyes met. If there were other people around her, they faded away. She couldn't hear them, couldn't see them.

Then her stomach growled again. Jacob signaled for the server. "Let's get you some food before you fade away before my eyes."

"I'm not some insubstantial miss who's going to fade away."

"No," he said, turning to look at her. "You're perfect to me."

❧

The moment the words slipped out, Jacob wished he could call them back.

"I wish somebody else felt I was perfect," she muttered.

"Yes, can I help you?" the server asked.

He wanted to send her away, but he'd called her over. Besides, Mary Katherine was hungry, and so was he.

They placed their order, and then he looked back at her. She was tracing the circle of condensation on the wooden table left by her glass of water and frowning.

"What was that about wishing somebody thought you were perfect?" he asked her quietly.

She was distracted as Jamie and Ben got up.

Jacob glanced up at them.

"We want to go look at the bakery case," Jamie told them.

Mary Katherine looked relieved to see them leave. "The bishop stopped by the shop after you dropped me off," she said quietly.

"The bishop visited the shop?"

She nodded.

"Well, I never thought about him doing that. Was he buying a gift like I did?"

She gave a derisive laugh. "Hardly. He came to tell us that he didn't like what we were doing. I think he was especially displeased by what I do."

"You?"

"Some of our things are too modern. Not Plain enough. We're supposed to be representing the Amish with traditional crafts, he said."

"Really?" He sat back, trying to absorb what she said.

"I love what Grandmother has encouraged us to do. Naomi and Anna and me, I mean. I'd hate to think that it's causing a problem for her."

"What do you mean? Is he threatening to go to the church elders about it?"

She shook her head. "He didn't say that today. But I'm afraid that's the next step."

Shaking her head again, she sighed and leaned back in the booth. "I wonder what Daniel's bishop in Florida is like?"

❦

The minute Jamie walked into her apartment with Mary Katherine, Jamie kicked off her shoes and walked over to collapse on the sofa.

"I'm going to put the leftover pizza in the refrigerator," Mary Katherine told her. "Unless you want another piece?"

"No," Jamie said with a moan. She put her arm over her face. "I feel sick. I think I ate too much."

"You're not the only one," Mary Katherine told her. "Maybe I should wrap the pieces in aluminum foil and put them in the freezer."

"Good idea."

When Mary Katherine returned to the living room, Jamie wasn't lying on the sofa anymore. The bathroom door was closed, and when she heard the toilet flush, she knew where her friend was.

Then the door opened, and Jamie appeared, leaning dramatically against the jamb. "I feel so sick. I can't seem to keep anything down lately. Why I thought I'd get away with pizza—especially stuffing myself with it—is beyond me."

"Is it the flu? It's going around."

Jamie's face contorted. "I don't think so. I'm—I'm scared to death I'm pregnant."

She said it with such bitterness and despair, Mary Katherine was shocked. A *boppli*—baby—was eagerly looked forward to by the Amish. Well, they weren't perfect, she reflected; occasionally there were couples who anticipated their vows, who married and had an early baby.

"Think? You haven't gone to the doctor?"

"I can't afford it," Jamie said, returning to the sofa to flop onto it and cover her face with the afghan.

"Then you should at least take a pregnancy test from the drugstore."

Jamie pulled the afghan down, revealing her face. "How do you know about this?"

"I'm Amish. Not ignorant," Mary Katherine told her briskly. She stood and pulled her purse strap onto her shoulder. "Then that's the first thing you need to know. The drugstore is probably still open. We'll go get a pregnancy kit."

"I think I'm going to throw up again." Jumping up, Jamie bolted for the bathroom and slammed the door.

This wasn't looking good, thought Mary Katherine. She walked over to the door and knocked on it. "Are you okay?"

"Yeah."

"I don't want to leave if you're not okay."

The toilet flushed, and water ran in the sink. Jamie opened the door. She was wetting a washcloth. "All better now."

"I'll go by myself. You don't seem to be in any shape to go."

"Thank you," Jamie told her.

She looked wan, but her voice was heartfelt.

Mary Katherine started for the door. "Is there anything else you need?"

"Chocolate," Jamie said in a muffled voice as she wiped her face with the washcloth. "A couple of pounds of chocolate."

"Chocolate never cured anything," Mary Katherine told her, but she couldn't help smiling a little.

"It never hurt, either."

Mary Katherine was holding two pregnancy kits—wondering which was better—when she felt someone watching her. She turned and someone—a man—darted behind a display of cereal.

Shrugging, she turned back to her study of the kits. One promised that fewer mistakes were made with it and that it could detect a pregnancy earlier than any other tests on the market. She checked the price. It was two dollars more, but she figured it was worth the price.

Satisfied, she walked to the checkout and was digging in her purse for money when she realized that everything had gone silent. Glancing up, she saw that the clerk and two staff members were standing there, staring at her.

She felt a moment's twinge, then dismissed it. They didn't know her, and she didn't know them. And most importantly, she wasn't wearing her Plain clothes. They probably thought she was *Englisch,* so no one in her community would ever know that she'd bought a pregnancy kit.

She quickly handed over the money, got her change, and held out her hand for the package safely hidden now in a plastic bag.

Hurrying back to Jamie's apartment, she thrust the package into her friend's hands. "There. You can find out now."

Jamie stared at the package as if it were a snake.

"Well, I thought you'd want to find out right away."

Lifting her eyes, Jamie shook her head. Her lips trembled. "I do. But I'm scared everything is going to change if—if—"

Mary Katherine hadn't ever been faced with something like this. But she could see Jamie's terror, could almost feel it. She'd never even thought of what might happen if she got pregnant outside of marriage because she'd been so determined to avoid dating until she figured out where she belonged.

But fear—she'd known fear, and she saw it now. So she did the only thing she could think of. She reached out and hugged her friend.

"Let's just get it over with," she murmured. "The sooner, the better. Then we'll talk about whatever you need to do."

Jamie's breath hitched, and she nodded. "Okay." She backed up. "Thanks."

"The instructions say it's really easy. That it's hard to get the results confused."

"Really?" Jamie's laugh was more an exhale of air than a sound of mirth. "Well, that's good to know." She rubbed at her forehead. "It's just been such a difficult semester. I took on too many classes to get out sooner, then I had my hours cut back at work. My roommate moved out. I'm scared I won't have my rent money this month. And I let myself get talked into—" she stopped and blushed.

Mary Katherine hugged her again. "Everything will work out."

"I don't know how." She turned and walked toward the bathroom with slumped shoulders and closed the door behind her.

"I'll pray for you," Mary Katherine whispered.

Mary Katherine took a seat on the sofa and did as she'd told Jamie she would do: she prayed for peace, and for guidance, for her friend.

She realized at that moment that she had turned to God for the first time in a long, long time. She'd asked Him for peace, for guidance—things she hadn't asked Him for herself. And she'd asked, believing that He was listening to her when she hadn't felt that way for months and months.

⊷⊶

The next day, Jacob sat in his kitchen, brooding over a cup of coffee while he waited for the oven timer to go off.

He couldn't forget Mary Katherine's question from the night before: "*I wonder what Daniel's bishop in Florida is like?*"

Why had the bishop picked now to visit the shop and make his comments to Leah? Mary Katherine had been so upset. Jacob didn't see anything wrong with what they created and sold at the shop, and he didn't think anyone else in their Plain community would.

And it didn't make sense that if the bishop wanted Mary Katherine to join the church, he would be critical of her. Then again, he was an authority figure who didn't go around trying to be liked. Instead, he was looked on as being someone who saw to it that the *Ordnung*, the unwritten rules, were strictly obeyed.

Mary Katherine had been so upset with the bishop she told Jacob she had left the shop for a walk to cool off.

He could only wonder if she'd view what had happened with the bishop as just another reason she shouldn't stay in the Plain community. The timer dinged, and he rose to pull the baking pan from the oven. Setting it on top of the stove, he used a toothpick to check to see if it was done. Satisfied that there was no uncooked batter on the toothpick, he turned off the oven.

The pan was still warm when he knocked at his sister Rebecca's door a little while later.

He heard yelling through the door, and then it was opened by one of his nephews.

"*Mamm! It's Onkel* Jacob!" he yelled.

She held her hands over her ears and winced. "*Danki, liebschen.* Next time please use your inside voice. Now go back to your homework."

Jacob watched him drag his feet back to the kitchen. He remembered the days of homework and winced. Then he realized that his sister was standing there rubbing at the small of her back, an expression of pain on her face. He stepped inside and closed the door.

"I brought you a peace offering." He held out the coffee cake.

She took it from him and sniffed at it. "Smells good. *You* made it?"

"*Ya.* Here, let me carry it into the kitchen and you sit down. You look exhausted."

"Well, if you go around saying things like that, it's no wonder you're not married," she told him with a trace of tartness.

"I'm sorry, but—"

She held up her hand. "Never mind. You try being pregnant for nine months and see how good *you* look."

He felt himself pale. "That's not funny."

Yawning, she leaned against the chair of her oldest and watched her do her sums. "What I wouldn't do for a nap."

He looked around the table. His nieces and nephews were busily working on their homework. Such quiet, well-behaved children, he couldn't help thinking. Even the youngest, a four-year-old boy who was the spitting image of his mother, was quietly coloring a blue squirrel within the outlines of a coloring book.

"Tell you what," he said, placing the coffee cake on the kitchen counter. "How about I watch the *kinner* so you can lie down?"

She walked over to him and thrust her face uncomfortably close to his. "Jacob, don't be joking about something like that with an overdue pregnant woman."

Jacob backed up. "I wouldn't joke about that. I meant it."

"You have the time to babysit my five little monsters? Well, four. One of them went to town with his *dat*."

"Four, five," Jacob said, shrugging. "Doesn't matter. I'll watch them." He frowned when he saw her trying to suppress a smile. "What?"

"You'd be surprised," she told him dryly. "But I'm going to take you up on your offer. You won't think it's so easy after you do it."

Now she was making him uneasy. "I never said it would be easy. I learned never to say that anything you or any other woman does is easy."

"So, is the coffee cake safe to eat?" she asked, breaking off a piece and trying it.

"Well, that's pretty good."

She pulled a roll of aluminum foil from a kitchen drawer and covered the top of the pan with it. "This is dessert. No one gets it until after supper."

"We can't have some now?" Mary asked. She gave Jacob a winsome smile. "It's hours and hours until supper."

"And we're starving," her six-year-old brother added.

"You had cookies and milk and fruit when you came home from *schul*," his mother reminded them.

"Hours ago," John said with a nod.

"Ignore them," Rebecca told Jacob. "They're little eating machines."

"*Kinner* get hungry," he said, shrugging. "I remember those days."

"You still eat like them." She waved a hand at the oven. "Supper will be ready in an hour." She sighed. "Nap. I can't remember what a nap feels like."

Jacob kissed her cheek and then gently pushed her toward the stairs. "It means sleep. Now go. No worrying about anything."

"You've never taken care of them. You've never taken care of a single *kind*."

"No playing with scissors," he whispered in her ear. "No running screaming around the house. No fighting. And definitely no more snacks, especially coffee cake."

"How bad can it go?" he heard her say as she left the room. "I'll be right upstairs if you need me," she called over her shoulder to him.

"We won't need you," he said. "Right?" he asked his nieces and nephews.

"Right!" they chorused.

"It's babyish to take a nap," John said once she left the room. "I haven't taken a nap in years."

Probably why she needs one, Jacob couldn't help thinking. While they were behaving now—were, in fact good *kinner*— he wasn't so naïve that he thought they were angels.

But it was just an hour. What could go wrong in an hour? And maybe this was a way to see how he'd be as a father. It was a logical step after thinking of Mary Katherine as his choice of *fraa*, his wife, after all. He was going to find a way to convince her that she belonged here.

That she belonged with him.

10

Shh!" Jacob hissed at his nieces and nephews. "We have to be quiet so your *mamm* can get some rest."

Everyone quieted down again. For about five minutes.

He was exhausted. Homework had been done twenty minutes ago, and after the *kinner* finished, they had run around the house like little wild things while he raced after them trying to stop them. Then there had been the begging for snacks, which he'd had to turn down. A contest to see who could do the most jumping jacks was next. And on it went.

He got them quiet, sank into a chair, exhausted, and heard the telltale creak on the stairs that told him Rebecca was coming down.

"Now you've done it," he muttered and looked up to see his sister shaking her head at him. "Sorry."

"For what? I slept like a log." She bent down to kiss his cheek. Then she turned to her children. "No thanks to you monsters. I can see by the way your *onkel* looks so tired that you ran him ragged."

They had the grace to look penitent. "Sorry, *Onkel* Jacob," they said as one.

The youngest tugged at his hand. "Sowwy," she said, looking up at him with big blue eyes.

Jacob reached down to pick her up. "I forgive you."

She grinned and kissed his cheek.

There was a faint noise that sounded like water being spilled. Jacob pulled his gaze away from his youngest niece and couldn't believe what he was seeing.

"*Mamm!* You're going potty!" one of the *kinner* cried.

Rebecca sighed as she stared at the puddle at her feet. "I just mopped this floor yesterday." She looked up at Jacob. "My water broke."

Jacob stood and set Lizzie down. "You're having the baby. Rebecca, you're having the baby."

She laughed and patted his cheek. "It's okay. Yes, I know, I'm having the baby. But don't look so scared. It's not going to plop out onto the floor any second."

"I don't know anything about having a baby."

"Maybe you better sit down before you fall down," she suggested, laughing.

He sat.

"Mary, go get the mop. Luke, run down the street and get your *grossmudder.*"

Jacob watched his sister take charge and became ashamed of his behavior. He took her by the shoulders and eased her into the chair he'd been sitting in. "Should we call 911?"

"Why?"

"To take you to the hospital."

She waved her hand at him and tried to rise from the chair, but he kept his hands on her shoulders, preventing her from standing. "No, silly. I have my *boppli* at home, remember?"

"But—"

"When *Mamm* gets here, I'll have her call the midwife. And don't worry, she'll stay in the room with me, so you don't have to worry about helping deliver a *boppli*."

He crouched down and held her hands. "Are you okay?"

Shrugging, she nodded. "I wondered a couple of times today if I was having back labor. Figured I'd find out soon enough if it wasn't. Now, don't worry. I have very easy deliveries."

The oven timer buzzed. Jacob turned it off and used potholders to get the roast out and place it on top of the stove. He inhaled the delicious aroma and turned back to Rebecca, frowning as he watched her rub her swollen abdomen.

"Should I make you something to eat?" he asked her, feeling clueless.

She shook her head. "Can't eat now that I'm in labor."

The front door opened. "*Mamm? Grossmudder* isn't home."

Rebecca waved a hand at the refrigerator. "Jacob, the midwife's number is there under the magnet. She needs to be called."

"*Schur.* First, let's get you up to bed." He held out his hand and helped her to her feet.

"The *kinner* need supper," she protested.

There was something he could do to help. He could feed his sister's children. He didn't have to feel helpless.

"I'll do it. After you lie down." He turned to the children. "I'll be right back."

"My labors have been getting shorter," she told him as he helped her up the stairs, his arm around her waist. "I figure if I have another couple *kinner*, it'll take no time at all to deliver."

He felt faintly sick. "Rebecca?"

"*Ya?*"

"Shut up. You're scaring me."

She laughed and walked into her room, sinking down on the bed. "One thing you can do for me."

"Anything but deliver a *boppli*."

"Help me with my shoes?"

"Of course."

"I haven't seen my ankles in months," she told him as he drew off her shoes and covered her with a quilt.

"They're still there."

"Ha ha."

When he walked back into the kitchen, he warned the children to stay away from the stove—and the coffee cake—and went to call the midwife. She promised she'd be right over.

He got the children to wash their hands, then with questioning found out their supper routine. One child set the table, another poured glasses of water, a third helped fill a basket with bread and set out butter and spreads. The littlest put a paper napkin on each plate and then climbed into her seat and waited patiently.

The midwife walked in, said a quick hello to everyone, then hurried up the stairs.

Jacob carved the roast and placed it on a serving plate, spooning potatoes, carrots, parsnips, and celery around it. He sat in his brother-in-law's seat, and they said a prayer in thanksgiving for their meal. Then he suggested that they all pray for their *mamm* and the *boppli*.

"They're going to be *allrecht*, aren't they, *Onkel* Jacob?"

He nodded. "God is always watching over us." He prayed silently that all would be well.

There was no loud talking like before as the children passed bowls and filled plates and began eating. Jacob helped Lizzie put a small amount of everything on her plate. None of the children whined about eating something they didn't like. He knew his sister insisted eating what was served was part of being grateful for God's bounty.

The plates cleared, the children looked expectantly at the coffee cake that had been promised for dessert.

"Maybe you should wait and have it in the morning for breakfast," he suggested tongue-in-cheek.

"We want it now," Luke said. "Please," he added as an afterthought.

"But it's to eat with coffee," he teased them.

"I like coffee," Lizzie piped up so loud her mother probably heard her upstairs.

They all laughed. "You don't drink coffee," Jacob told her.

"But I'd like it," she said in a hopeful voice.

Jacob got a knife and cut the cake into small squares, secretly pleased that he'd made something they were looking forward to.

The cake was immediately stuffed into mouths and crumbles of cinnamon sugar decorated their faces.

"It's very good," Luke said, and each of them nodded.

They looked eagerly at the pan. He glanced at it. There was enough left for another small serving for each of them. None for their mother, but she was rather busy right now.

"Okay, one more piece," he said, cutting squares. "I guess we can consider it a kind of birthday celebration, since a new *bruder* or *schwesder* is arriving tonight."

The front door opened just then, and his brother-in-law and oldest nephew rushed into the room.

"Am I in time?" Saul asked, sounding out of breath.

"I don't know," Jacob told him, wiping cinnamon sugar off Lizzie's chin. "The midwife's in with her. I'm just grateful I didn't have to go in there." He shuddered.

"I'd better get upstairs." Saul took the stairs two at a time.

Jacob fixed a plate for his oldest nephew and settled him at the table to eat it. He wrapped another plate for Saul and put it in the refrigerator. The table was cleared, and the two oldest girls washed the dishes. Jacob swept the floor and then took out the trash.

"What next?" he asked.

"Baths. I help *Mamm* with giving baths," his oldest niece said.

His sister's house ran like a well-oiled machine, Jacob couldn't help thinking.

He glanced at the staircase. His brother-in-law's question made him wonder if he should have asked if the midwife needed anything. Dragging his feet a little—he was a single *mann*, after all, so how could anyone expect him to think of such a thing?—he went up the stairs and knocked on the master bedroom door.

The midwife opened the door. Jacob remembered that his mother had told him she had delivered him and all his siblings.

"Can I get you anything?" he asked her. "Do Rebecca or Saul need anything?"

"Why, what a sweet boy you are," she said, beaming. She rubbed at her forehead with the back of her hand. "I was just about to come down for a cup of tea while Saul sits with Rebecca."

She walked downstairs with him and sat at the big table while he fixed her a cup of tea and placed the last piece of coffee cake before her.

"I can fix you a sandwich if you're hungry."

"*Nee*, I'm fine. So you're taking care of the *kinner*, are you?"

"They about did me in," he admitted with a grin. "But please don't tell Rebecca. She'd never let me hear the end of it."

"You're just not used to it," she told him as she sipped her tea. "Once you have your own, it'll be easier."

The front door opened, then closed. "I'm here!" his mother called out. She rushed into the kitchen. "I came as soon as I heard."

"Where have—" Jacob started to ask, and then he caught himself. "You weren't home."

His mother nodded. "Has she had the *kind* yet?"

The midwife shook her head. "I think it'll be another hour or so."

"You're usually right. I'll go on up."

The midwife followed her a short while later, and Jacob listened to the quiet. It was a different kind of quiet than at his house, he mused and smiled at such a fanciful thought.

He glanced at the clock. Time had flown. It was after ten. When he'd first realized that he'd need to stay until Saul got home, he'd unhitched his buggy and put his horse into an empty stall in the barn. Luke had gone out and fed him after supper. The best thing would be to sleep on the sofa. Travel at night in a buggy wasn't the safest thing, and besides, he suspected that if Rebecca's labor went much later, his brother-in-law might appreciate him getting the *kinner* ready for *schul* tomorrow morning.

So he locked up and returned to the kitchen and fixed a new pot of coffee. He sat at the table and listened to it percolate on the stove and soon found the rhythmic sound was lulling him to sleep. Telling himself he'd just rest his eyes for a moment, he put his head down on his arms on the table and waited for the coffee to brew.

Jacob woke to a sound he couldn't identify for a moment. The coffee had stopped perking, and it was twenty minutes later than when he'd last looked at the clock. He listened and then he heard it again.

The thin, reedy sound of a newborn echoed down the stairs. He'd never been this near to a baby being born . . . a few times he'd held a niece or nephew a few hours after birth. But he'd never been in the same house, heard the first cries. The sound filled him with awe.

He thanked God for the sound of new life entering the world, one he had a blood connection with. One day this new *kind* would play with his other nieces and nephews, exhaust him with playing as the *kinner* had done tonight. Maybe play with one of his own *kinner* on his farm.

He sat back and praised His creation.

∼୧ඛ

The minutes ticked by like hours.

The directions had said the test would only take a few minutes, but time seemed to stretch out. Finally, the bathroom door opened.

"It's negative." Jamie sagged against the doorjamb.

Mary Katherine let out the breath she hadn't realized she'd been holding. "Are you okay?"

Jamie pushed her hair back from her forehead. "Yeah." She straightened and walked to the kitchen. "I need something to drink."

Mary Katherine hoped she didn't mean alcohol. When Jamie pulled a diet soda from the refrigerator, she was relieved.

"Want one?"

She shook her head. "I don't understand why you were throwing up."

"Must be stress," Jamie said. She took a long swallow of the soda. "My stomach's never handled it well. I guess I jumped to conclusions." She gave a short laugh. "Well, I wouldn't have if I hadn't let Robert talk me into bed that last night when he came over."

Sinking into a chair at the tiny kitchen table, she ran the cold can of soda across her forehead. "I might not have shown much intelligence in dating that guy, but I've learned my lesson. I'm not going through that kind of scare again."

"I wish you wouldn't talk like that," Mary Katherine said quietly. "It bothers me when you say you don't think you're smart. You're in college—"

"And not doing so well right now."

"Well, if it was easy, everyone would go."

Jamie's eyes widened. "Wow. You don't mince words, do you?"

Mary Katherine shrugged. "I don't know how to play games with words. I'm Plain, remember?"

"You know, we wouldn't have become friends if we didn't have a lot in common." Jamie traced the condensation on the can with her finger. She laughed. "I mean, I know we come from two different worlds, you with your *kapp* and uptight hair and me with my purple streaks in my hair and clothes that are unusual for the most extreme *Englisch* person. But we share one thing, don't we?"

"What?"

"We've both had to struggle with self-esteem." She stared sadly at Mary Katherine.

"My self-esteem is fine." Mary Katherine stood.

"Uh-huh. Sure." Jamie yawned. "I am so beat."

"Maybe you can get some sleep tonight."

Jamie put her half-finished can of soda in the refrigerator and turned off the kitchen light. "Listen, since my roommate moved out, why don't you sleep in her room instead of on the sofa? There's some clean sheets in the bathroom closet."

"The sofa was fine last time."

"The bed'll be better this time," Jamie said over her shoulder. Then she turned and hugged Mary Katherine, surprising her. "Thanks for being such a good friend."

Mary Katherine shrugged. "No biggie," she said, using one of Jamie's favorite expressions.

"It's a very big deal." Jamie stood back. "Listen, I was wondering if I could go with you to church this week? It's a church Sunday, right? I mean, you keep saying I'm welcome to come."

"You are."

Jamie walked over to the mirror that hung on the wall near the front door. She fluffed at the purple streaks. "I'll tone this down a little. Wouldn't want to give your bishop a stroke if he stops by."

She might be restless and unsure if she wanted to stay in her community sometimes, but in her worst moments, Mary Katherine didn't wish a stroke on anyone. "*Danki*," she said with a straight face. "You wouldn't want that on your conscience."

⁂

Everyone was polite. It wasn't the first time an *Englischer* guest had shown up at church, after all.

But Mary Katherine noticed how many glances were directed toward her friend. She hid her smile as she watched the little girl who looked to be about four who was sitting on her mother's lap a few seats away. The child's eyes were wide as she sucked on her thumb and stared at Jamie.

"Imagine if I hadn't covered up the purple," Jamie whispered before the service started.

"I think she's fascinated because your hair is so curly," Mary Katherine whispered.

Jamie shifted, looking like she was already uncomfortable. "I didn't count on the seats being this hard."

"Aren't they the same everywhere?"

"How would I know? I'm not in church often." She glanced around. "I guess since yours is held in a home, somehow I thought there'd be more comfortable chairs."

"They don't have enough recliners," Mary Katherine told her tongue-in-cheek.

Jamie rolled her eyes and elbowed her. But there was laughter in her eyes. Mary Katherine was glad to see her friend in a better mood after the tension of thinking she was pregnant.

"Three hours, huh?"

Mary Katherine looked her in the eye. "*Ya*," she drawled.

Because she had a guest, Mary Katherine found herself seeing the service through her eyes. She didn't know what an *Englisch* service was like—well, she knew one thing. They were led by a church official, whereas here, members of the congregation—lay ministers—spoke. Today, one of them talked about his understanding of the book of Luke.

She watched Jamie frown in concentration as part of the service was delivered in High German. Translating wasn't an option—even if she whispered, it could disturb those around them.

Then she realized that Jamie was looking around. When she looked at her, eyebrows raised, her friend had the grace to blush. It was her guess that Jamie was curious as to where Ben was.

"I made it," Jamie said with some pride when the service was over. She watched as the men and boys began turning the benches around and into tables. "What's going on?"

"We have a snack before everyone heads home."

Jamie grinned. "Cool. Sometimes they have a potluck at a church I attend in town."

"I should go help with the food. You don't have to . . ." she trailed off. "Maybe you want to go look for a certain person."

"I'm sure Jacob will come say 'hi' if he's here."

"Don't even try to tell me you're looking for Jacob," Mary Katherine said dryly. With that, she left her friend and joined the women in the kitchen.

Her mother was there, slicing a loaf of bread. She looked even quieter and paler than she had the last time Mary Katherine had seen her.

"Are you all right? You look tired."

"I'm fine."

For some reason, Mary Katherine didn't think so. As much as she didn't want to talk to him, she decided to go in search of her father. He was standing talking with some other men when she found him on the front porch, and he finished his conversation before he left them and walked toward her.

"*Mamm* doesn't look well."

"It's just her arthritis. She's getting old. We all are." He started to move away, but she shook her head. "What?" He sounded irritable with her.

"I'm worried about her."

He frowned. "Then maybe you should stop by and help her sometimes."

Mary Katherine stiffened. "You know I work six days a week."

"Most of us do," he said.

She wanted to say that he made it difficult for her to want to go to the house when he was there. But she'd been raised to be respectful to her parents. It was too deeply ingrained in her, no matter how he behaved.

Turning, she walked back into the house and started toward the kitchen. Jamie walked toward her carrying a slice of bread covered with Amish peanut butter.

"This is amazing," she said, licking her lips. "Who came up with the idea of putting marshmallow crème in peanut butter?"

Mary Katherine managed a laugh. "I don't know. But it's good, isn't it?"

"You mean it's *gut*," Jamie said, using the Pennsylvania *Dietsch* pronunciation. She grinned.

Naomi came rushing up to her. "Mary Katherine, your mother's ill."

"Go get my father," she said as she ran into the kitchen.

Leah and Anna were gathered around her mother in the kitchen. Her face was white, and she was pressing her hand against her chest.

"Pain in my—chest," she said with effort.

"Someone call 911," Mary Katherine called over her shoulder.

"*Nee*, I don't need that!" her mother insisted, but her voice was weak. "No fuss!"

"When are you going to think you're worth the trouble?" Leah asked quietly. "What if you're having a heart attack?"

"Women don't—" Miriam broke off, then fought to continue, "women don't have heart attacks."

Leah muttered beneath her breath. "You're wrong. We need to get you to the hospital."

Miriam closed her eyes and then opened them. "Oh, *allrecht*," she said. "Isaac is going to think it was a waste of time. And money."

"Never mind about *Dat*," Mary Katherine said firmly.

"How dare you talk about me that way," he thundered behind her. "Leave us!"

"Fine," said Mary Katherine. She rushed past him, blinking back sudden tears.

Someone grasped her arms. "Mary Katherine?"

She blinked. "Jacob! *Mamm's* sick."

There was a commotion at the door what seemed like hours later. "The paramedics are here. Come on, let's go out on the porch while they take care of her. Come on."

He led her outside to a chair, made her sit, and knelt in front of her, holding out a clean handkerchief. "Calm down. They're taking care of her. I'll take you to the hospital. We'll go as soon as—" he stopped as the door opened and the paramedics pushed a gurney with Miriam on it onto the porch. Mary Katherine's father walked alongside it, carrying his wife's coat and purse.

"Let me get your coat and we'll follow," Jacob told her. "I'll be right back."

∽✑∾

Jacob sat with Mary Katherine in the hospital waiting room. Her mother had gotten help just in time—the paramedics said her heart had stopped in the ambulance, but they'd gotten it restarted. One of them had told Mary Katherine that her father had gone white and not spoken the rest of the ride. A surgeon had been waiting to perform a bypass when her mother arrived.

Jacob watched Mary Katherine, and with every hour that passed, she seemed to be withdrawing deeper inside herself right in front of him. He hated to see the change from the happy, confident young woman she'd been before her mother had suddenly become ill.

He might have blamed it all on her mother's current hospitalization. But he'd noticed Mary Katherine tensing when her father entered the surgical waiting room . . . then it was almost as if a shadow came over her, and she seemed to shrink inside of herself. He didn't know exactly why, but he had the suspicion that more was going on here than he understood. The doctor stuck his head in the door and took her father and grandmother with him to talk to them. When Leah returned, she sat and began telling Mary Katherine how her mother was doing. Jacob excused himself to walk to the cafeteria to get them all coffee.

"Jacob! Wait!"

He turned and saw Naomi and Anna coming down the hall. "They won't let us see *Aenti* Miriam tonight, just *Onkel* Isaac and Grandmother, maybe Mary Katherine. We're going to go call a driver to take us home and come back tomorrow."

Jacob wasn't waiting to see Miriam, and he certainly would have preferred not being watched by Isaac as they sat in the waiting room. But he wanted to be there for Mary Katherine.

They got coffee for everyone and carried it back to the waiting room. Leah accepted hers gratefully and urged a cup on Mary Katherine.

A nurse appeared and told Isaac that he could see his wife.

"We'll see if the doctor will allow you to sit with her for a few minutes later on," she told Mary Katherine.

Leah leaned forward and squeezed Mary Katherine's hand. "I know you're worried. But it's in God's hand, *liebschen*."

Mary Katherine wrapped her arms around her grandmother. "I'm so sorry, I'm just thinking about myself. She's my mother, but she's your daughter."

"It's *allrecht*," Leah murmured, rocking her granddaughter and patting her back. Her eyes met Jacob's.

"Why don't you and Jacob go take a walk and stretch your legs?" she suggested. "It's going to be hours before we're allowed to see your *mamm*."

Mary Katherine started to object, but then she looked at Jacob, searching his face for something.

He didn't know what to say, so he just held out his hand. "Come, we'll just take a short walk. Maybe get something to eat. Leah will make sure you're called if you're needed."

She might have turned him down, but Leah briskly steered her toward Jacob, like a mother bird might push a chick from the nest.

They walked past the nurse's station, past rooms of patients, and got into the elevator. It stopped at the maternity floor, and the doors opened. A nurse pushed a woman in a wheelchair inside. She held a newborn in her arms, something all the occupants immediately noticed. A bunch of balloons was tied to one armrest. The woman reached out to grab them back, then giggled when they floated toward the doors as they started to close.

Mary Katherine glanced at the baby and smiled, then turned to Jacob. "I'm sorry, I forgot to congratulate you on being an *onkel* again. Someone told me at church."

He smiled. "It was quite an exciting evening. I'd never been around Rebecca or my sisters before when they had their *boppli*—not that I was in the room when she had it—" he shuddered as the elevator stopped at the main floor and they stepped off.

"Just like a *mann*," she teased. "What are you going to do when your wife is having your baby?"

"That'll be different," he said, indicating that they should proceed down the corridor.

"Why?"

"Well, first, it won't be my *sister*," he told her. "And who wouldn't want to be there together when your child is born?"

Her steps faltered, and he stopped, wondering if he'd said something too personal. She cleared her throat and looked around. "Where are we going?"

"We haven't eaten since breakfast. Neither of us got a snack at church. I thought we could have something to eat and then go back up and check on your mother."

He could see that she was torn but out of consideration to him agreed. As they walked down the line, she chose a salad, but he'd known her for years and knew what she liked, so he added a chicken salad sandwich to her tray.

"You don't know when you'll get a chance to eat again," he told her when she protested. He added a carton of milk to her tray at the drink station.

They sat at a small table in a corner of the cafeteria. The place was nearly empty. Two women in scrubs at a nearby table ate their meals silently, looking too tired to talk. A woman with a fussy toddler calmed him by scattering a breakfast cereal on her tray and letting him pick the rings up and stuff them into his mouth. She sipped from an extra-large cup of coffee and stifled a yawn.

"It's really nice of you to stay with us—"

"It's what a friend does," he said, waving away her thanks. "Besides, where else could I get a meal like this?"

She looked at the beef cubes and limp noodles on his plate and couldn't help laughing. "Yes, that's worth all your trouble."

"You are," he said quietly. "Now eat. You'll need to keep your strength up."

༄

A slight noise woke Mary Katherine.

She blinked, not sure what had awakened her. Then she realized that her mother's eyes were open and she was looking around the room. Her head turned on the pillow, and she smiled weakly.

"Cold. What day is it?" she asked, shifting in her bed.

"Tuesday." Mary Katherine stood to unfold the extra blanket at the foot of the bed and spread it over her mother.

"So tired."

"I thought you'd never wake up," Mary Katherine said, biting her bottom lip to keep from crying. "You'd come to for a while and then go back to sleep." No matter what the nurses had said about this being normal post-surgery, Mary Katherine had worried.

Her mother patted her hand. "I'm *allrecht*."

Mary Katherine saw her look around the room. "Why aren't you asking where *Dat* is?"

"I can't imagine he'd want to sit around here," her mother told her. But her tone held no censure.

"If we'd listened to him, you wouldn't be here," she blurted out, her hands clenching at her sides.

"Now, Mary Katherine—"

She took a deep breath and forced herself to relax her hands. "I'm sorry," she said quickly. "I don't want to get you upset."

"It's my own fault. I ignored how I was feeling. I knew something was wrong."

When she reached for the cup of water on the tray next to her bed, Mary Katherine moved quickly to help her.

"You can't blame him. He never gets sick, so he doesn't understand it when others do."

"Well, you're not going to be able to keep to that schedule he's so fond of when you get back home."

"We'll manage."

Mary Katherine didn't like how wan she looked. "Are you hungry?"

Her mother shook her head. "Just tired." She closed her eyes, then opened them. "Just so tired."

"Rest, then. I'll be right here."

"You should go home," her mother began.

She was fighting a losing battle to keep her eyes open. Mary Katherine watched as she lost the battle, and slept.

Sinking back down into the chair she'd occupied since her mother had been moved to a regular room, Mary Katherine felt exhaustion steal over her.

Something moved at the periphery of her vision. Her grandmother stood in the doorway, gesturing at her. Getting up, she tiptoed over to the door.

"How is she?"

"She woke up a little while ago, but then she went back to sleep."

Her grandmother held up a brown paper bag. "I brought you lunch." She threaded her arm through Mary Katherine's and pulled her out of the room. "*Kumm*, let's go sit outside and eat. You've been cooped up here for days."

They went outside on a small patio and sat at a table, but instead of taking the food from the bag, her grandmother reached across it and took Mary Katherine's hand.

"She's going to be fine, *liebschen*," her grandmother said. "You need to come home and get some rest."

"I thought I was going to lose her," Mary Katherine said, tears welling in her eyes. "I feel so guilty. If I'd gone by to see her more often, I might have noticed that she wasn't well. But he—" she stopped.

"Your *dat* didn't make it easy, did he?" She sighed. "But Miriam has to take some of the blame, too. She never spoke up. She made excuses for him every time we talked. Even when she knew you were moving out, she wouldn't speak up and tell him she thought he was being too stern with you."

She shook her head. "He's the head of the house as a *mann* should be, but I don't believe that *God* ever meant for women to be treated the way he treats his wife and daughter. Your grandfather never behaved like that at all."

"'Browbeaten,'" Mary Katherine said. "Jamie used that word when we talked about our fathers sometime back."

Leah sighed, picked up the bag, and started withdrawing items. "You see, it's not just Amish fathers who can be too stern with their daughters. Jamie has told you that her father is the same way. If I'd told you that *Englisch* fathers did this, you might never have believed me."

"I always believe you," Mary Katherine told her staunchly.

"Then you will believe what I tell you next," she said, meeting her granddaughter's eyes. "You know what you need to do."

Mary Katherine rested her elbows on the table and put her forehead in her hands. "Yes."

Leah patted her back. "It's the right thing to do. 'Honor thy father and mother, which is the first commandment with promise.'"

She handed Mary Katherine a paper-wrapped sandwich, a bag of potato chips, and a can of her favorite soda. When she pulled out a cookie the size of a saucer, Mary Katherine couldn't help laughing.

"You even brought the big chocolate chip cookie," she said, shaking her head.

"I was prepared to bribe you," her grandmother told her, reaching over to hug her. "I didn't think it'd take the big cookie, but I wasn't taking any chances. Shall we bless our food?"

Mary Katherine looked at the spread that her grandmother had brought to her, remembering the things she loved. She thought about how her grandmother had brought up a difficult subject but had not tried to lecture her or tell her what she should do. And she felt regret.

"I haven't thought much about how you feel," she said, her eyes welling with tears again. "I thought about losing my *mamm*, but it would be even more awful if you lost a child."

Leah patted her hand. "You thought of your mother and that's as it should be. I'm fine."

"I'm missing work—"

"You're not to think of that," she said quickly. "Naomi and Anna are covering for you and everything is going well."

"The doctor says he thinks *Mamm* can go home soon," Mary Katherine said as she unwrapped her sandwich. "I'm not looking forward to moving back in, but it'll just be for a short time."

When her grandmother made a slight movement of distress, Mary Katherine's heart sank. Sure enough, when she looked up, she saw her father's stiff back as he turned and walked away.

"He heard me," she whispered.

Her grandmother nodded. "I'd have told you if I'd seen him in time." She sighed. "Well, they say that eavesdroppers never hear good of themselves. Why don't you go talk to him, and I'll wait for you?"

Mary Katherine wrapped up her sandwich and got up. With feet that felt like lead, she went to find him.

⁓❧⁓

To her surprise, her father wasn't in her mother's room.

"I sent him out to see you and *Mamm*," Miriam told her. "Did you miss him?"

Mary Katherine nodded but decided her mother didn't need any details.

"Maybe you can catch him. He was just here a few minutes ago."

"We'll see each other tomorrow."

Miriam straightened her covers. "I can't wait to get home. It'll be good to sleep in my own bed, see my garden."

"You can't work in it for a while."

"Everything will die if it's not tended," Miriam said, her fingers becoming agitated on the covers. "I need to water the plants and—"

"I'll take care of it until you can."

"But you work and you live—"

"I'm going to come and stay with you for a while until you feel better."

Relief swept across her mother's face but was just as swiftly gone. "Oh, how can you do that? You and your *dat* don't get along . . ." she trailed off, looking worried.

"We'll manage." Mary Katherine didn't know how, but that was her concern, her problem.

"Listen, I'm going to go back out and finish my lunch with Grandmother. Do you need anything before I go?"

Miriam shook her head. "Would you mind if I said I want to take a nap? I'm feeling really tired."

"It's time you said what you need," Mary Katherine told her. She leaned down and kissed her mother's cheek. "Maybe I'll go back to the shop with *Grossmudder* for a few hours and see you later this afternoon?"

"Tomorrow," Miriam said with more firmness. "Tell *Mamm* I said I'll see you both tomorrow when I get to go home."

"Bossy lady," she teased. "Sweet dreams."

❧

It felt so good to be back at the shop. Mary Katherine walked into the space filled with brightly colored fabrics and crafts and just stood for a moment, absorbing it.

Naomi and Anna rushed at her, hugging her and asking rapid-fire questions about her mother.

She absorbed their love and their chatter, so grateful for their warmth and concern.

"I'm fine, and *Mamm*'s doing better and getting out tomorrow," she said, answering their first two questions. She pulled off her coat and headed for the back room to hang it and her purse up.

Then she turned back to Naomi and Anna. "And I'm going to move back into my parents' house for a while."

She heard disbelieving squeaks out of her cousins.

"Grandmother! You can't let her do this!" Anna wailed.

Leah walked into the room and hung up her things. "She needs to take care of her mother. You'd do the same if it was your mother."

"But it means she has to be around her father again!" Anna shivered.

Secretly, Mary Katherine agreed. But what could she do? The only way she could care for her mother was to be in her house, and that was where her father lived . . .

"It'll be all right," she said, trying to convince herself. "It's only for a short time."

They shared their afternoon cup of tea, the "Back in 10 Minutes" sign on the locked front door of the shop guaranteeing an uninterrupted break. It was a welcome one after the last few days of tension at the hospital.

"You've been so happy since you moved in with *Grossmudder*," Naomi said quietly, her eyes filled with compassion.

"You won't talk about why you were so miserable," Anna said, looking stormy rather than compassionate. "That tells me that it was really bad. And *Onkel* Isaac barely looks at you when he comes here to see *Grossmudder*."

"It doesn't matter. It's just for a little while." She turned the mug in her hands around and around. "*Mamm* needs someone to take care of her."

"But your father is—"

"No!" Mary Katherine said sharply. "He didn't think she was sick up until the time they carried her out of there in an ambulance."

"But now that he's seen that he was wrong, he'll be better. He'll take good care of her."

Mary Katherine shook her head. "I can't take that chance." She looked into the tea she hadn't touched, then up at her grandmother.

"We'll all help," Leah said firmly. "Bring meals, help with chores."

"That's understood," Naomi said. "And her friends will, too."

"She hasn't got many friends. Not many people wanted to be around *Dat*."

She got up, went out into the shop, and turned the sign to "Open" before unlocking the door. Straightening displays helped her feel calmer, but it was only when she sat at her loom that she felt she could really breathe for the first time since her mother fell ill.

Taking up her shuttle, she began weaving the pattern she'd left days ago . . . what felt like years ago. And barely noticed the tears slipping down her cheeks.

⟋⟍

Bright and early the next morning, Mary Katherine let herself into her parents' house. She called out to her father just in case but knew that he'd gone to the hospital with her grandmother.

The living room was still fairly neat. There were newspapers next to her father's favorite chair that he'd obviously read and then left for someone else to pick up. Sighing, she did so on the way into the kitchen.

Her breath caught when she saw the kitchen. She should have expected it, but still . . . didn't a grown man know how to wash a dish? Scrub a pot? Ugh! Wipe up after a spill in the refrigerator?

She went upstairs to put her things in her old room and found that nothing had been changed. After she'd unpacked, she walked into her parents' room. It didn't feel entirely comfortable to be in it, but she wanted to make sure it wasn't a mess like the kitchen downstairs. The bed wasn't made. She might have fainted if it was, she told herself. On the way to the clothes hamper she picked up her father's trousers, shirts, and socks.

No wonder her mother looked tired so often. Mary Katherine had forgotten how much her mother did for her father—she was obviously picking up after him like he was a small *kind*.

After a little tidying up of the bedroom and bathroom, she went downstairs and searched through the refrigerator and freezer to find something to cook for dinner. Her mother might be ready for some home cooking after hospital food. And she had no idea how much she might have to do for her mother when she first came home, so making sure a meal was cooked ahead of time was best.

She found a frozen container of vegetable soup, put the contents in a pot on the stove, set the flame low, and covered it. It wouldn't take long to thaw and then warm. Using a recipe from the wooden box on the countertop, she mixed a pan of cornbread and set it in the oven to bake. Thinking ahead to the next meal—especially since it seemed everything was frozen, she put a package of pork chops out to thaw.

A glance at the clock had her frowning. Where were they? Had the doctor decided her mother needed to stay longer? She walked into the living room and looked out the window, but there was no sign of her parents and grandmother.

Turning back, she had a thought as she stared at the sofa. Maybe she should put a blanket and pillow on it for her mother to rest before dinner. Nodding, she looked in the linen closet and found a quilt and an extra pillow. There, that looked welcoming, she thought. While she didn't think she'd ever seen her mother lie down in the daytime, now was the time to start since she was recuperating.

She heard the front door open and rushed into the living room. Her grandmother was helping Miriam inside.

"I got worried they decided to keep you another day," she said. After giving her mother a big hug, Mary Katherine began unbuttoning her coat.

Her mother laughed and batted at her hands. "I'm not a child."

Mary Katherine's hands stilled on the button. "No, you're not," she said seriously as she blinked hard to keep from crying. "But you'll let me take care of you a little, won't you?"

"Now, now," her mother said, holding Mary Katherine's face in her hands. "I'm going to be just fine."

"Doc says so," her father said brusquely as he shut the front door and headed for the kitchen, not looking at Mary Katherine. "Did you make some coffee?"

Mary Katherine opened her mouth to make a retort but caught the warning look in her grandmother's eyes.

"I wasn't sure when I should start it," she said in a milder tone than she might have if her grandmother hadn't given her the look. "Here, sit on the sofa for a minute, *Mamm*, and I'll make the coffee."

She took her grandmother's and mother's coats and hung them on pegs in the kitchen. Her father was opening the oven door and peering inside.

"Be careful, don't—" she began but he was already doing what she had feared he would do—letting the door slam shut.

Sighing, she carried the percolator over to the sink to fill it with water. Hopefully, the cornbread wouldn't collapse the way a cake might. If it did, she supposed she'd have to find some regular bread or crackers to go with the soup.

"I'm warming up *Mamm's* vegetable beef soup for dinner," she said as she placed the percolator on top of the stove.

He merely grunted and headed for the bathroom.

Shaking her head, Mary Katherine couldn't help thinking how little things had changed. She returned to the living room and was a little relieved to see her mother lying on the sofa, the quilt draped over her knees, her back propped up with pillows. Her color was better than it had been at the hospital, although it still concerned Mary Katherine.

"Are you hungry? I'm warming up some of your vegetable soup," she told her mother. "And the cornbread is almost done."

"That sounds *wunderbaar*," her mother said.

"Then a nap," Leah said firmly. "And there'll be no arguing."

"I won't be arguing today," her mother said. "I'm feeling weak as a kitten."

The back door slammed, and her father came into the room a few minutes later. He held a mug of coffee. "Dinner ready yet?"

The oven timer went off.

"Good timing," Leah said brightly, getting to her feet and helping her daughter to hers. "I'm hungry. Let's go eat."

Mary Katherine followed them into the kitchen. While her father had barely acknowledged her presence, maybe this wouldn't be so bad.

But she couldn't help a feeling of dread as everyone settled around the table and she thought about the time when her grandmother would be leaving them that evening.

᪐

Jacob stood on the porch of Mary Katherine's house—well, the house of her parents—holding a casserole.

He felt a little silly. He didn't know any Amish man who'd ever done such a thing. Men helped each other with carpentry, with plowing or harvesting.

Not with a casserole when someone had been in the hospital.

What was next? He'd be attending a quilting or a social visit of some kind? But this was the perfect excuse to stop by and see how Miriam was doing.

Well, if he was honest with himself, he was here to see Mary Katherine, not her mother. He hadn't seen her for more than a week—not since her mother had been admitted into the hospital.

Mary Katherine opened the door, and he watched her smile bloom on her face.

"*Gut-n-owed.*"

"*Gut-n-owed.*"

"I brought this." He held out the casserole. "It's just a tuna casserole."

"I love tuna casserole."

"Mary Katherine, who is it?"

The brusque voice of her father made her flinch and her smile fade.

"It's Jacob," she called back into the house.

Her father came out of the kitchen and regarded Jacob. "Thank your *mamm* for the food."

"Actually, I made it, not my mother."

Her father frowned at Jacob. "*You* made it?"

Jacob nodded.

"Men don't cook."

Shrugging, Jacob held out the casserole. "Well, I'm learning. It isn't fair to expect my sisters or my mother to be making all my meals."

Her father grunted and accepted the casserole. "A man your age should be married and have a *fraa* to cook for him."

Jacob glanced at Mary Katherine and saw her trying not to grin.

"Yes, well, I don't think a man should get married to have someone cook for him."

"Mary Katherine, pour your friend a cup of *kaffe*," he said as he turned to carry the casserole into the kitchen.

She lifted her brows at him, and Jacob nodded. "*Danki*, I'd love one." He took off his coat and hat as he walked, and she took them from him to hang them up.

The scent of coffee filled the kitchen. It smelled a lot better than what he brewed. He'd have to get her recipe.

He bit back a chuckle. Now he sounded like a *fraa*, thinking about asking for a recipe. Taking a seat at the table, he watched Isaac pull a fork from the silverware drawer, then peel back the foil covering the casserole. He scooped up a bite, put it into his mouth, and chewed. Swallowing, he gave Jacob a disbelieving look.

"How is it?" Jacob asked him.

Isaac shrugged. "Well, I wouldn't toss it to the pigs."

"High praise indeed," Jacob told him dryly.

They looked to the stairs when they heard them creak as Miriam descended.

"Jacob! What a nice surprise. Did you come to join us for supper?"

"He came *with* supper, *Mamm*."

"I see," she said as she walked into the room. She stopped next to her husband. "Looks like you want supper early."

Jacob rose and pulled out a chair for her. She still looked too pale to him.

Isaac glanced at the clock and nodded. "Sounds *gut* to me. I don't see anything else started."

Mary Katherine started to say something and then stopped. She took the casserole and put it on the top of the stove, covering it again with foil to keep it warm. Then she poured three cups of coffee and set them before her parents and Jacob.

"I'll just put together the rest of the meal. It won't take any time."

Jacob watched her move around the kitchen, opening canned pickled vegetables and tomatoes from her mother's garden. She dumped two big jars of peaches in a baking dish, mixed up a batter and poured it over the top of the peaches, and then set the mixture in the oven to bake.

Isaac shifted in his chair and seemed to glare at his daughter. "What's taking so long?"

Mary Katherine set a plate of sliced, just-baked bread on the table. "Everything's ready. I'll get some plates."

Miriam pushed back from the table. "I can help—"

"Absolutely not," Jacob said.

"But—"

He put a gentle hand on her shoulder to stop her as he got to his feet. Reaching into a cupboard, he withdrew four plates and set them on the table.

"You still remember where things are stored from eating with us years ago," Miriam said with a fond smile.

Nodding, he reached into the silverware drawer for forks, knives, and spoons. "You made some wonderful meals. I'd have been here every night if my own *mamm* hadn't said I was making a pest of myself."

Miriam's expression turned dreamy. "I always wondered if you and—"

She pressed a hand to her chest as a pan clattered on top of the stove.

Everyone looked at Mary Katherine. Her face red, she picked up an empty metal baking pan from the floor. "Sorry."

Seating herself at the table, she served the casserole. Jacob watched for her reaction as she put a forkful of the casserole in her mouth. She liked it—he could tell from the way her eyes half-closed as she chewed appreciatively.

"The recipe called for crushed potato chips on top, but I didn't have any so I used crushed cracker crumbs."

"Imagine having a *mann* who can cook," mused Miriam as she helped herself to a slice of bread. "Imagine how nice it'd be to have someone to help occasionally."

"It's a woman's job to cook," Isaac muttered, spooning up another healthy serving of casserole.

"But a wife sometimes helps in the fields, and you always said that's a *mann's* job," Mary Katherine pointed out.

He shot her a look Jacob would swear could have burned a hole in her. "No smart mouth from you."

Finished with his meal, he let his fork drop to his plate. "Is the dessert done yet?"

"No, there's a few more minutes left."

"Your mother would have had it ready," he said, scooting back from the table and standing abruptly.

Mary Katherine flinched at the harsh sound of his chair being scraped back on the wooden floor.

"I'm going out to the barn," he told them. "Got to check on Ned's foreleg." He glanced at Jacob. "I'll be back in a few minutes."

Grabbing his jacket, he pulled it on and left them, slamming the door behind him.

The noise was as loud as a gunshot in the quiet room.

Jacob glanced furtively at Mary Katherine. She sat, pale with two spots of color burning on her cheeks. Her mother looked just as miserable.

What he'd just observed explained a lot about Mary Katherine, Jacob thought. He had another piece of the puzzle to understanding the complicated, conflicted woman that she was. He got up, brought the coffeepot to the table, and refilled their cups.

"Don't know what he was thinking, leaving me with two lovely ladies," Jacob said gallantly.

Mary Katherine gave a short laugh. "*Schur*, Jacob," she said, rising as the oven timer went off. "It's the peach cobbler that's not safe from your attentions."

11

*N*aomi, Anna, and her grandmother showed up the next afternoon.

When Mary Katherine opened the door, they stood smiling, their arms loaded with bags and boxes. And parted to show another visitor.

"Jamie!"

She grinned and threw her arms around Mary Katherine. "I asked if I could come along."

Glancing around, Jamie lowered her voice. "Thought we'd beard the lion in his den."

"You're safe. He's in the barn."

They crowded into the house.

"My, my, it's a party!" Miriam exclaimed from her seat on the sofa.

"I hope you're up to it," her mother told her, leaning down to kiss her cheek.

Naomi and Anna bent to kiss their aunt and carefully hug her.

"This is Jamie, Mary Katherine's friend," Leah said.

"*Ya*, I saw you at church that day I got sick."

Jamie shook her hand. "I'm glad you're feeling better."

"Someone's been taking very good care of me." Miriam pulled her shawl closer around her shoulders and smiled at Mary Katherine.

She patted her mother's shoulder. "How about we have some tea with whatever's in that bakery box?"

There was a chorus of agreement.

"Let me help you," Jamie said. "I feel like I haven't seen you in ages."

Maybe it was her imagination, but it seemed to Mary Katherine that there was an exchange of glances among the women.

"I wanted to talk to you alone," Jamie said without preamble as they entered the kitchen. "I hope it's all right with you."

Mary Katherine tilted her head and studied her friend standing there and chewing on a purple painted fingernail in a nervous gesture unlike her. "What's going on?"

"Well, I went by the shop to see you, and I caught them when they were really busy."

"That's good. There was a bit of a lull for a while."

"I love that place. You know that." She laughed nervously. "Sorry, I'm babbling."

"A bit. What's going on?"

"Well, I started helping this one customer. You know, I was telling her about your things while she was looking at them, and she bought two pillows. And a throw you made. Oh, and one of those adorable cupcake hats that Anna makes."

Jamie took a deep breath and blurted out, "So your grand-mother hired me."

"Hired you?"

She nodded. "Just for ten hours a week. Until you come back."

"Did you lose your job?"

Jamie shook her head. "Remember, they cut back my hours. So I was thinking about finding something, and before I could, it just happened."

"That's wonderful!"

"You're sure? You're okay with it? Really?"

Mary Katherine's heart went out to her friend. "You were worried? Why? I know you aren't trying to take my job."

Jamie threw her arms around her. "No! Never! I just love hanging there. It's such a cool place. I feel so creative when I'm there."

Standing back, Mary Katherine considered her words. "Why didn't we ever think of that?"

"Of what?" Jamie flung herself into a chair.

Going to the sink, she filled the teakettle, thinking hard. "You should talk to my grandmother—"

"Talk to your grandmother about what?"

She spun around to look at Leah, who'd walked into the kitchen. "You should have Jamie show you her portfolio from her classes. I think some of her things would be perfect for the shop."

"Didn't I tell you that she'd be fine with your helping at the shop?" Leah smiled at Jamie. "And yes, I'd love to see your portfolio."

The teakettle whistled. Mary Katherine took it off the flame and started filling cups.

"What's taking so long?" Anna, impatient as always, demanded. "We've been waiting and waiting!"

"It's been less than five minutes," Naomi pointed out dryly. "Here, let me carry those out to the living room. We're insisting on *Aenti* Miriam staying on the sofa."

"Longest time I've ever seen her sit down in her own home," Leah muttered. "Where is Isaac?"

"He went into town for supplies." Mary Katherine loaded the cups onto a tray and carried it out into the living room.

Her mother must have heard her. "They haven't had a single fight," she told Leah. "I'm proud of her."

Mary Katherine was carrying a bottle of Pepto-Bismol in the pocket of her dress . . . But she wasn't going to tell her mother that. She served her a cup of tea with a dollop of cream, just the way she liked it, and exchanged a look with her grandmother that said, "As if I'd fight with him around her."

Anna opened the bakery box and took out cream horns.

"You remembered my favorite from that little bakery near the shop!" Miriam exclaimed, taking the horn Anna placed on a plate and handed her. "This is worth getting sick for."

Leah looked over the tops of her glasses.

"Well, maybe not quite," Miriam admitted with a twinkle in her eyes. "But it's worth it to have Mary Katherine here."

She smiled at her mother but found herself dreading her father's return.

"So, tell me all the latest news," Miriam said, wiping the whipped cream from her lips with a napkin.

"You mean the gossip," Anna said mischievously. She leaned forward. "Naomi is seeing someone."

"Anna!"

Leah gave Anna a stern look. "Now, don't tease. You know that's private."

"Why's dating so secret?" Jamie asked, debating one of the little tea cakes Leah offered from another box. "I never understood that."

Mary Katherine lifted her shoulders and let them fall. "It's just our way." As much as she wanted to know, she tried to repress her questions.

Naomi shook her head. "If I don't tell you, Anna will drive me crazy," she said.

Anna sniffed, then laughed. "You're right."

"John has been coming around the shop," she told them. "John Zook." She smiled shyly. "Things have really been moving fast. We've seen each other every day for the past two weeks."

"Well, I'm away for just a little while and look how things change," Mary Katherine said. She looked—really looked—at her cousin. She'd never seen her so happy.

But every day?

She glanced at Anna and saw that her expression had sobered. Their eyes met. Anna nodded and frowned slightly.

Naomi was telling her aunt how John had brought her a carved wooden keepsake box for her birthday.

"That sounds expensive," Miriam told her. "Are you sure you should be accepting such expensive gifts from someone you're not even engaged to?"

Naomi bit her lip, glanced at her grandmother, then blurted out, "I don't think it'll be much longer. Before we're engaged, I mean. John said he got a crush on me the minute he came to the community six months ago. Now that we're seeing each other, well, he doesn't see any point in delaying."

"Delaying what?" Miriam asked, looking at her expectantly. "Delaying what?" she asked again when Naomi just blushed.

Mary Katherine stood. "I'm going to go boil some more water." She looked at Anna. "Maybe you can help me."

Anna laughed. "Like you need help boiling water?"

"You can bring the dishes into the kitchen," she told her, giving Anna a meaningful look.

Anna started to say something and then caught the drift. "Oh, okay." She picked up the dishes and followed Mary Katherine into the kitchen.

"Now," Mary Katherine said. "We barely know John. What do you think of him?"

Mary Katherine was beginning to feel like taking care of someone meant that you wore a path in the floor going to answer the front door.

"I could get that," her mother said as Mary Katherine rushed to the front door to keep her from doing just that.

When she opened it, all she could see was a big bunch of cut flowers. Then it lowered, and she saw Jacob smiling. "*Guder mariye.* These are for you."

"Me? You mean my mother."

He thrust them at her. "No, you."

"But we're just friends."

"Friends can give friends flowers."

She put a hand on her hip. "Who said?"

"Me." He continued to hold them out to her. "They're to celebrate spring. It's been a long winter, and the last couple of weeks haven't been easy for you."

"Mary Katherine? Who is it? Invite them in, it's cold outside."

Jacob stepped inside. "*Guder mariye,* Miriam. Good to see you again."

"*Kumm,* have some *kaffe.*"

He shook his head. "I have something to do first."

With that, he ducked out the door, and Mary Katherine shut it behind him. She looked out the window and watched him walk to his buggy. He reached in and withdrew a flowering bush and set it on the ground, then pulled out another and another. Mystified, she watched him carry them up to the house.

"What's he doing?"

She jumped. "You scared me!"

Miriam smiled. "What's he doing?" she repeated.

"I don't know."

They heard the clump of boots behind them. Mary Katherine turned and saw her father approaching. Her glance fell, and she saw that he'd tracked in mud from the back door. Honestly, couldn't the man wipe his feet? She couldn't believe how much extra work he made for her mother . . . well, for *her* the past couple of weeks, as she wouldn't let her mother do anything.

But she wasn't going to say anything if she had to bite holes in her tongue.

"What's he doing here?"

"I don't know."

"Is he courting you?" he asked her bluntly.

"Isaac! You know that's not our business."

He grunted and left the room.

Miriam watched him go, then turned to Mary Katherine. "Is he courting you?"

"*Mamm!*"

She laughed, and Mary Katherine felt a shaft of happiness shoot through her. It was the first time her mother had done so since she'd gotten sick . . . really, the first time Mary Katherine could remember in a very long time.

Maybe it hadn't been such a bad thing to come back here in spite of the way her father treated her.

"I'm going to go find out what he's up to." Mary Katherine went to the kitchen, got her shawl, then marched outside.

"What are you doing?"

"Figured I'd bring these for your mother and cheer her up. Might be hard for her to do her spring garden planting in the shape she's in."

Mary Katherine could only stare.

He looked up at her. "Pick your chin up off the ground," he told her dryly.

"I'm sorry," she said, walking down the stairs. "I'm just surprised. It's very nice of you."

"It'll do her good," he said quietly. "And the sooner she's better, the sooner you'll be out of there."

"I—" She didn't know what to say.

"But it's going to snow again, so we'll leave them on the porch for her until we can plant them."

"You're sure it's going to snow again?"

He lifted his head in the way so many of the farmers she knew did, taking in the sky and clouds and the smells on the air. "*Ya.*"

"Did you consult that weather site, too?"

Grinning, he nodded. "And some of the other farmers I know. Always best to consider all the sources. Why, I hear some people even pay attention to a groundhog. When I was in town one day, I saw a news show on television and everyone was watching a show about it. Name was Phil."

"Whose name?"

"The groundhog. He's from Punxsutawney."

"Did it talk?"

He laughed. "No, although the television surely had a lot of make-believe on it." He scooted a potted plant over a few feet. "Does this look good?"

She glanced over at the window and saw that her mother was still standing there looking out. "I think this is something *Mamm* should decide."

"True. Is she up to it?"

"I think it'll do her good," Mary Katherine told him. "She loves her garden."

"I know. I've often seen her working in it when I ride past."

"Be right back."

"What's going on?" her mother wanted to know when Mary Katherine came inside.

"You'll see." Mary Katherine fetched her mother's coat and scarf.

"Well, so I'm actually being allowed outside?"

Mary Katherine rolled her eyes. "I haven't held you prisoner." She helped her mother into her coat.

"You keep telling me to rest."

"Because you need to."

"You just buttoned me into my coat like I'm a little girl."

She stared at her mother for a long moment, and then she laughed. "I did, didn't I?" She hugged her. "I'm just glad that you're better. It was a scary time when you got sick."

Miriam patted her back. "I'm fine. I intend on being around for a long time."

"Good."

"Your *dat*, too."

Mary Katherine shivered. "Come on, let's go tell Jacob what you think of his gift."

Miriam oohed and aahed over the bushes as she walked around the porch. She pointed out that the pots of daffodils would look pretty nearer the door, and then she went inside, saying she'd make coffee.

"You lie down!" Mary Katherine called after her. She turned and found Jacob grinning at her. "What?"

"You don't think she's going to listen to you, do you?"

"Probably not," she grumbled.

"I see where you got your stubbornness."

"I'm nothing like her."

"No?"

"No," she said with conviction. "We're nothing alike. She won't speak up to my father about anything."

He looked at her for a long moment.

"What?"

He just continued to look at her.

"Go ahead and say it."

"Say what?"

"You obviously want to say something, and you won't." She folded her arms across her chest as much from feeling defensive as to keep warm.

Jacob stopped. "Look, I understand that you want to keep the peace while you're here so you don't upset your mother. And I'm all for being respectful of your parents. But that night I had supper with the three of you . . ." he trailed off, then he looked directly at her. "It wasn't right the way he was treating you, that's all. I'm sorry."

"You don't have to feel sorry for me," she told him stiffly, feeling her cheeks redden with embarrassment.

"I didn't say I felt sorry for you," he said, his tone sharp. "I was sorry that I didn't tell your father that it was wrong to treat you that way. I didn't want to upset your mother or make things worse. But it was wrong of me not to speak up. When we witness such an action, we have a responsibility to speak up."

Mary Katherine sat down on the stairs and wrapped her arms around her knees. "*Mamm* never spoke up," she said, staring at the ground. She lifted her gaze. "I know she loves me, but she never spoke up when he was treating me badly."

He came to sit on the stair beside her. "Did he ever hit you?"

She shook her head.

"But sometimes words hurt more than hands," he said quietly.

"I remember when I was a girl I thought you had the most wonderful parents." Realizing what she'd blurted out, she glanced over her shoulder to make sure her mother wasn't behind her, listening. "I've grown closer to *Mamm* since I've been here, and I'm grateful for that. But I wish things had been different."

"Then maybe things might have been different for us as well."

Surprised, she jerked her head up to stare at him. "How?"

"Think about it, Mary Katherine. Think about it."

He got up to walk to his buggy, leaving her to stare after him.

"Is she sleeping?"

"Shh!"

"Don't shush me."

"Well, be quiet then!"

"I'm awake," Mary Katherine said without opening her eyes.

"You were snoring."

She opened her eyes and glared at Anna. "I don't snore."

Anna giggled. "You do."

"Don't tease," Naomi said.

"Stop acting like the older sister, Naomi."

"Stop acting like the younger one, Anna."

Mary Katherine groaned. "Stop acting like—like bickering *kinner*." She yawned and stretched. "Thanks for letting me sleep, you two." She frowned when she saw the time. "But you shouldn't have let me sleep so long."

"The shop was quiet." Naomi opened the refrigerator, took out a plastic container, and opened it to reveal sandwiches. She set it on the table. "You looked tired."

"I tried to get everything done so *Grossmudder* wouldn't have much to do today. *Mamm's* getting better, but she still needs a lot of help."

"I brought in a casserole so you could take it home with you," Naomi told her as she carried a pitcher of iced tea to the table. "It's in the refrigerator."

"*Danki*, it'll be nice not to cook tonight."

Someone knocked on the front door.

"Did you put the 'Closed' sign on the door?"

"Yes. People don't read. Maybe if we ignore them, they'll go away."

But the knocking not only continued, it became more insistent.

Naomi started to rise, but Anna stopped her. "I'll go."

Mary Katherine chose a sandwich and placed it on her plate. "Thanks for bringing this in."

"It's the least I can do." She bit into an egg salad sandwich. "When do you think you'll be back for good?"

"Next week, I hope. After *Mamm* goes to see the doctor."

Anna returned, frowning. A young man followed her into the room.

"Who was—oh, it's you! What are you doing here?"

Mary Katherine watched Naomi's face light up. This must be John, she realized.

"Brought you a little gift," he said, bringing a bouquet of roses from behind his back with a great flourish.

"Oh, you shouldn't have," Naomi said, burying her face in the blooms. "But they smell wonderful." She gazed at him adoringly.

Anna cleared her throat, and Naomi blinked and shook her head.

"Oh, sorry," she said to Mary Katherine, and she blushed. "This is John. He used to live over in Franklin County. John, this is my cousin, Mary Katherine."

"Hello." He immediately turned back to Naomi.

Naomi found a vase in a cupboard, filled it with water, and arranged the roses in it.

Mary Katherine surreptitiously studied John. He was handsome, but she didn't think that he seemed as warm as Jacob.

"Would you like a sandwich?" Naomi asked him. She held out the plastic box to him.

"Thanks," he said, and took two.

She placed a plate before him and got up to get another for herself.

Anna picked up the box and handed it to Mary Katherine. "Quick, get yours before he gets his hands on it," she whispered.

Mary Katherine elbowed her, but there was no need to worry—Naomi and John appeared engrossed in each other. "You want tuna or peanut butter and jelly?"

"I know you love PB & J. You take it."

They took their sandwiches and began eating.

"So, John, what do you do?"

"Do?" He pulled his attention away from Naomi.

"For a living."

"Oh, I'm a carpenter."

"What are you doing in town today?" Naomi asked him.

"We finished the job early," he said, swallowing the last bite of his sandwich. He looked into the plastic box and appeared disappointed when he found it empty.

Naomi placed half of her sandwich on his plate, and he took it eagerly.

"I thought I'd see if you could take the afternoon off," he said, reaching over to pick up her glass and take a drink of her tea.

"Oh, sorry, I should have gotten a glass for you," she said.

"This one's fine," he said, taking another sip.

Anna glanced at Mary Katherine. She gave her a warning glance. It was obvious that Anna didn't like John, but she needed to be polite. Later, they could talk about whatever was Anna's problem with the man.

"Oh, I'm sorry, I can't do that," Naomi told him.

"Why not? You said last night it's been slow the last few days."

"Yes, but—"

"You don't mind, do you?" he asked Anna and Mary Katherine.

"It's not up to us," Anna told him. "It's up to our grandmother."

"So ask her," he said, wiping his mouth on a paper napkin. "Got anything else to eat?"

"Some cookies." Naomi brought the cookie jar to the table and spread some on a plate. "Grandmother's not here today. She's helping *Aenti* Miriam."

"Well, an hour can't hurt." He took a handful of cookies and stood, grasping Naomi's hand and drawing her to her feet. "You two can hold down the fort, can't you?"

"Sure," Anna said sarcastically. "You two just go on."

"You're sure?" Naomi hesitated.

Mary Katherine glanced at Anna, and then she nodded. "We're sure."

John was already pulling Naomi out of the room, she laughing and protesting that she needed her jacket. She managed to grab it, and a few seconds later, they heard the sound of the bell over the front door as they left.

"Okay, so why don't you like him?"

Anna poured them more cold tea. "It's not that I don't like him. It's just that he's moving so fast and . . ." she hesitated. "I don't know, he's moving so fast and coming on so strong."

Anna sighed. "Naomi really likes him. She's not the type to be flighty or make bad decisions . . ." she trailed off. "I guess we'll see."

"I'll go open up," Mary Katherine offered.

"Are you sure?"

She nodded. "You and Naomi gave me a break earlier."

"Great," said Anna, reaching for a book she kept on a nearby shelf.

Mary Katherine went out to the front door, turned the sign around, and unlocked the door. She remembered how Jacob had seemed to pursue her two months ago when Daniel returned to town. And then when she'd insisted that she wasn't interested in dating, he'd backed off abruptly.

But he was looking more and more attractive to her lately, she thought, biting into the cookie she'd brought from the kitchen. Oh, not just physically, either—Jacob seemed to understand her better than anyone she knew. She wasn't used to that.

Be careful what you ask for, she told herself. Well, she hadn't asked for it, for him. She'd actually been pretty vocal about not wanting a *mann*. She'd felt too restless, too undecided about getting baptized. It wasn't a good time to think about dating.

But there was Jacob, seeming to insidiously make himself a part of her world, subtly making her look at who she was and what she wanted.

And—that question he'd asked as he left before she had time to answer—about what might have happened to the two of them if her father hadn't made her feel so unloved.

What would have happened? she asked herself now.

Young women in her community talked a lot about God setting aside a man for them. She'd seen enough of them match up with one and marry. She'd been so caught up in her restlessness, her indecision about whether this was the place for her, that she'd never thought a complication like Jacob would appear.

Complication. She smiled and shook her head. Wonder what Jacob would think of being called a complication?

12

$\mathcal{A}$ pounding on her bedroom door woke her. "Mary Katherine!" her father bellowed.

She scrambled from her bed and opened the door. "What is it? Is it *Mamm?* Is she sick?"

"She's downstairs, fixing breakfast, while you laze in bed! If you're here to help, then help!" He turned and stomped downstairs.

Furious at the way he'd behaved—she'd been up late trying to finish a project that had been commissioned—Mary Katherine dressed and hurriedly bound her hair in place, donning her *kapp* as she raced downstairs.

"*Guder mariye*," her mother said with a smile as she turned from the stove, a spatula in her hand. "I was hoping you'd sleep in. I'm making French toast. Your favorite."

Mary Katherine blinked. Apparently, her mother hadn't heard how her father had awakened her.

"Sit down and let me finish that," she said, reaching for the spatula.

"No, I want to do it," her mother said, refusing to let go of the spatula. "I'm enjoying being back in my *kich.*"

They had a brief, friendly struggle over the utensil, and then Mary Katherine released it.

"Where's *Dat*?"

"He went out to the barn for a minute. I told him to come right back, breakfast is nearly ready."

"I'll go get him." She was so revved up, she didn't even think to take her shawl. The weather was cool outside, but she didn't care.

She pushed open the barn door. It was dim inside, but she easily found her *dat* wiping the side door on the buggy.

He did nothing inside the house, but the buggy, like the inside of the barn, was spotless. Somehow, that just made her angrier. Her mother needed help, but he stuck to thinking he only needed to do the routine tasks that he'd always done. Not only did he barely acknowledge her presence, he'd never once said he appreciated anything . . . far from it, he'd even been abusive to her this morning.

"Breakfast ready?" he asked, as if nothing had happened.

"Not yet. I wanted to talk to you," she said, fuming when he returned his attention to the buggy.

"*Dat!*"

He turned and straightened. "Don't use that tone to me."

"Then don't be rude to me!"

"The Bible says to honor thy parents."

"And it also says, 'And ye fathers, provoke not your children to wrath, but bring them up in the nurture and admonition of the Lord,'" she responded evenly.

His eyebrows went up. No doubt he was surprised. The women of the house had never spoken up to him. But the way that honoring your parents was so consistently stressed had bothered her so much that she'd looked it up in the Bible. Several times. Now she knew what she'd just recited by heart. She didn't think God would make the mistake of urging children to honor parents while not giving those parents instruction in behaving well toward their offspring.

"I have cooked and cleaned and—"

"Done as you should," he interrupted her.

"Let me finish!" she cried. "And I am glad to do all those things for my mother, for she's shown me love as a parent should. It's good that I did all those things without expecting any thanks, because I would never get them from you. I haven't said anything to you up until now so I wouldn't upset my mother. But the time to stay silent is gone. I will not be spoken to as you just did when you woke me up so rudely—"

"I'll speak to you as I wish in my own home."

She drew herself up. "No, you will not speak to me that way or you may not speak to me at all. It's no good for either of us if I let you treat me that way, walk all over me the way you have my mother."

"Your mother has not complained—"

"No, and she'll end up dropping dead if she continues like that," Mary Katherine said, spacing her words slowly and carefully. "She can't do and be what she used to be. So if you have any love for her in that selfish heart of yours, then you'll start lending a hand to this woman who's been at your side for so many years."

The anger drained out of her, leaving her feeling exhausted and empty.

"She doesn't need me anymore but she needs you. She needs you to show her that she's your *fraa*—your partner and not your slave. I'm going back to *Grossmudder's* to live."

She turned and stalked out of the barn and didn't stop at the house. Instead, she turned down the drive and kept walking and walking, and when she reached the end of the drive, she stepped onto the side of the road toward town.

A rumble overhead drew her attention to the sky. A cloud as dark and stormy as her mood hovered overhead.

She sighed and shook her head. Wasn't that always the way when you let yourself build up a bad mood? But surprisingly, she felt lighter now that she'd said what she'd wanted to her father. It wasn't right to leave without saying something to her mother, but she'd had to do it. She'd stop by after work and apologize—but just to her mother, not her father!

A car and a truck passed, but no one stopped. Rain began falling, large, cold drops that plopped on her head and ran down her face and her shoulders. Then a deluge poured down from the heavens.

Drawing her sodden shawl closer, she wondered if she'd ever felt more miserable. She shivered. Great. Was pneumonia next?

She heard the clip-clop of horse's hooves behind her. Edging closer to the right side of the road, she glanced behind her and squinted, trying to see through the curtain of rain.

A man stuck his head out the window of the buggy. "Mary Katherine! Get in!"

"Jacob?" Water squished in her shoes as she walked back to the buggy he'd pulled off the road and stood staring at him inside.

"Get in! You're soaked!"

"I'll get everything wet and muddy."

"I don't care! Get in!"

She did as he said and watched the water run down her skirt onto the floor of the buggy.

"What are you doing out in this?"

"It wasn't raining when I started." Well, she hadn't exactly looked up at the sky, but . . .

"Where were you going?"

Anywhere away from my father, she wanted to say. "To work."

He gaped at her. "You can't have been thinking to walk that far and with no jacket."

She shrugged.

Jacob reached into the back seat for a blanket and wrapped it around her shoulders. "You're shivering."

"I know," she said, her teeth chattering.

"I was driving past your house—your parents' house—" he corrected, glancing back at the road before pulling onto it again. "Your mother was trying to hitch up their buggy."

She closed her eyes and leaned against the seat. "Oh, no!"

"She was arguing with your father when she was doing it. She looked so upset. I stopped to see if I could help, and she asked me to look for you."

"That's nice of you. I'm sure you had a lot more important things to do than go looking for me."

"I can't imagine what they might be."

Mary Katherine sighed. "What a day *Dat's* having."

"What do you mean?"

She pulled the blanket closer and wondered when she'd feel warm. "We had a little argument. From what you said, my *mamm* had some things to say to him as well." She glared out the window. "It was a mistake to go there."

"Do you really believe that?" he asked quietly. "Your mother needed you."

Leaning back, she closed her eyes. "I know." She sighed. "You're right. I'm not sorry."

She opened her eyes and looked at him. "I wish I knew why things happened sometimes."

"Maybe you're supposed to forgive him." He held up his hands when she opened her mouth. "Whoa, wait a minute before you yell."

The rain was coming down harder. He pulled into a parking lot and turned to her. "I'm sorry he wasn't the kind of father I had, that many of us had. He's a hard man who only knows his way."

He was silent for a long moment. "If you don't feel sorry for him now, maybe you will one day."

"Sorry for him!" She stared at him in disbelief. "Why would I ever feel sorry for him?"

"Look at what he lost."

"What has he lost?"

He turned and looked at her, then away. "You," he said.

꩜

The rain drummed down on the top of the buggy, and the windows fogged up, enclosing them in their own world.

He knew they shouldn't be alone together, but visibility was near zero and people didn't watch out for Amish buggies in the best of driving conditions.

Her shivering had stopped. "Are you getting any warmer?"

She nodded. "Can we go now?"

He shook his head and gestured at the windshield. "Not a good idea. We need to wait out the rain. You can't have been in a hurry to be somewhere if you were walking."

She gave a half-laugh. "I was too angry at my father to think about how far it was to town. I just started walking." Her eyes narrowed. "What's so funny?"

Apparently, he hadn't been able to hide his smile. "I was just thinking I hope I never get you that mad at me."

She couldn't help it—she laughed. "No, even your brother didn't get me that mad with his pranks when we were scholars."

Looking down, she grimaced. "I look a sight."

Mary Katherine wasn't like other girls. She didn't have a trace of artifice, didn't know how to fish for a compliment. In fact, she'd never looked lovelier to him. She had beautiful skin, and now, damp from the rain, it seemed to glow. Her hair, drawn back and tucked into a bun under her *kapp*, was escaping in long tendrils around her face. It made him remember how she looked with her hair hanging loose around her face, all glorious and touchable—he hadn't been able to look away that night he'd seen it down.

What would she have thought if he'd touched it that night?

What would she think if he touched it now?

They sat so close in the small buggy. So close. He could smell the rain on her, the faint scent of something flowery she'd washed her hair with. Her slender hands clutched the blanket over her wet clothes. He'd just caught a glimpse of how they'd clung to her slender figure before she'd climbed into the buggy.

If he thought about how desirable she'd looked then, he'd need to stand in the cold rain.

Deliberately he forced his attention away. He swiped at the moisture on the inside of the windshield. The rain was clearing.

Just in time. He didn't think he could be trusted not to cross the line from friend to someone who wanted more from her.

"It's letting up," he said. "Where shall I drop you?"

"I can't go into work like this," she said. "If you could take me home, I'll change and call a driver."

"I'll wait for you and give you a lift into town. I'm picking up some supplies for planting."

"Spring planting's coming soon, hmm?"

He nodded. "I can't wait."

A short time later, they pulled up in front of her grand-mother's house. Raindrops clung to the grass that was coming to life after the winter. The air was swept clean.

Jacob was glad that the faint scent of flowers from Mary Katherine's shampoo left the buggy with Mary Katherine.

She was back quicker than he expected, having changed into a dress the color of morning glories, her hair still a bit damp but parted and neatly done under a fresh organdy *kapp* tucked under her black bonnet.

Another buggy rolled past, and a man leaned forward to look into theirs.

Mary Katherine made a face as she climbed inside. "Ugh. Did you see who that was?"

"No, who?"

"The bishop."

Jacob shrugged. "Well, he didn't see anything to be concerned about. I waited in the buggy for you. We didn't go inside."

So why did he feel the tips of his ears burn? No matter what he thought, he hadn't acted on it. That was what was important. Right?

Pulling his hat lower on his head, he checked the road and got the buggy rolling along toward town.

$\approx$

Mary Katherine thought about the bishop frowning at them as he passed.

Nothing had happened, just like Jacob had said. He hadn't gone into the house. Hadn't done anything inappropriate in the buggy.

But he kept giving her sideways looks . . . looks that she'd have to be really unobservant to miss.

She had to admit that she looked at him sometimes. She might have said she wanted to be only friends with him because she felt so restless, so conflicted.

But Jacob was a handsome man, one whom she'd watched grow from a cute boy that other girls had flirted with in *schul* and at singings, to the man who'd expressed interest in her not that long ago.

And he was the man who had—despite what she'd said—agreed to be her friend, and she was beginning to realize she felt closer to him than anyone else.

He glanced over at her now, and she saw the warmth in his eyes. No, it was more than the warmth of friendship. She'd never seen desire in a man's eyes, but she recognized it now.

The buggy suddenly seemed to be smaller, warmer . . . more intimate.

Her emotions were on a roller coaster. She'd gone from being rudely awakened to shouting at her father to being rescued from a thunderstorm by Jacob. And he was giving her looks that were those of a man who wanted something from her that was deeper, more—so much more—than friendship.

She shouldn't be surprised. He'd been honest with her in the beginning about wanting more but had accepted her saying she wanted only friendship. Maybe, though, he hadn't been honest with himself.

He glanced to the left when a car passed them, then he focused on the road ahead. She studied his profile, and her gaze settled on his mouth. Had he ever kissed a girl? she wondered.

Stop that! she told herself sternly. You're not supposed to be thinking about things like that.

But has he?

She'd never kissed a boy, of course. And it wasn't just because she hadn't found any of the boys to her liking.

Who wanted to take the chance of falling in love with someone and marrying and then finding that he'd turn into a tyrant like her father was? Because she was sure that he— her father—hadn't started out that way. She didn't think her mother would have married him if he'd been that way as a young man.

What had her parents been like as young people—the age she was right now, the age that Jacob was?

This is what made things so hard for her . . . you had to be so sure of things, and that's the last thing she was. You had to be sure you wanted to join the church because if you changed your mind afterward, you were shunned in this community. If you married in the Amish church, it was forever. Forget divorce. It just wasn't done.

How could you be sure of anything when decisions were so big and the consequences huge?

She jumped when Jacob touched her hand. He reddened and pulled it back.

"Don't let what happened upset you."

She realized that he meant the argument with her father.

"I'm not."

"*Schur* you are. I know you."

He said it so confidently. It must be nice to be that way, she thought. The only time she really felt that she knew what she was doing, knew who and what she was, was when she sat in front of her loom.

She couldn't wait to get back to it. She did her best thinking when she worked on it, and it wasn't just thinking about the pattern. Jacob had told her once that walking the rows in his fields made him feel connected to the people in his past and to the God in his present. When she ran her hands over the fibers, she felt closer to the person she'd become this year since she broke free of her life at her parents' house.

Maybe this time as she sat before her loom she'd see if she could talk to God.

And maybe He'd listen to her.

❧

The "Closed" sign was still on the door when Mary Katherine got to the shop.

Funny, it felt like so many hours had passed since she'd argued with her father.

She unlocked the door, and as she walked inside, her grandmother came from the back room.

"Why, Mary Katherine, I didn't expect to see you today." Leah welcomed her with a hug.

"I didn't expect to come in today." She stepped back. "*Grossmudder*, I can't go back to my parents' house. I can't!"

"I know."

"My father was just—" she stopped. "Wait a minute. What do you mean you know?"

"I stopped by to check on Miriam not long after you left." She sighed. "Have you had breakfast, child?"

Mary Katherine felt like pouting. "No. And *Mamm* was making French toast when I left. My favorite."

Leah patted her cheek and smiled. "I'll make you some for breakfast tomorrow. In the meantime, let's go to the back room and you can have what I brought for lunch."

Mary Katherine told her what had happened over a tuna salad sandwich.

"I'm not sorry for what I said," she told her grandmother as she rose to get a soft drink from the refrigerator. "But I don't like that it got my mother upset."

She sank into her chair and rolled the can in her hands. "I wish I hadn't gone off angry. Now I have to go back and get my things. I'd just leave my clothes, but I was working on some pillows for an order."

Sighing, she popped the top on the can and took a sip. "Well, it serves me right for getting angry. I was trying so hard not to say or do anything until *Mamm* was well enough for me to leave."

"Like mother, like daughter."

"What?"

"That's what your mother's been doing for years. Keeping the peace."

"Are you saying it's wrong to keep the peace?"

Leah leaned over and picked up the cookie jar. She took off the lid and offered the contents to Mary Katherine.

"The Bible tells us to submit to our husbands, but that doesn't mean ill treatment. Your mother let your father rule the house like a tyrant."

She closed her eyes as if she was in pain, and then she opened them. "But even when she was willing to accept that treatment, it doesn't mean he should extend that to his child."

Mary Katherine reached over to cover her grandmother's hand with hers. "It's the best thing that ever happened to me. The day you invited me to come work here, and to live with you."

Leah smiled. "It was a very good day for me, too." Her smile faded, and her expression grew troubled. "I wanted you to be happy, to do the kind of work you have such a talent for. But you're still restless, still . . . feeling unloved, aren't you?"

"I'm not—" Mary Katherine began.

But her grandmother's words rang true. So true. Her shoulders sagged as she acknowledged the truth.

Her grandmother reached to clasp her hands. "I'm sorry that your father never loved you the way you needed, and in her not speaking up you felt abandoned by your mother, too.

But I think you're forgetting something, dear one. I think you're forgetting Whose child you are."

"I'm the child of Isaac and Miriam."

Leah smiled slightly. "You're God's child, dear one. If He loves you, how can you feel unloved?"

She shook her head. "If He loves me, why didn't he make my parents show me more love? Why didn't He take me away sooner?" There was ingratitude in her voice, but she didn't care.

A noise drew their attention. Anna and Naomi appeared in the doorway.

"Mary Katherine! I didn't know you were coming in today!" Naomi cried, rushing forward to throw her arms around her.

"It's good to see you," Anna exclaimed, making it a group hug.

Mary Katherine met her grandmother's gaze over the shoulders of her cousins. "*Ya*, we love you, and He loves you, too."

❧

Her mother was sitting on the front porch when she arrived that evening.

Mary Katherine climbed the stairs, sat in the rocking chair next to her mother, and watched her stitching closed the top of one of her pillows.

"You didn't have to do that."

"I'm enjoying it," her mother said. "It feels good to be doing something." She knotted the thread and snipped the ends with a pair of scissors.

Holding up the pillow, she brushed at a stray thread and smiled. "Beautiful pattern. Maybe I could commission you to make me a couple of them for the living room?"

Taking the pillow from her, Mary Katherine looked it over. "You have the neatest stitching. I can never do this kind of job. How about we make a deal? I weave the pattern and you assemble the pillows? It sure would speed up the process."

Her mother held out her hand. "Deal."

Mary Katherine tucked the pillow into the carryall with the other completed one.

"So this is what you were doing after all the cooking and housework and taking care of me was done for the day."

"It was relaxing."

Her mother snorted. "*Schur.*"

"Where is *Dat?*" Mary Katherine asked, casting a glance around.

"He's gone to talk to Abe Yoder." Miriam set her chair rocking. "I think he needs to talk to another man after the women pecked at him today, don't you?" She turned and grinned.

She hadn't realized her face had been stiff until her mother's words hit her and she laughed. It felt like the tension in her face was cracking.

Her mother's grin faded. "I shouldn't joke about it. It's not respectful." But her grin reappeared. "I gave him an earful after you stormed off." She paused and looked thoughtful. "Hmm, stormed off . . . in a storm."

Mary Katherine grimaced. "Bad pun. And I got really cold and wet. That'll teach me to do such a thing."

Her mother rocked and stared off into the distance. "You were right to stand up for yourself today." Glancing at Mary Katherine, she nodded. "Your father told me what he said to you and what you said to him." She sighed. "I know that you young women think some of us older wives are—what's the term?"

"Doormats?"

Miriam winced. "Yes. Doormats. In trying to do as the Bible says and submit to our husbands, well, sometimes maybe we lean too much into our own understanding, *ya*?"

Mary Katherine thought about Miriam's words, remembering how the Bible said not to lean into your own understanding . . .

"Well, it's done, and maybe your father will think on what we've both said. I'm hoping that he knows that if we didn't love him we wouldn't try to help him understand he can be a better man if he changes a little."

"I don't know," Mary Katherine said. She gestured at the table between them. "I'm afraid I think *Dat's* like that table. He can't change."

"Well, I believe in miracles," Miriam said, looking more serene than Mary Katherine had ever seen her. "If I didn't, I might not have stayed with your father all these years in spite of what the *Ordnung* says about marriage and divorce."

She smiled as she watched the wind ruffle the purple spears of the hyacinths Jacob had planted a few feet from where they were sitting on the porch. "Maybe you need to believe in the miracle of love yourself, *ya*?"

13

Mary Katherine walked into her bedroom at her grand-mother's house and felt the weight of the world slip from her shoulders.

She unpinned her *kapp*, undressed, and hung up her clothing. After she slipped into a nightgown, she climbed into the narrow bed and felt herself melt into its softness.

She hadn't fully relaxed at her parents' house—even though she'd slept in the same small bedroom there that had been hers from the time she was born.

Rain pattered against the window, drops illuminated by moonlight as they slid down the glass. She burrowed under the quilt and felt so grateful to be here after being soaked earlier in the storm . . . grateful, period, for being back here in what had become a real home to her.

Her room was plain, as she was. Her Bible lay on the small table next to her bed, along with a battery-operated lamp if she wanted to read. Some of her earliest projects decorated the room—a pillow with a slightly crooked pattern deemed not good enough to sell, a small purse embroidered with violets. A basket with fabric balls that she and Anna had had fun making sat on a nearby dresser. Emily, the faceless doll her grandmother had made for her when she was a little girl, sat propped against a small wooden box her grandfather had fashioned for her before he died. The doll wore a dress made from a scrap left from one of Mary Katherine's own dresses years ago. She supposed she should put away such a childish toy, but the doll made her remember the love that her grandmother had put into making it.

The whole room reflected the love her grandmother felt for her, from the walls she'd painted herself to the quilt she'd stitched for the bed. Even the rag rug on the wooden floor was handmade by her grandmother.

She fell asleep to the music of the rain.

Something woke her. She lay in her bed and wondered what it was, then heard it again. It sounded like the rain had the night before, pattering against the window glass. But when she turned her head, she saw that the rain was gone and the sky was blue and cloudless.

Getting out of bed, she winced as her feet hit the cold wooden floor. She went to look out the window and saw Jacob standing on the grass below. He tossed a handful of pebbles that hit the glass and then waved when he saw her.

"Come down!" he mouthed, gesturing with his hand.

She hesitated, and then she drew the curtain and flew around the room, gathering her undergarments and clothing to dress.

Mere minutes later, she ran down the stairs and joined him outside. "What are you doing here?"

"I wanted to see you. Let's go for a ride."

"Where?"

"Anywhere you want to go."

"Far away," she said, gazing past her grandmother's farm to the town that lay miles away. "I want to go far away."

When she glanced back at him, wondering why he hadn't responded, she saw that he looked sad. She didn't want him to be sad but she yearned for something . . . something she didn't know how to find. Didn't even know how to express to herself, let alone to him.

"Where are you going?"

"Hmm?" she turned and looked at him. "What?"

"Where are you going?"

Fog swirled around her, like the clouds of doubt that had surrounded her for so many months now. She stuck out her arms, trying to part the fog so she could see him, touch him, but it was impenetrable.

"Come back," Jacob called. "Don't go away!" His voice faded.

She'd wanted to leave but not like this, cut off from seeing him, hearing him.

But she couldn't have that—whatever it was out there—and have him, too. He was rooted here and couldn't leave. Wouldn't leave.

She woke, her cheeks wet with tears, and realized she'd been dreaming.

❧

"You're being awfully quiet," Anna said. "What's wrong?"

Mary Katherine examined the weaving on the loom before her. She sighed. "Do you ever feel like nothing's as good when you make it as when it's in your mind, your imagination?"

Anna walked over and took a seat. She pulled her knitting needles from a nearby basket, and the familiar clacking noise began.

"Yeah. I think it's like that with anyone who does something creative. Especially artists," she said, holding up the muffler she was creating.

Laughing, Mary Katherine undid the last two rows she'd woven. "I'm not an artist."

"No? I think you are. And you're also a perfectionist."

Mary Katherine looked at her cousin. "That's the pot calling the kettle black. I've seen you unravel baby caps that look fine to me."

"Hey, they have to be as perfect as what I make for anyone else." She smiled. "Maybe even more so. They're going to be worn by someone who's considered pretty much perfect, wouldn't you say?"

"Yes, I suppose."

"I guess you're glad your mother's doing better."

Mary Katherine nodded. The new row she'd added still didn't look right.

"So you can go back to seeing Jacob again."

That got her attention. "Jacob's a friend."

"Uh-huh."

Leah walked past with a bolt of fabric. "Anna, are you teasing—" she paused. "Or shall I say *needling* Mary Katherine again about Jacob?"

"Nice pun, *Grossmudder*," Mary Katherine said.

Grinning, Leah nodded and walked to the cutting table.

"But I'm a big girl," she said. "I can deal with Anna."

Anna giggled. "Go for it, Cousin."

Mary Katherine picked up a ball of yarn and tossed it at her. Anna neatly caught it on one of her knitting needles.

Was it possible to achieve perfection? she wondered. Not just in creative work, but as a person?

Anna jumped up, dumping her knitting in the basket beside her chair when a customer entered the shop.

Leah walked past with the bolt of fabric to return it to its shelf. She took Anna's chair when she returned. "So, what's got you looking so thoughtful?"

"If we're made in His image, why aren't we perfect?"

Her grandmother raised her brows. "Well, that's an interesting question."

"Deep for me, right?" Mary Katherine grinned.

"You've always been 'deep,'" Leah said. "Always seeking, always questioning."

"Not an easy child, right?"

Leah's smile was kind. "I'd rather have a child who's looking for answers than an easy one who just accepts everything."

Mary Katherine laughed. "Well, you got that in me, didn't you?"

"It doesn't make for an easy life though, does it, dear one? It's why you struggle so with your decision."

Sighing, Mary Katherine nodded.

Leah smoothed her hands over her skirt. Mary Katherine noted that her grandmother's hands were still beautiful, not lined or rough, even though Leah cleaned her own house and worked in her kitchen garden.

"It has occurred to me that you may be overthinking some things," Leah said slowly. "Maybe you're thinking with your head instead of your heart."

Mary Katherine rested her own hands—usually so busy—in her lap. "How can I overthink something so important? The decision is one you make for a lifetime."

"The church or marriage?"

"Well—both."

"I guess it's a matter of just what you think you'll find in the *Englisch* world that you've been seeking here and haven't found."

She considered that. "You mean, make a list?"

Leah laughed. "You might be a creative person, but you're very practical, you know that?"

"Can someone be Amish and not be practical?" Mary Katherine teased.

"Ah, so you consider yourself Amish?" Leah returned seriously.

"I—uh . . ."

"And I would ask you what you think you'll find in a man that isn't in one you already love?"

Mary Katherine threw up her hands. "Why is it that you and Anna and Naomi seem determined to pair me with Jacob?"

Leah just smiled that wise smile of hers. "I wonder."

❧

It was Jacob's favorite season.

He knew many farmers preferred late summer or fall, when they reaped what they'd sowed, when they harvested the crops they'd toiled over for so long.

But there was something about spring that made it his favorite. A whole world of possibilities stretched out in front of him . . . He could change everything out—rotate his crops. Plant seed for new varieties. The weather was never certain, but he never shrank from a challenge—not with God on his side.

For the longer he farmed, the more he came to depend on Him and acknowledge His will and His wisdom in his life.

He walked his fields and every so often found himself glancing out at the road, wishing that Mary Katherine would visit as she had that day after she'd taught that class. Now that her mother was better and she'd moved back in with her grandmother, he hoped he'd see her happy again.

There was nothing better than Mary Katherine happy.

He couldn't figure out any excuse to go by her shop, and besides, it was coming up on a busy time for him again. Sighing when the only vehicle that passed was an *Englischer's* car, he went back to walking the fields.

Memories of working these fields often came to him as he walked them to check on the progress of the crop, to see what he needed to do to nurture it.

Amish children learned early how to farm, and most of them loved it. He frowned when he thought about how Mary Katherine didn't feel that way about it. It was easy to understand her dislike of farm work. Her father wasn't an easy man and seldom cracked a smile. Jacob figured that Mary Katherine, with her gentle nature and her artistic bent, had had a hard time of it being around such a critical man. Then, too, Isaac hadn't had a big, sturdy son to help him with the harder farm chores, only a rather delicate young daughter.

And Isaac considered it a waste of money to hire outside help.

Farm work was hard, no doubt, and not for the weak or squeamish or lazy. Definitely not for those who hated it. But he wasn't sure Mary Katherine hated it.

He was still hoping that she didn't really hate it, that she'd developed an . . . aversion to it because of her father.

And optimist that he was, he hoped he could work on that.

A glance at the position of the sun told him the approximate time. Clear skies and low humidity meant he and Ben would begin planting the seed the next day.

If he hadn't had his head bent, watching where he was walking, he might have missed the little clutch of violets pushing up from the earth.

He heard a car door slam and looked up to see Mary Katherine emerging from a car he recognized as one from Nick Brannigan's taxi business. A rush of pleasure shot through him. Acting on instinct, he plucked up the flowers and carried them with him. It was hard to keep his stride steady and not hurry too much.

"*Gut-n-owed*," she called as she picked her way through one of the rows.

"Stay there, don't get your shoes dirty!" he called.

The setting sun outlined her slender figure; the wind fluttered the skirts of her dress and the ties of her bonnet.

She smiled when he approached and held out the flowers.

"I found these just as I heard the car."

"They must be the first violets of the season. And white ones. You don't often find them." She raised them to her nose and inhaled. "Mmm, they smell so sweet. *Danki*."

"My *mamm* used to have the most beautiful garden out in front of the house."

They walked together to the front porch, and he gestured for her to have a seat.

"I helped her take the flowers and bushes to her new home when she remarried," he told her. "I knew I wouldn't have the time to keep it up. Maybe not even the knowledge to do so."

"You're a farmer. You couldn't make her garden grow?"

"I'm a crop farmer, not a flower grower," he said. "And she needed the things she'd nurtured. They were like her *kinner* to her."

"I had a little garden at my parents years ago. *Dat* didn't give me much time to work in it. Said it was more important to raise vegetables we could eat."

"My *mamm* always says a woman's soul needs flowers."

"What was it like growing up with so many females in your house?"

He leaned back in his chair and grinned. "Part of me wanted to be the big brother and protect them and part of me wanted to drive them crazy."

"Which did you do most often?"

"Drive them crazy, of course." He grinned.

She laughed. "I thought you'd say that."

"Don't worry, they did their share to me, too, ganging up on me because there were more of them. And Rebecca's done her share of giving me a hard time, too."

"I wanted to stop by and thank you again for bringing the flowers to my mother. She loves sitting out on the porch and looking at them."

"No need to thank me. Your mother invited me to supper so often when I was younger, she probably thought she had a second child."

"She loved doing it. Even though she never said much about it, I think she wanted more children. I'm sure my father wanted a son."

He nodded. "Some men do. Some are happy with what God wills."

A buggy rolled past, and one of his neighbors waved. Jacob waved back. "So, have you had supper?"

She shook her head. "I just came from the shop."

When she took a deep breath, Jacob wondered what she was about to tell him.

"It's last minute, but I thought if you hadn't eaten you might like to go for pizza."

Relief flooded him, but he didn't let on.

"Jamie and Ben are going," she said quickly.

He lifted his eyebrows. "Chaperones?"

She blushed. "Of course not. They—seem to be seeing a lot of each other."

He nodded. "I know. I'm not sure why."

"Jamie's a sweet girl—"

"I know," he said quickly, holding up his hand. "But where can it lead? He's Amish, she's *Englisch*." He paused. "Very *Englisch*."

"We've had *Englisch* join our church. Jenny Bontrager and Chris Matlock, remember? And it's worked out well for them." She shrugged. "Anyway, Jamie says he's just a friend."

"There's a lot of that going on lately," he said, rising and checking his pockets for cash.

"It's my treat for saving me from the storm that day."

"There's no need—"

"It's my treat," she told him firmly.

"Yes, ma'am," he said. "I'll go hitch up the buggy. Lock the front door for me?"

"Sure."

She stood and walked to the door, opened it, and turned the lock. After she closed it, she jiggled the doorknob to make sure it was locked.

Jacob started down the stairs and saw another buggy rolling past. Josiah leaned out his window and stared at them. Jacob waved, but all he got was a frown from the old man. Well, he wasn't surprised. He'd known Josiah all his life, and he'd seldom seen him without a frown. His mother had told him on more than one occasion that if he screwed up his face it might freeze that way one day. He'd heard other mothers say something similar. Jacob figured maybe Josiah's had done that.

***

Mary Katherine knew she was playing with fire.

So she was careful to sit as close to her door as possible. She didn't think she could ever forget how she felt sitting so close to Jacob, to feel that sexual pull. Although she'd never kissed a man, never even been as physically close to one as she had been that rainy day, she knew what went on between a man and a woman. After all, she'd grown up on a farm. Like she'd told Jamie, she was Amish, not stupid.

It was a heady feeling, knowing that a man wanted you.

It was scary, wanting him back.

She was so restless, so unsure of what she wanted now that she was old enough to be able to reach for it. Her work had almost fallen into her lap. Oh, she had worked for it, had studied it and practiced it and been humble enough to keep trying for perfection, and she knew she was very lucky to be doing it.

No, she didn't believe in luck. The Amish didn't. What a person did well—it was a gift from God to be humble about.

And she'd had the friendship of this man who understood her so well. That was a gift as well, to be understood. Only a few people had ever really understood her.

What if she was wrong about how he felt about her? She glanced sideways at him and found him watching her.

There it was again . . . that look of desire. She wasn't wrong about that.

And even her grandmother and her cousins thought he was the right man for her.

Had God dropped the man he'd set aside for her into her lap and she hadn't been watching, hadn't been listening to Him?

"You okay? You're quiet."

"Busy day. I'll be glad to relax. And eat lots of pizza." She glanced at the fields of a neighbor of Jacob's. "When do you start your planting?"

"Tomorrow." He glanced at her. "So Ben better eat lots of pizza tonight so he has energy, *ya?*"

"*Ya.*" She laughed.

The restaurant was crowded, noisy, and full of the delicious aromas that drew people in despite its being crowded and your almost needing to yell to be heard even when sitting in a tiny booth.

Mary Katherine exchanged a look with Jacob when they approached the booth where Jamie and Ben sat very close together. When Ben looked up and saw Jacob, he reddened and put distance between them.

"Look who I brought," Mary Katherine said lightly as Jacob gestured for her to slide into the booth before he seated himself.

"Glad you could come," Jamie said. "We ordered a pepperoni pizza. If that's not what you want, you can order one that you like. We can always take the leftovers from ours home."

"Ben, on the way here Jacob said you should eat lots of pizza to have energy to plant tomorrow."

Ben grinned. "I intend to."

A waitress came to place a pizza in front of them.

"I don't think there'll be leftovers," Jamie said, picking up a slice of pizza. "I intend to eat a lot of it, and I'm not planting tomorrow."

Mary Katherine chose a slice of pizza and began eating. It felt so good to be out with friends, not having to walk around tense at her parents' house. Normal. Things were getting back to normal.

They talked about jobs and local events and how nice it was that spring had finally come. Another pizza came and was demolished along with pitchers of soft drinks.

"I can't move," Mary Katherine said. "Why did I eat so much?"

"Let's go to the little girls' room," Jamie said.

"Why do they call it that?" Ben asked.

"Euphemism," they heard Jacob say behind them.

"Huh?" Ben said.

"You remember. Our parents and our teacher spent a lot of time teaching us about finding something different to say at times, like not taking the Lord's name in vain and choosing another word. Maybe Jamie didn't want to say 'restroom.'

Now, don't even think about taking that last slice. It's mine, remember?"

Jamie slipped her arm through Mary Katherine's as they walked toward the restrooms. "So great to hear your mom's doing well and you're back at your grandma's and the shop. So, when are you and Jacob going to announce your engagement? You call it that, right?"

"We're not getting engaged. Have you been talking to my cousins?"

"Of course." She went into a stall and shut the door. "So, when?"

Mary Katherine held her hands under the faucet and water began to flow. Such an amazing thing. You didn't even need to turn on the faucet. What would the *Englisch* think of next?

"Well?" Jamie called out.

"Can't hear you. Water's running."

The toilet flushed, and Jamie came out, pumped some hand soap, and lathered up. She glanced over. "Having fun?"

"The *Englisch* world . . ." she shook her head.

Jamie rinsed her hands, reached for some paper towels, and handed Mary Katherine one. She leaned back against the sink and met Mary Katherine's gaze. "You know, you're fascinated by stuff in my world, but I think you're just having a temporary dissatisfaction with things that have nothing to do with you really wanting to leave your community."

"Oh?"

"I've known a lot of Amish and the ones who leave . . . well, they're attracted to so many things. The technology. The freedom. Cars. Music. Sometimes alcohol and stuff like that. None of those things seem to interest you. I'm your only *Englisch* friend. And the fact that you're drawn to Jacob . . . well, you'll never find a great guy like that in my world."

"That's pretty cynical, don't you think? Just because your last boyfriend—"

"Let's not talk about him." She tossed her crumpled-up towel in the trash can, then took Mary Katherine's and did the same with it.

"So is that why you're attracted to Ben?"

"He's a friend."

"You looked pretty . . . friendly with him when we walked in."

"A close friend," Jamie said with a grin. Then her grin faded. "He hasn't joined the church yet, but he's a fish out of water like you. Well, guess we better get back before they wonder what we're up to. They had this funny skit on TV once where the men were trying to guess what women did when they spent so much time in the ladies' room," she told Mary Katherine on the way out of the restroom. "The guys figured we had a spa in here."

"A spa?"

Jamie patted her back. "Facials, massages, manicures. Fancy stuff. I'm just a working girl. I wouldn't know about all that."

"Me, either," Mary Katherine said. "This restroom is as fancy as I've ever seen."

It was dark by the time they left the restaurant. The stars were out, and the road was empty of cars.

"Cold?"

"I'm fine."

"Thank you for supper." He glanced over at her. "It's the first time I've been taken to supper by a woman."

"I remember a lot of girls hung around you when we went to *schul*."

He laughed. "Back then I didn't have much time for them. Not after *Dat* died."

"But that's been years."

"I guess I just had this sense that I'd know when the time was right." He glanced at her. "For a while there I thought that I might have misread something."

"Misread?" Her heart began thumping.

"I thought you were interested in Daniel. But you're not, are you?"

She shook her head, not entirely sure where this was going.

He glanced behind him and then pulled over. "Are you any closer to making a decision about joining the church?"

Then, before she could speak, he shook his head and waved a hand. "No, it's not right to ask that. I don't want to pressure you."

Her heart felt like it skipped a beat. "Not yet. It's such a big decision."

"Decision?" he asked. "Just one?"

14

Another church service, and God hadn't talked to her.

Mary Katherine sighed as she watched the women sitting around her get up and leave the room.

She supposed it was ridiculous to expect God to talk to her while others were—while the lay ministers talked and everyone sang and attention was generally on other things.

Maybe He just wasn't interested in communicating with her when she hadn't talked to him much in a long time. But she'd had a good reason. He hadn't listened to her when she'd been so unhappy on her parents' farm. She'd prayed and prayed and prayed, and the only reason she was out of there was because her grandmother had come to ask her parents if she could live with her and help her there and at the shop.

Funny, she thought now. It was the first time she'd seen her grandmother act . . . old and say that she needed help. But her grandmother still insisted on doing her own housework—Mary Katherine got to help only because she insisted—and any helping at the shop? She'd been encouraged to spend a lot of her time there working on her weaving.

"You're looking thoughtful."

Mary Katherine looked up and saw Jenny Bontrager smiling down at her. "I . . . guess."

"May I?" Jenny gestured at the chair beside her.

Nodding, she watched the other woman take a seat.

"I should help with the food, but I thought I'd say hello. I wanted to tell you that the pillows I bought from you are really pretty in my living room. I thought I'd order another set in blue for my friend, Joy."

"I'm so glad you like them. And thanks for the order. I can have the new ones to you in a week. Is that okay?"

"Two weeks is fine. They're for her birthday next month, so there's time."

Mary Katherine withdrew a notebook from her purse and jotted a note to herself about the order.

The bishop walked into the room, stopped, and looked at them over the tops of his wire-rimmed glasses, then walked out, his hands clasped behind him.

Jenny shivered, and then she grimaced. "I'm sorry, that was irreverent. No, make that disrespectful. He's the bishop, after all. But he just kind of scares me, he's so stern. I liked the bishop we had when I joined the church."

She tilted her head and stared at the doorway the man had exited through. "He reminds me a little of Josiah, the elder who wasn't very happy about me coming to this community or joining the church."

"The bishop isn't happy that I'm taking so long to join the church."

"But it's not like you're old!"

"True." She hesitated, then took a deep breath. "Can I ask you something?"

"Sure."

Before Mary Katherine could frame the question, Matthew, Jenny's husband, appeared in the doorway. She held up two fingers in some kind of signal he understood, and he left them.

"I'm sorry, this isn't a good time for you."

Jenny smiled. "It's a fine time. What's your question?"

"How did you make your decision to become Amish? I mean, you'd been *Englisch* all your life."

"I always felt very comfortable here." Jenny brushed at imaginary lint on the skirt of her dress. "My father grew up here, and though he chose not to become Amish and stay in the community, he let me come here during the summers to visit my grandmother."

Several men came in and began moving the chairs around for the snack that would be served.

"Let's go out onto the porch, shall we?"

Mary Katherine followed her there, and they stood out of the way of people coming and going.

"I fell in love with Matthew, the boy next door, so to speak, but I went away to college. Then I went overseas, was injured, and ended up back here."

She stared off at the fields, and Mary Katherine wondered what she was thinking.

"I came back to Paradise feeling like God had abandoned me. But then after a while it seemed like everything became clearer. While I was recuperating, it seemed like everything clicked."

"Especially with a certain man," Mary Katherine teased.

"Yes," Jenny said with a reminiscent smile. "But it's not an easy decision to change your faith to marry. Especially to this faith."

She glanced down at her Plain dress, then looked up as a buggy passed. "It was still a bit of a culture shock, even though I knew more about it than most *Englisch*."

She looked at Mary Katherine. "Joining the church is a big decision. It can't be done quickly or lightly. I think most everyone understands that. Don't let the bishop or anyone else make you feel you have to do it by a certain time if you're not comfortable."

"Anyone else?"

"The Amish grapevine is at work," Jenny said with a grin. "Jacob's a nice man."

Mary Katherine rolled her eyes. "Not you, too."

Jenny patted her arm. "Sorry, I couldn't help myself. I remember what it was like to have Matthew's sister put in a good word for her brother, too. I haven't known Jacob as long as you, but he seems like a very good man."

The door opened, and she brightened when she saw Matthew exit the house and walk toward her. "But she was right. My sister-in-law, I mean."

"Feeling *allrecht*?" he asked, his expression concerned.

Jenny covered a big yawn with her hand and then placed it on her rounded abdomen. "Yes, but I sure could use a nap."

"I'll get the *kinner* and the buggy."

He strode away, a tall, handsome man who reminded her a little of Jacob. She remembered that they were distant cousins, third or fourth, something like that.

"Anything else you want to ask me?"

Mary Katherine shook her head. "No. Thanks."

Jenny touched her hand. "No, thank *you*."

"Me? For what?"

"For reminding me of all I have to be grateful for now."

Mary Katherine jumped when she heard a squeal from the other end of the porch.

She looked up and saw a little boy who was the image of Matthew come toddling toward them with outstretched arms.

"There he is!" Jenny exclaimed, chuckling. "Mr. Mischief!" She turned to Mary Katherine. "He kept us up with teething pain last night and then was out of his crib this morning playing with the cat."

Mary Katherine sat there for a long time after Jenny left, thinking about what she'd said. Then she realized that she should have been helping the other women with the food.

But the bishop was probably still inside. Sighing, she squared her shoulders and headed for the kitchen.

"I think someone's looking for you," her grandmother told her as she entered the kitchen.

"Oh?" Mary Katherine's shoulders slumped.

"In there," Leah said, jerking her head toward the living room.

With a feeling of dread, she started out of the room.

"Here, take this with you." Leah handed her a plate.

"Like I'm going to be able to eat," she muttered.

"What?"

"Nothing."

But when she walked into the room, instead of the bishop, she found her mother laughing and talking with her next-door neighbor.

"We came in late, so we sat in the back," her mother said. "I saw you talking to Jenny. Such a nice woman." She glanced at the plate in Mary Katherine's hand. "That looks good. Lizzie, we should get something to eat."

"This is for you." She handed her the plate and kissed her on her cheek. "What would you like to drink?"

"That iced tea looks good," she said, jerking her head toward the woman at the next table who was drinking it. "Are you going to join us?"

"Sure. Let me go get your tea and some food for myself."

Her mind on the surprise, she didn't see someone in front of her until she ran into him.

"Oh, sorry!"

"No problem," Jacob said, grinning. "I was just looking for you."

"I'm getting my mother something to drink," she told him.

His eyebrows went up. "She's here? I'll go say hello. Then maybe we can talk?" He turned, then glanced over his shoulder, and there was that look on his face—that look he'd been giving her—before he strode away.

Her face felt warm as she moved toward the kitchen.

The kitchen was crowded with women preparing the meal. Her cousin Naomi stood at the counter pouring glasses of iced tea.

"Can I get some iced tea for my mother?"

"*Schur.*"

"Naomi!" A young man stuck his head in the doorway. "Let's go. Now."

"John! Say hello to Mary Katherine."

Looking reluctant, he moved closer. "Hello." He turned to Naomi. "Let's go."

"I'll be just a few more minutes," she said, handing Mary Katherine the glass of tea. "Why don't you wait on the porch?"

"Five minutes," he said and turned on his heel.

"He wants to take me to lunch in town," Naomi explained, shrugging. "Tell your mother I said hello. I'll stop by later this week to see her."

"Okay." Mary Katherine watched as Naomi hurried out of the kitchen.

After she fixed a plate of food, she picked up the glass of tea that Naomi had prepared but forgotten to give her. Anna hadn't particularly cared for John, and he certainly wasn't growing on Mary Katherine.

She found it hard to have a conversation with her mother when one person after another had to welcome her back after her absence, but it did Mary Katherine's heart good to see that her mother had been missed. Through the years, Miriam had been overshadowed by her husband's stronger personality; now, with him out of town on some errand, not being rushed off as was his habit to do after church, she clearly enjoyed the attention and knowledge that she'd been missed.

What Mary Katherine noticed was that few people asked Miriam about her husband's absence. Maybe it was because they knew the reason. Mary Katherine might not get along with her father, but she derived no pleasure in the fact that he didn't seem to get along all that well with others. It was sad, really.

"So you were talking really seriously with Jenny," her mother said when there was a lull in people stopping by to talk to her.

Mary Katherine found herself thinking about what Jenny had said.

Miriam cleared her throat. "That was a hint."

"Oh, sorry. We just chatted about this and that."

She was grateful when someone interrupted them and let her thoughts drift again. Maybe God hadn't talked directly to her. But maybe He'd put Jenny in her path today to talk to her instead. It was something to think about.

Her grandmother had once said that there was a reason why we weren't put on Earth by ourselves. We're supposed to learn something from other people, and they from us, she'd said.

She was in this community for a reason, she was coming to realize, even as it had caused a restlessness in her. This faith-filled community had shaped everything about her—given her stability, loving relationships—well, all but the one with her father. Here she'd grown up with a man who was a friend, then a best friend who understood her better than anyone she knew. A man who wanted a deeper relationship with her but was willing to set aside his own needs so that she could make her own decisions about faith and about their spending the rest of her life with him.

She relaxed and breathed in the peaceful atmosphere of after-church here in the house of one of her longtime friends, and when Jacob walked into the room and his eyes searched for her, she smiled and lifted her hand.

And felt the restlessness leaving her like the tide on a shore.

There were some things that couldn't be avoided. People, actually.

Apparently, the bishop was one of them.

He showed up again at the shop a few days later and was closeted with her grandmother in the back room for nearly half an hour. When he came out, he was frowning and her grandmother was smiling as she walked behind him.

Mary Katherine bit her lip so she wouldn't smile when the man turned and her grandmother quickly changed her expression.

"Think about what I said."

"Oh, I will," Leah told him pleasantly. "Thank you for stopping by."

Leah waited until he left, went to the store window to assure herself that he had walked out of sight, then turned back to her granddaughters, who were anxiously waiting to hear what had happened.

"He came in to grumble again about how he didn't think we were looking like we offered traditional Amish crafts and goods."

"My work, in other words. He means my work."

"Well, it doesn't matter whose things he's talking about," Leah said, smiling now. "He came in to grumble, but he can't do more. I'd heard he went to others in authority in the church, and they didn't agree with him. So we have nothing to worry about."

Mary Katherine breathed a sigh of relief. She'd been so upset when he came into the shop the first time and complained. She remembered what Jenny Bontrager said at church two weeks ago, about how she liked the last bishop better than this one, and had to agree.

Now she wondered if Jenny had heard about the bishop's visit and was trying to send her a subtle signal that things did change, even in their community.

Well, it didn't really matter. She felt easier about it all. Going to her loom, she sat and began working again.

"I think this calls for a celebration," Leah announced.

"Celebration?" Anna, Naomi, and Mary Katherine said at the same time.

"What kind of celebration? We close early?"

Leah chuckled. "No, Anna. We can't really do that. We wouldn't want to disappoint anyone who was visiting the area and intending to stop by here, would we?"

Anna pouted, but she shook her head.

"So then what do you have in mind, *Grossmudder*?" Naomi asked.

She smiled. "I think we should have supper out. In a restaurant. The four of us."

"Really?" Anna's voice rose in a squeak.

"Really. My treat."

Anna glanced at the clock. "It's four o'clock."

"Too early to close," Leah said with a smile as she walked behind the counter and took out the day's receipts to add.

"But we could get the early bird special," Anna said persuasively. "Save you some money."

Leah laughed and shook her head. "It's so kind of you to think of my pocketbook. We'll close at 4:30."

Anna pumped a fist in the air. "Yes!"

Naomi looked at Mary Katherine. "Thank goodness the bishop isn't here to see that. He'd faint."

Without being asked, the cousins straightened displays, swept the floor, and emptied wastepaper baskets. When their grandmother emerged from the back room with her coat over her arm, her purse and the day's deposit in her hand, her eyebrows shot up.

"Well, perhaps I should treat us to supper more often."

"You should," Anna told her with an impish smile. Then a shadow fell over the door. "Oh, no, a customer!" she cried. "Quick, lock the door, and we'll go out the back way!"

"Don't be silly," Naomi told her. "It's a man. He won't stay long. Probably just here to pick up thread for his wife."

The door opened, and in strolled Daniel. "Hello, ladies!"

"Daniel! I thought you went back to Florida?"

"Came back for a visit. Are you closing?"

"We're going out for supper," Leah told him. "Would you like to join us?"

He brightened and nodded. "That would be wonderful."

They walked to a nearby restaurant that was frequented by locals and tourists alike. Maybe Mary Katherine was imagining it, but Daniel seemed to maneuver things so that he sat near her.

She wondered about that. The last time she'd seen him— when he'd been here to sell his parents' property—he'd acted as though he was interested in her.

Leah asked him about his mother, and he passed along a message from her. Naomi asked if he'd met a friend of hers who was vacationing in Pinecraft. And Anna wanted to know if the ocean was warm enough to swim in.

Daniel had questions of his own. "So, I hear you and Jacob are dating," he said quietly while the others gave their orders to a waitress.

Mary Katherine stared at him, surprised. "Who did you hear this from?"

"I hear things."

"All the way down in Pinecraft?"

He shrugged. "Been back for a few days."

"What are you having tonight, sir?"

Daniel picked up his menu. "You order, Mary Katherine."

When it was his turn, he flashed the waitress a charming grin. "Sorry, I was too busy talking to look at the menu. I'll have the baked chicken special."

"S'okay," the waitress said, smiling as she took his menu.

He turned back to talk to Mary Katherine, but Anna— always inquisitive—had questions for him. Florida sounded so exotic to her, she said. She wanted to know more and asked him endless questions about Pinecraft.

She wasn't the only one. Naomi was asking her own questions, Mary Katherine noticed. Glancing at her grandmother, Mary Katherine wondered if she should switch seats with her sister so that they could talk.

Daniel glanced at her, and she thought he looked a little frustrated. Dessert was ordered—no one passed up dessert here—and when the time came for the check to be presented,

Mary Katherine looked up from talking to Anna and discovered Daniel gone.

"Ready to go?" he asked when he returned.

"We're waiting for our check," she explained.

"It's taken care of."

"But *Grossmudder* was treating us," Anna said.

"It's my treat. My parents gave me a nice little present for taking care of selling their property," he said.

"Well, *danki*, Daniel," Leah said. "That is very nice of you."

"Does this mean we get another dinner to celebrate?" Anna asked as she followed them out of the restaurant.

"You were celebrating?" Daniel held the door open. "Is it somebody's birthday? It's not Mary Katherine's."

"The bishop decided not to give us any problems—" Anna began.

"Anna!"

She covered her mouth. "Sorry."

Daniel glanced at Mary Katherine, but she shook her head. Her grandmother didn't have to remind *her* that such things weren't to be discussed.

They walked back to the shop, arriving a few minutes before their driver was scheduled to arrive.

Daniel put a hand on her arm and drew her aside. "Could I see you tomorrow?"

"I'm working."

"Lunch," he said, his eyes direct on hers. "Everyone has to eat lunch."

Their ride pulled up to the curb.

His fingers tightened on her arm. "Please?"

"Why do you want to talk to me?"

"Just let me take you to lunch and talk?"

"Mary Katherine, are you coming?" Anna called.

"Be right there!" She looked at Daniel. "Fine. I'll meet you at noon at the place we just ate at."

⟡

Anna rested her chin on Mary Katherine's shoulder as she sat before her loom. "So, what does Daniel want?"

"To talk. That's all."

"Talk? About what?"

"I have no idea. I guess I'll find out when I talk to him."

Anna moved to throw herself into a nearby chair. It took only a minute before she was reaching for her ever-present knitting. "I think he's still interested in you."

Mary Katherine worked on a couple of rows, sliding the shuttle in and out.

"Mary Katherine!"

"What?"

Exasperated, Anna stared at her. "Say something!"

"I know you love a romance, but he could be here just to talk about something with me."

"Uh-huh."

Mary Katherine glanced at the clock. "Time to go."

"I want to hear everything when you come back!" Anna called after her.

"Me, too," said Naomi as she opened the door for her.

"You, too?"

"Me, too." Naomi grinned. "Have a nice lunch."

Daniel was waiting for her at the restaurant. He rose to seat her, and she saw that ice water and a menu were already at her place at the table. He wasn't wasting any time.

So she wouldn't, either.

"What is it you want to talk about?"

"Are you or are you not dating Jacob?"

She rolled her eyes. "You know it's no one's business if I am."

"It's mine."

The waitress came with her order pad, and then left them alone.

"How do you figure it's your business?" she asked him.

He reached over and took her hand. "You know I'm interested in you."

"But I told you before you left that I wasn't interested," she said, trying to be gentle.

"While I'm here I thought I'd see what's going on with you." He looked up when he was served a soft drink. "What was Anna talking about last night? About the bishop?"

"It's not really something I can discuss." She twirled her straw in her glass of iced tea.

"Likely poking his nose in things he doesn't need to. I know about him the same way I know about you and Jacob." He leaned forward. "Why don't you come to Florida for a visit? See what it's like where I live? You might want to stay."

She rested her chin on her hand, her elbow on the table, and stared out the window of the restaurant. "You know, the last time you were here I was feeling pretty restless. Actually, up until recently that was true. I didn't know if I even belonged here. But I'm not feeling that way anymore."

"What changed?"

"I think I was still hurting over the way my father was," she told him.

Her food was served, and she thanked the waitress but didn't immediately begin eating. "I didn't think God had listened to me. I was so mixed up I didn't even see what was in front of me. Who was in front of me."

"Jacob," he said heavily.

Even though dating was considered very personal, something that wasn't shared as she knew it was in the *Englisch* world, she felt he deserved to know. She saw his look of disappointment and felt bad, but didn't know what to say. Finally, she nodded.

"A lot of people come to my town for a break from the winter weather," he said. "But then they leave. I'm starting to wonder if I'll ever find a wife."

She reached across to take his hand. "I'm sorry. But you know, God's set aside a woman for you. He'll bring the two of you together when it's time."

He squeezed her hand. "You're a sweet woman, Mary Katherine. I kept thinking about you and decided to come back and see if you and Jacob were engaged."

Someone appeared at the side of the table. They looked up and saw Hilda, the mother of a schoolmate of theirs.

"Why, Daniel, I thought you'd gone back to Florida!" she exclaimed.

"I did. Just making a quick visit back," he told her. "How's Lizzie?"

Mary Katherine quietly withdrew her hand, but the woman saw and a speculative expression crossed her face.

"Married and has two *kinner* already," she told him.

"That's nice," he said, but there wasn't a lot of enthusiasm in his voice. "Tell her I said hello."

"I'll do that."

She left them, and Mary Katherine picked up her fork and tried her chicken salad. It was excellent, as usual. She glanced over at Daniel, who was picking up his hamburger.

Evidently, he wasn't so lovesick for her that he couldn't eat, she thought, trying not to smile. Not that she'd wanted him to be.

Well, maybe she did. But just for a few minutes. She couldn't help feeling flattered that two men were interested in her. She was only human, after all.

Very human.

15

$\mathcal{J}$acob watched Hilda drive away in her buggy and wondered if she knew just how devastating what she'd said had been to him.

He knew she didn't have a mean bone in her body, that she hadn't come to deliberately upset him. But she'd felt he should know. Daniel was back in town, and she'd seen him holding hands with Mary Katherine in a restaurant at lunch.

There had to be some explanation. She'd called him and said that she was going out to supper with her grandmother and her cousins and so couldn't go for a drive with him. She promised to stop by later in the week, and he had looked forward to it ever since.

He walked to a rough wooden bench at the edge of the field and sat down. Taking off his hat, he wiped his forehead with a bandanna, then tucked the bandanna back into his pocket. He watched Ben walking toward him carrying an insulated jug and two plastic cups.

A flock of birds flew overhead. "Guess they're hoping we'll drop some seed," Ben said.

He passed Jacob the cups and poured their water. "So what did Hilda want? I'm guessing it wasn't good. You don't look happy."

"She said I deserved to know."

"Nope. Doesn't sound good." He gestured for Jacob to move over and sat beside him.

"Said Daniel was back in town and she saw him holding Mary Katherine's hand."

"Hilda loves to gossip. Always has."

Jacob glanced at him. "But she wouldn't tell an untruth."

"Well, there has to be an explanation. You're going to ask Mary Katherine about it, right?"

Jacob glanced at him and nodded. "Of course. And we're not engaged. She can see whoever she wishes."

He felt Ben pat his back awkwardly.

"I'm sorry. But you need to ask Mary Katherine about it. Wait until you talk to her."

His throat was dry, and it hurt to swallow. "It's all my fault."

"How do you figure that?"

Jacob looked at him. "I knew Daniel was interested in her the last time he came to town. It made me realize she meant more to me than I thought. So I decided to pursue her. She said at first she only wanted to be friends, but lately . . ."

"Lately she feels more for you. I've seen it."

"You have?" Jacob looked at him. "You're not just saying that because you think I want to hear it?"

Ben drew back and looked affronted. "I wouldn't do that."

Jacob sighed. "No, you wouldn't."

He tossed back the last of the water in his cup and then set it down. "It's what I get for tampering with God's will," he muttered. "Maybe He planned for Mary Katherine and Daniel to be together."

"Well, you know what they say."

"Best-laid plans?"

"No, I was thinking, 'If you love something, let it go. If it comes back to you—'"

A flock of birds flew overhead, interrupting him. He raised an imaginary shotgun and fired.

"What—?"

"Oh, sorry," Ben mumbled, looking embarrassed.

Jacob stood and flexed his shoulders to work out the ache. It was a good ache, one that came from hard work. But his muscles hadn't been used like this since harvest. He'd be grateful for a hot shower later and one of the meals he'd frozen last week. He knew the first days back to the all-important planting were going to be exhausting, so he made up some simple casseroles—with recipes from his mother and his sisters—and all he had to do was put one in the oven.

Then he suspected that he'd be sitting around thinking about why Mary Katherine had been with Daniel at the restaurant.

Sighing, he stood. "Let's get back to work while we still have some daylight."

❧

The bishop's home office was as austere as the man himself.

Aside from shelves filled with volumes of books ranging from several editions of the Bible to histories of the Amish, there was little decoration. The big wooden desk he sat behind held a jar of pencils, a desk blotter with a calendar, and the biggest Bible she'd ever seen.

He was dressed very formally in the kind of Sunday suit he wore when visiting the services in the homes of the people of the community.

"So, how can I help you, Mary Katherine?"

"I've come to tell you I want to join the church."

She was surprised that he wasn't surprised but instead stared at her intently over steepled fingers.

"Do you think you're ready? It seems to me that you are still in rebellion."

"Rebellion? I don't know what you mean. I've been uncertain whether I should join and I finally made my decision."

He shook his head. "I'm not as certain that it's the decision you should make."

She hadn't expected this. Oh, she hadn't thought he'd give her some kind of big rousing welcome, but he was telling her no? She took a deep breath. "Why is that?"

Placing his hands on the desk, he leaned forward. "It seems to me that you've had too much exposure to the *Englisch* world. There have been a number of incidents that demonstrate this. One," he said, ticking off a finger, "you were seen coming out of Jacob's house—"

"I did NOT go into—"

"Do not interrupt!" He gave her a quelling look. "Two, you spoke disrespectfully to your father. And three, you were seen sitting with Jacob in his buggy beside the road."

"Well, I had no idea you listened to gossip and half-truths," she told him, trying to keep her voice level.

Color rose in his thin, lined cheeks. "That's impertinent, young lady. I am the arbiter of correct behavior in this community."

"My behavior has been above reproach," she said, sitting up straight. "I simply locked the door for Jacob that day while he hitched his horse so we could go for a ride. And yes, we were riding home one evening and pulled off to the side of the road to talk. But nothing happened. And so far as my father—I had no idea he complained to you but I don't believe what I said to him is anyone's business but ours."

"He came to me to seek advice on whether he had been incorrect in how he behaved in his home. I advised him that he had not."

Mary Katherine sighed and shook her head. "I'm sorry to hear you say that. It just isn't right the way he treats my mother or me."

"It's a *fraa*'s role and a dutiful daughter's role to—"

The beginnings of a headache began to pound behind her eyes. Stay calm, stay calm! she warned herself. You have to go through this man to get what you want and deserve.

"Bishop, I'm here to begin the process to join the church." She met his gaze unflinchingly. There was no way she was going to be goaded into an argument with him. But there was also no way that she was going to be deflected from her goal. She was going to start the preparations to join the church.

"Are you taking this step to pursue a relationship with Jacob? To marry him?"

"I'm taking this step to become a member of the church and have a relationship with God. That's the most important reason."

He subsided into a silent study of her. If she hadn't grown up with the man who was her father, he might have been able to intimidate her. Perhaps he might have even been able to do that a year ago. But not anymore.

Finally, with a begrudging air, he opened a big book that looked almost like a ledger, and made notes with a ballpoint pen. He rustled in a file for some papers and handed them to her.

"These outline your course of study." He stood. "That will be all."

With that, she was done. She'd set in motion one of the biggest decisions of her life.

She couldn't wait to tell Jacob. Then she'd tell her grandmother and her cousins. Oh, and her mother. And Jamie. A whole list of people.

But Jacob was the most important one. Jacob.

❧

Jacob was hitching up the buggy when he heard a car in the drive. He looked out and saw Mary Katherine paying the driver, then turning to look for him.

He felt conflicting emotions rush through him. On the one hand, his heart leaped with joy at seeing her when he hadn't for a few days. But he felt dread, too. Had she come here to tell him that she'd decided on Daniel?

If she was going to tell him she wanted to be with Daniel, it not only meant the end of his own plan to ask her to marry him—it meant that he'd probably never see her, as she'd be moving to Florida. Of course they'd live there since Daniel loved it so much. Jacob was losing more than a possible wife . . . he'd be losing his best friend.

He sent his horse back into its stall in the barn. Poor horse. He'd thoroughly confused it by making it think it was going to take him for a ride—something it loved to do—but he couldn't do anything about that.

Mary Katherine looked as she had before her mother had fallen ill—happy, a smile on her lips, her stride confident and energetic as she waved and walked toward him.

She stopped close to him, so close, then frowned. "Were you going somewhere? I saw you hitching up the buggy."

"I was going to your grandmother's house to talk to you."

Now that she was closer, he saw how her blue eyes sparkled, how her cheeks were flushed rose-pink.

"I wanted you to be the first to know. I—"

"I already know," he blurted out.

"You do? How could you? I just came from—"

"Someone saw you with him."

"Oh. I guess the Amish grapevine's working better than usual. But I could have just been going in to talk to him about anything."

"You were holding his hand."

She stared at him. "Holding his hand? What? Why would I want to hold his hand?"

"Because you're in love with him."

"In love with him? Are you *ab im off*—crazy?" She shook her head as if to clear it. "Why would I hold the bishop's hand?" She made a face. "I'm not even sure the bishop's wife wants to hold his hand."

They stared at each other. "What are you talking about?" he asked her.

"What are YOU talking about?"

"Someone stopped by to tell me that you were holding hands with Daniel at a restaurant in town the other day."

"Me?" She was so surprised that her voice came out in a squeak.

Then the light went out of her eyes and her smile faded. She frowned. "You thought that I was flirting with Daniel, didn't you?" she asked in a dull voice. "You thought that I would do that to you?"

He didn't know what to say. Spreading his hands, he shrugged. "I was coming in to talk to you about it."

"Why?" she asked in a bitter tone. "It seems to me that you've already made up your mind."

She spun around and started back down the drive, her back stiff and straight.

"Mary Katherine!"

She shook her head and waved her hand, but she didn't slow, didn't turn.

"Where are you going?"

"Home!"

"Let me give you a ride!"

She waved her hand at him again, still not turning, and her stride was carrying her away from him. He made his feet move and he ran after her, grabbed her arm, and spun her around to face him.

"Look, I'm sorry, it gave me a bad moment, and I was coming to talk to you."

She tried to shake off his hand, but he wouldn't let her. Her eyes were filled with angry tears. "Let me go! I'm not going to justify my actions because you have some petty jealousy of Daniel!"

"But he pursued you last time he was here. How do I know he's not doing it now?"

"It doesn't matter what he's doing. I haven't done anything wrong. Of all the stupid, immature—"

"I know it!"

She stopped struggling and her shoulders sagged. "You've just ruined one of the most important days of my life!"

Jacob must have been so surprised at what she said that he let her go, because she was able to pull from his hands and run from him. A buggy was coming up the road and when she ran toward it, it stopped. He couldn't see its occupant, but Mary Katherine must have known whoever was in it because she nodded and climbed inside.

He stood there at the end of his drive, breathing hard from the exertion of running after her, angry with himself for letting petty jealousy over another man cause them to argue.

She'd said he had ruined one of the most important days of her life. In their miscommunication she'd thought he'd been talking about the bishop . . . there could be only one reason she'd gone to talk to the bishop . . . one reason she'd considered it one of the most important days of her life.

She must have gone to make arrangements to start instruction in joining the church. And the fact that she'd come to tell him made him realize that she was thinking of a future with him, not another man.

He threw his hat to the ground and cursed his stupidity.

The minute she got home, she slammed the door, then winced. She should have walked home. Maybe then she'd have gotten rid of some of her pent-up energy. Tears still burned behind her eyelids, and emotions bubbled up inside her.

"Is that you, Mary Katherine?"

Her grandmother came out of the kitchen, wiping her hands on a dish towel. "Oh, my goodness, what's the matter?"

Mary Katherine swiped at the tears on her face with her hands. She'd managed not to cry when she hitched a ride with a neighbor, but from the minute she'd climbed out of the buggy, the tears had run unchecked down her cheeks.

Leah dropped the towel and rushed to her side. "Are you hurt? What happened?"

"I went to see the bishop—"

"What did he say? I'll have a word with him!"

"No, no, he didn't hurt me," Mary Katherine said quickly. "It was Jacob!"

"Oh, you quarreled with Jacob." Leah put her arm around her and led her to the kitchen. "Come on, I'll fix you a cup of tea and we'll talk about it."

She shook her head. "You can't cure everything with a cup of tea."

Leah squeezed her shoulders. "No, of course not. It's the talking that goes with it."

She led Mary Katherine to a chair and pushed her gently into it before going to fill the teakettle and set it on the stove.

"Did you have supper?"

Mary Katherine rubbed her forehead and slumped in the chair. "No, first I went to see the bishop, and then I went to see Jacob."

Leah went still and walked over to sit in the chair next to her. "It just sank in. You said you went to see the bishop. What about?"

Chiding herself for not remembering what was most important here, Mary Katherine sat up straighter and reached for her grandmother's hands. "I made plans to take instruction today. I'm joining the church."

Leah closed her eyes, and when she opened them, they were brimming with tears. "Oh, *danki*, God! I hoped—oh, how I hoped and prayed," she broke off and dug in the pocket of her dress for a tissue.

Mary Katherine got to her feet and hugged her. "I never meant to worry you about my decision."

"You didn't. Well, not really." She smiled. "I love what my friend Phoebe says: 'It's arrogant to worry. God knows what He's doing.'"

Her grandmother might deny that she'd worried. But Mary Katherine could feel the trembling in her grandmother's ᵇ It was relief.

When she withdrew her arms, her grandmother stood and bustled around the kitchen, taking out the leftovers from supper and warming them, setting a plate before Mary Katherine and pouring them both a cup of tea.

"Jenny's grandmother," Mary Katherine mused. She propped her elbow on the table and put her chin in her hand. "I guess that's where Jenny gets some of her wisdom. Things she said helped me make my decision."

"Hmm, so is Jenny the only one with a wise grandmother?"

For a moment Mary Katherine was afraid she'd hurt her grandmother's feelings, then she saw the twinkle in her eye.

"No, I, too, have a very wise grandmother."

Unsure if she could eat, Mary Katherine took a bite or two to satisfy her grandmother that she was eating, and then she held the cup of tea in her hands and found comfort in the warmth of the mug.

Her grandmother watched her with kind eyes. "Now tell me, dear one. What has Jacob done to upset you? Wasn't he happy that you'd gone to the bishop?"

Tears welled up again. She set the cup down. "He was upset with me. So upset. Someone had told him that they saw me holding hands with Daniel the other day."

A thought struck her. She remembered being uncomfortable with the way Daniel had taken her hand. She'd hoped no one she knew would see them. And then someone had walked up. Frowning, she tried to remember who it had been.

Hilda! she realized. Hilda had passed by them, recognized her, and stopped to chat for a minute. She remembered how the woman had looked pointedly at Daniel holding her hand.

"What?" her grandmother prompted.

"It was Hilda who saw me with Daniel. She just had to tell Jacob!" She rubbed her aching temples with her fingertips. "She's not a teenager. Why would she tattle like one?"

"Some people just enjoy gossip," Leah told her. "She could even have been misguided and thought she was warning him. There are people like that everywhere, I expect. I don't think she's a happy person. She can't be, really, can she? Happy people don't say things to people to hurt them."

"You talk like Jacob's the only one who got hurt."

Leah shook her head. "No, he's not. I know you're hurting, too."

"This is why I didn't want to get involved with someone." She pressed her hand to her chest. "It wasn't just because I didn't know what I was going to do about joining the church. It just hurts too much to love someone, to place your trust in someone and have them throw it back to you. It hurts too much!"

"So you love Jacob?"

The pain in her chest became sharper as she nodded. She wondered if it was possible to have a heart attack like her mother when she was only in her twenties.

"Give him a little time to cool off," Leah advised. "Sometimes even the best of men don't think before they speak."

The pain and pressure eased as Mary Katherine thought about what her grandmother said, and she found her righteous anger returning. "Oh, I'll give him some time," she muttered darkly. "Because maybe I need to cool off, too!"

She stood. "My head is pounding. I'm going to take something and go to bed early."

"Eating something might help."

Leaning down, she hugged her grandmother. "Sorry, I can't eat right now. I'll stick it in the refrigerator and have it later if I'm hungry."

Her head still hurt the next morning, and it provided a good excuse for her being quiet at work.

Customers came and went, exclaiming over the products. Mary Katherine was happy to see that they were buying after a bit of a slump earlier in the month.

Now that spring was coming, Anna hummed as she worked on the display window. Mary Katherine smiled at the darling little Easter bunny hats with big floppy ears crocheted in pastel yarns for babies and at the knitted sweaters with baby chicks and such. Draped on a rocking chair were nine-patch quilts with squares of flowered prints made by Naomi and the women who contracted their work to the shop. Amish dolls sewn by Leah were seated round a tiny table, enjoying tea from porcelain cups decorated with violets. Pots of daffodils, hyacinth, and tulips completed the display and gave the shop a cheerful look and fragrance.

Everything said rebirth, renewal.

But Mary Katherine had the same old feelings of rejection and lack of confidence she felt after one of her father's critical tirades. She sighed.

"You did it again."

She looked at Anna. "Did what?"

"You sighed."

"No, I didn't."

"Did too."

"Did not."

Naomi tossed down the quilt she'd been working on. "The two of you sound like children."

"Do not," said Anna.

Rolling her eyes, Naomi marched over to Leah, who was standing near the front window, looking out.

"They're behaving like children," she told her grandmother.

"Am not," Anna called over.

But Mary Katherine saw her trying to hide her smile.

"Why don't you go take a walk while it's slow?" Leah suggested.

"Are you sure?" Naomi chewed on a fingernail and glanced out the window.

"When did you start biting your fingernails?"

"Hmm?" Naomi looked back at her, then down at her hands. She hid them in the pockets of her skirt. "I don't know. I think I'll go for that walk. I won't be long."

Mary Katherine watched Leah gaze after Naomi with a frown.

"What is it?"

"She seems a little edgy, but whenever I ask her about it, she says she's happy." Leah paused. "Very happy." She looked at Mary Katherine. "And how are you feeling?"

"Is something wrong?" Anna asked, looking from one to the other.

"I'm fine."

"What's the secret?" Anna wanted to know. "What don't I know?"

Mary Katherine rolled her eyes. "How to stop being a pest."

Anna stood. "It's not right to keep a secret. We're supposed to all love each other and take care of each other."

"But you keep secrets," Mary Katherine pointed out. "You won't talk about what happened with—"

"Stop prying!" Anna retorted. With that, she flounced out of the room and shut the back room door with more than a little enthusiasm.

Leah threw up her hands.

"Look who I ran into," Naomi said as she walked into the shop a little while later.

Jamie strolled in wearing hot pink streaks in her hair, a mile-long scarf in rainbow colors wrapped around her neck, and a short plaid dress.

"Well, *guder mariye*, it's good to see you. How are classes going?" Leah asked her.

"Great. Thanks so much for working with my schedule this week."

She walked over to look at what Mary Katherine was weaving on her loom. "I like the pattern. What's it going to be?"

"Tote bags with leather handles from Sam. He has a leather shop."

"Neat. Say, we're still on for tonight, right?"

"Tonight." Mary Katherine searched her memory. "Oh, tonight." She bit her lip and blushed.

Jamie pretended to scowl. "Oh, tonight," she mimicked. Flopping into a nearby armchair, she pulled out the knitting she kept in a basket. "Well, good thing I don't get my feelings hurt easily."

Mary Katherine must have made some movement because Jamie glanced over at her and tilted her head. "You okay?"

She nodded. "Just had a bad headache most of today."

"Well, then, a nice, relaxing evening with the girls will cure that."

"Girls?"

"Naomi and Anna are coming, too. Won't that be fun?"

"*Schur.*"

"Wow, the enthusiasm." Jamie glanced up at Leah as she walked by with a bolt of fabric. "Leah, would you like to come over to my apartment tonight, have some pizza, and watch a movie?"

She smiled and shook her head. "No, thanks. I'm looking forward to a quiet night and a book."

"Peeeet-za," Jamie teased.

"Definitely not pizza before I go to bed," Leah said with a laugh. "You young people don't get heartburn from such things, but people my age do."

"Stop talking like you're old," Anna said. "I don't like to hear you talk like that."

"Well, I seldom do, so you're safe. But pizza and a late night—no, I grew out of that a long time ago." She turned to Anna. "Will you help me get together the deposit?"

"If I must," Anna said, sighing melodramatically. But as she passed them, she winked. Her moods—when she had them—were mercifully short, Mary Katherine couldn't help thinking.

Mary Katherine wanted to beg off. She was in no mood to be with anyone else. She just wanted to go home, hide under the covers, and feel sorry for herself.

"Come on, do you good to get out," Jamie murmured.

Maybe it was her imagination, but she thought she saw sympathy in Jamie's eyes.

"What do you know?" she asked her. "Have you heard the gossip, too?"

"I talked to Ben today. He's worried about you and Jacob."

16

"Men!" Anna shook her head.

"Tell me about it," Jamie said. "And here I thought they were better in the Amish community than the ones I know. Why, Ben—" she stopped when she realized that Mary Katherine, Naomi, and Anna perked up.

"What about Ben?" Anna wanted to know.

"Nothing. He and I are just friends," Jamie said quickly.

"That's what Mary Katherine said about her and Jacob," Naomi observed. "But now here she is crying because we asked her if she and Jacob had a fight."

"I don't want to talk about it," Mary Katherine told them. "It hurts too much."

"It'll help to talk it out," Jamie said. "Really."

"It just doesn't make any sense."

Jamie laughed derisively. "Men don't, but go ahead."

"He knew how I felt about him but the minute he heard gossip he believed I was going to go off with Daniel." Angry now at the memory, she pulled a tissue from the box Jamie had brought to her at the first sign of tears.

She blew her nose. "And he has no reason to be jealous of Daniel."

"Sometimes men don't need a reason," Naomi said quietly.

"Well, he just ruined yesterday."

"By fighting with you?"

Mary Katherine nodded. "I had this good news to tell him, and he just ruined it all."

"What is it?" they clamored. "What is it?"

The doorbell rang.

"Oh, honestly!" Jamie exclaimed. "Hold that thought!"

Picking up her purse, she went to the door and looked through the security peephole. "What—?"

"Don't open it if it's not someone you know!" Naomi called to her.

"Oh, I know this person!"

When she opened the door, Ben stood there with a long-stemmed rose atop two pizza boxes.

"I told you this was Girls Night In," she said, frowning at him. "You're not charming your way in with a rose."

"I do my own charming," he told her, leaning forward to kiss her on the tip of her nose, startling her. "But the rose is from Jacob. It's for Mary Katherine, and there's a note attached."

"He better not be here, lurking in the hallway," she warned, stepping out into the hall to survey it.

"He's not. Anyway, here are your pizzas." He shoved it into her hands. "I'll see you tomorrow. Lunch and a movie?"

"Sure. How much do I owe you?"

"It's on me. Or maybe Jacob. Maybe I'll make him pay for delivering everything."

Leaning in the doorway, he waved to them. "'Night, ladies. Enjoy the pizza!"

Jamie shut the door. "Well, that was clever." She looked at Mary Katherine. "If Jacob had been out there, would you have wanted to see him?"

She shook her head. "No."

Jamie held out the note and the rose. "Here."

"I don't want it."

Her eyebrows went up when Jamie tossed them into her lap. "Don't take it out on the flower. Enjoy it—it doesn't deserve to go in the trash can."

Sighing, Mary Katherine opened the note. She read it quickly. Jacob apologized and asked to see her. She frowned. She wasn't ready to forgive him. Shoving the paper into her pocket, she lifted the rose and sniffed its rich perfume. When she realized she was brushing its petals against her cheek, she stopped and blushed.

Jamie smirked. "C'mon, everyone, grab a plate and let's eat." She carried the pizzas into the kitchen and opened them up. Breathing in the scent, she grinned. "I've heard of doghouse flowers—you know, the ones guys send after they've done something they need to apologize for. But I never heard of doghouse pizza. Guess there's a first time for everything."

Each of them took a plate piled with several slices of pizza and a can of soda into the living room. Anna won the right to choose the movie—a DVD of *Tangled*—and soon Rapunzel was letting down her hair, song filled the apartment, and everyone became absorbed in the story.

Mary Katherine was reminded of that night in the pizza place when she'd dressed in *Englisch* clothes and left her hair loose—no tightly drawn bun, no pristine *kapp*. Jacob had seemed to be fascinated by her hair, staring at it.

The fairy tale played on. The one on the television screen, that is. She wasn't so sheltered in her community that she didn't know about fairy tales. She'd read a number of them in books that she'd checked out from the library bookmobile. Maybe she'd even had a few girlish dreams of a handsome man falling in love with her.

But in the end, she was too practical to really believe in them. She didn't understand the *Englisch* fascination with such. Wasn't it better to look at love the way the Plain people did? You didn't wait for some handsome stranger—you dated the boy you'd grown up seeing in church, in *schul*, at singings and other social events. You knew you'd be his partner in his life's work—and he in yours if you chose to work as well as raise your *kinner*—so you made certain that your love ran true and deep and it wasn't just some story you'd made up about him.

Just how true and deep had Jacob's love been for her? she asked herself. If you loved the way you should, you didn't jump to conclusions about the other person. Did you?

Jamie got up from the sofa to get more pizza. "Something wrong with yours? I got pepperoni, your favorite," she whispered.

"I'm not very hungry," she confessed.

"Come on, let's go into the kitchen and talk."

"Shh," Anna hissed, her attention on the television set.

Mary Katherine got up and followed Jamie into the kitchen. "I really don't want to talk anymore. It just hurts too much."

Jamie gestured at a chair and took a seat. "I want to try out something I learned in Psych class this semester. Psychology class," she explained.

She narrowed her eyes. "You don't cut up animals in that class, do you?"

Jamie laughed. "No, that's biology and we do it on the computer. No animals are harmed in biology class at the college—actually, in a lot of those classes in other colleges and high schools."

She took a deep breath. "Okay, let's do this little experiment. When's the last time you felt this bad? Who hurt you?"

"You know the answer to that," Mary Katherine said. "My father."

"So you're feeling like you did something wrong when you didn't?"

Mary Katherine nodded, not sure why Jamie was asking such questions.

"You said once you didn't want to date because you weren't sure if you were going to join the church. But do you think maybe you were afraid of being hurt by a guy? I mean, if you didn't feel loved by your own father . . ."

She was right, of course. Although she'd really said as much to Jamie, Mary Katherine knew it was true for her, too. Sighing, she nodded.

"Do you think you overreacted?"

Mary Katherine stared at her. "You're not saying I shouldn't be upset with Jacob?"

"No, no, of course not. I'd tell him to his face he was a jerk. Anyone who sees the two of you together can see that you love him." She patted Mary Katherine's hand. "And anyone can see that the man is head over heels in love with you. I think he's a little insecure and maybe jumped to conclusions, reacted to that nosy woman."

"What's he got to be insecure about?"

"I don't know. But from what you told me, it sounds like he is. I think you should ask him about it." She grinned. "Maybe not until you cool down. But you owe it to yourself to find out and then see if the two of you can work it out."

"You're right. And you're right about another thing. Remember you said I really didn't want to leave the community, because I *was* Amish? Well, I'm going to take instruction to join the church."

Jamie didn't even blink. "I knew it!" She clasped Mary Katherine's hands and squeezed them. "It feels like a good decision?"

"It feels like a good decision."

She glanced at the pizza box. "I want another slice of pizza, but I guess that would make me a little piggy, wouldn't it?"

"*Ya*, a little oinkette," Mary Katherine agreed with a straight face.

Jamie stared at her and then she laughed. "So, the little Amish girl is starting to get her sense of humor back. That's a good sign. "

"I'm not little, but I'm an Amish girl," she said, grinning. "We'll see how it goes with the Amish boy when I talk to him. I don't intend to be a pushover just because I love the man."

"You go, girl!"

Anna came into the kitchen. "Have you guys eaten all the pizza?"

"Not even close. And there's ice cream in the freezer. I think we should celebrate, don't you?"

"Celebrate what?" Naomi asked as she put her empty plate in the sink.

"Mary Katherine taking classes to join the church."

"Oh, I always knew she'd do it," Anna said airily.

"Oh, you did, did you?"

"Of course. What kind of ice cream?"

Jamie winked at Mary Katherine as she got up to look in the freezer. "There's Rocky Road and butter pecan."

"Rocky Road," said Anna.

"Butter pecan," said Naomi.

"Mary Katherine?"

She grinned at Jamie and her cousins. "I think I'd rather have butter pecan than Rocky Road."

Jamie hugged her and handed her the carton of ice cream. "Smooth roads ahead, huh?"

"*Ya*," Mary Katherine said fervently. "Please, God, smooth roads ahead."

❧

Her mother wasn't home when Mary Katherine stopped by.

She checked inside the house and the barn and discovered both her parents were gone. When she'd talked to her mother the day before, she hadn't said anything about plans, but then again, Mary Katherine hadn't said she was going to drop by.

She supposed that was what she got for assuming that her mother was just waiting for a visit.

Disappointed, she bit her lower lip and decided to wait around a little while. As she sat in the rocker on the front porch, she thought about how she'd sat with Jacob on his porch and absorbed the serenity of his farm.

The plants he'd brought her mother were still ranged around the porch. The warming spring breeze brought the heavy sweet scent of the hyacinth drifting to her and made the yellow heads of the daffodils and narcissus nod.

It wasn't planting or harvesting she'd disliked or any of the work, really—well, she could be very happy if she never had to milk another cow. What she'd grown to hate was being under the harsh, overly critical scrutiny of her father.

Restless, she decided to make good use of her time. Going to the barn, she found a shovel and set about digging holes in the flowerbeds and planting the spring flowers.

A half hour later, all of the plants had been de-potted and set into the holes she'd dug, and the rich, fertile soil patted around them. She sat back on her heels, smiling at her work.

She turned at the sound of a buggy pulling into the drive. As the vehicle moved forward she blinked, when she saw that her father was in the front seat but it was her mother who held the reins.

Interesting. She didn't think she'd ever seen her mother drive the buggy when she was accompanied by her father.

Her mother stopped Ned, the horse, handed her husband the reins, and climbed out of the buggy. "Mary Katherine! I didn't expect you."

She stood, and her mother's eyes widened as she caught a glimpse of the flowers. "Why, look at what you've done!"

"I hope you don't mind."

Her mother kissed her cheek. "Of course not. I'll be busy enough with my kitchen garden soon."

"Did I put them where you wanted? Because I can move them—"

Miriam bent to touch the cheerful face of a purple pansy. "Don't you dare. They're perfect." She straightened. "Can you stay for supper?"

Mary Katherine shook her head. "Not tonight. I—" she brushed at the dirt on her hands. "I need to do something. Maybe another night."

"Well then, come inside and clean up. Leave the shovel and the pots. I'll have your father store it all away later." Her mother put her arm around Mary Katherine's shoulder to lead her inside.

"I have something to tell you first."

Miriam stopped walking and went very still, then turned and stared, stricken, at Mary Katherine. "What's wrong? *Mamm*?"

"*Nee*, she's fine."

"You." Her arm fell away from Mary Katherine's shoulder, and she sank down on the porch steps. "You've come to tell me that you're going to leave." Her lips trembled.

"*Nee*," Mary Katherine said, and she sank down on the steps beside her mother and took her cold hands in hers. "Just the opposite. I talked to the bishop about joining the church."

"You did what?" Her eyes wide, Miriam pressed her fingers against her lips, looking as if she was afraid of what she was hearing. "But I thought—"

"I took the advice of someone I know, and things started getting clearer. And I also didn't let the bishop keep me from where I belong."

Miriam threw her arms around her and hugged her. "Oh, thank you, God!" Tears flooded from her eyes. "I don't have to lose you."

Something moved in her chest. "You were afraid you'd lose me?"

Miriam nodded. "It was God's will that I had one *kind*, one precious daughter. I just didn't know how I'd bear it if—if—" Sobs shook her slender body as she searched the pockets of her dress for a tissue. Finding one, she wiped her eyes and took a shaky breath. "I feel like God's given me my daughter twice."

Mary Katherine felt a rush of guilt. Oh, she knew her mother loved her, but she'd been so caught up in her own feelings, she hadn't thought how her mother would feel if she left. She realized she'd thought of her mother as . . . her mother, not a person with her own fears and insecurities and wishes.

The front door opened. "Miriam, supper's ready—" He stopped when she turned and he saw her tears. "What's wrong?" He looked at Mary Katherine. "Have you upset your *mamm*?" he thundered.

Miriam jumped to her feet, and it must have been a case of too much, too soon, for she swayed on her feet. Isaac rushed down the steps and clasped her around the waist.

"No, no, I'm fine," she insisted.

After a long moment, he released her, but she stayed in the circle of his arms. "Our daughter here just told me she's joining the church. She's joining the church, Isaac!"

Their eyes met, father and daughter, and the glare faded from his. "Really?"

"Really," she said, nodding. She frowned when she remembered what the bishop had said about her father going to speak with him, but when she opened her mouth to say something, he shook his head, glanced at her mother, and then sent her a silent message.

They'd never communicated properly, but in that instant she understood that he didn't want to talk about it then because it would upset her mother.

"That's *gut* news," he said in his usual brusque tone.

So it wasn't the enthusiasm her mother had displayed. Well, her *dat* had never displayed emotion like her *mamm*. Sometimes, growing up, she'd wondered why she got the parents she had—well, parent, mostly. Her father was so harsh, so critical. If God truly loved her, why hadn't He given her a father who'd love her like He supposedly did? Didn't the Bible say we were made in His image?

And her *mamm*. She had always reminded Mary Katherine of a scared little mouse, scurrying around looking anxious about pleasing her *mann*.

"Mary Katherine says she can't stay for supper," Miriam was saying. "She has something she needs to do. Maybe some*one* she needs to see," she said coyly, glancing at her daughter. "She needs to wash up before she goes."

She debated telling her mother that she wasn't going to see Jacob—that they'd fought and she was hurting. He wasn't just the man she'd fallen in love with. He'd become her best friend.

Afraid she was going to burst into tears, she went into the bathroom to scrub her hands, and when she came out she found her parents discussing something in tense, hushed whispers.

"I just put Ned up," her father was saying.

"Well, get him out again. This is your daughter we're talking about," her mother hissed back. "I don't want her walking so far when it'll be dark soon."

Not wanting to appear to be eavesdropping, Mary Katherine made her steps heavier and louder so that her parents looked up and immediately stopped talking.

Sub sandwiches from a local shop were waiting on the table, and some of her mother's homemade soup sent out a delicious aroma as it heated.

Something felt very off here . . .

"Supper's ready," her father had said.

Okay, the sandwiches were bought, but the man who always said buying food out was a waste had obviously done so, and had set the table and warmed the soup while her mother sat on the porch with her.

What was going on?

"Your father is going to drive you where you need to go," her mother told her, lifting her chin.

Mary Katherine looked at her father and he nodded.

"I'll get Ned hitched up," he said in his usual brusque tone.

"You don't have to—"

"Your mother wants it that way," he told her, and he left them.

Since when had what her mother wanted mattered to him? Mary Katherine wondered. But she didn't say anything. After a long day at work she wasn't really interested in a long walk and didn't want to strap her budget even further than it was. When her mother had been recovering, Mary Katherine had often had to hire Nick or one of his cab and shuttle company's drivers to visit her at the hospital and then drive her home later.

Her mother impulsively hugged her, and then she cupped Mary Katherine's cheeks and gazed into her eyes. "Now, don't you two kill each other, all right?"

"I can't promise anything," Mary Katherine muttered.

She climbed into the buggy and sat as far from him as she could, wishing the buggy was bigger. They rode in silence for a time, and then she turned to him.

"Why was *Mamm* driving earlier?"

He glanced at her, then back again at the road. "Said she wanted to."

"And supper. You were making supper, weren't you?"

"Never happy, are you? You wanted me to help, and when I do, you criticize." He frowned.

"Well, I *am* my father's daughter."

He pulled the buggy into a drive and turned to her. "What is that supposed to mean?"

She folded her hands on her lap and lifted her chin. "When I stopped by to see the bishop about joining the church, he told me that you went to him to complain about me."

"That," he said, calling to Ned and getting the buggy back on the road.

"That!" she sputtered. "That!"

"I didn't go to complain about you," he said after a moment. "I went to him for advice. After you stormed out."

"Advice? From him?" She huffed out a breath and shook her head. "I can just imagine what he said."

He lapsed into silence, and she sat there and seethed.

Jacob's farm came into view. It was almost halfway between her childhood home and her grandmother's—what had become home for her. That hadn't been lost on her. She'd once thought about how convenient it would be to visit both homes . . . although she'd imagined back then that there would be few visits from her parents—at least from her father.

At first she thought it was a trick of her imagination, the fact that the light was fading, that she saw Jacob walking his fields. Maybe she thought she saw him because she wanted to.

But as the buggy passed the farm, she saw that it was, indeed, Jacob, standing there in his newly sown fields. Her fingers tightened on the window of the buggy as she saw that he stood there, gazing into the far distance.

Again, it had to be her imagination that he looked lonely. Perhaps it was just that she wanted to believe that he missed her as she missed him. He seemed so confident, so self-possessed, especially at home here on his farm he loved so much.

"Do you want me to stop?"

"No!" she said quickly, wincing when the sound reverberated in the small buggy. "No," she told him in a quieter tone.

From the corner of her eye she saw Jacob turn and catch sight of the buggy. Their eyes met.

"Your *mamm* seemed to think you'd want to."

"Well, she was wrong." Mary Katherine stared straight ahead.

"He's waving to you."

"Doesn't matter."

He hesitated but kept the buggy rolling.

"What is it?" she asked, sensing something.

"Your mother was hoping you'd want to be dropped off to see Jacob. Said something about hearing you two had had a disagreement."

"It's more than a disagreement." She forced herself not to look back at Jacob.

"It's none of our business. But I don't like to go back and tell her I didn't do one of the few things she's asked me to do in all the years we've been married."

Thoughtful, Mary Katherine studied him. "Tell her I'm going to go talk to Jacob. I'm just not ready yet," she said slowly.

"He's a good man."

This was the most she could remember her father saying in years. Most dating—the older folks often liked to call it courting—was done quietly, without telling the parents until the time came to announce the upcoming wedding. Her grandmother and her cousins knew that she and Jacob were seeing each other and that they'd had a falling out, but that was it.

She'd avoided Jacob for days, ignoring the rose and note apologizing for hurting her and asking to speak to her that he'd had delivered to Jamie's apartment, the messages he'd left for her at her grandmother's house. She didn't know how to resolve the argument they'd had. If a man didn't trust what you had together, what you were to each other, how could you fix that? Jealousy, envy, these were things that weren't familiar to her. Shouldn't be familiar to her. They had no place in a relationship.

She'd sensed there was a little tension between the two men but never guessed that Jacob would suspect Daniel of being underhanded and trying to draw her away from him.

When her father stopped the buggy at her grandmother's house, she got out. Just as she was shutting the door, she saw her father watching her.

"I didn't listen to his advice," he said. "The bishop's," he explained, turning to stare out his window. "He told me I was the head of the home, that I was right to try to quell your rebellious spirit, to have you and my *fraa* defer to me and serve me in that office."

She started to make an angry retort, to say that she bet he liked being vindicated in his tyrannical ways by the religious leader of the community. But before she could, he bent his head and said something she couldn't hear.

"What?"

"I went home, feeling pleased that he'd backed me up," he said, looking up and meeting her eyes. "I found my *fraa* lying there pale and ill on the sofa, crying that she'd lost her only *kind*. She blamed me and said things she'd been holding back for years."

Sighing, he stroked his beard and looked thoughtful. "So my religious leader is telling me I was correct, that he supported me, and that I was doing what God had decreed the roles of men and women should be. But I had my *fraa* blaming me for losing us our only *kind*."

Emotion seemed to overcome him. He jerked on the reins, and the buggy began moving away.

Mary Katherine watched it roll down the road until she couldn't see the reflective triangle on the back any longer. She walked up the steps and sank into a rocker, not ready to go inside yet.

Light spilled out the window of the front door as her grandmother peered out. She opened the door. "I thought I heard someone out here. Why didn't you come in? Did you lose your key?"

Rising, Mary Katherine shook her head. "My father just dropped me off. I was thinking."

Leah draped her arm around her. "Come inside and let's talk about it."

She shut the door behind them. "I kept your supper warm. And no telling me that you're too upset to eat. You need to eat."

17

*J*acob got a polite smile but nothing more from Mary Katherine after church later in the week.

He wasn't surprised. She'd been avoiding him for some time, and he never found her at home the several times he had gone to her grandmother's. He couldn't just drop everything and run into town to see her at the shop.

He'd been so surprised to see Isaac driving his buggy past his farm with Mary Katherine sitting beside him earlier in the week—even more surprised when she didn't return his greeting and stared stonily ahead as they passed. But he couldn't blame her. He knew the blame rested solely on himself.

"I want to talk to you," his sister, Rebecca, said to him.

He'd seen that look in her eye before. She'd given it to him right before she and her sisters and their *mamm* had stopped dropping off cooked food for him. What could she do to him now?

He lifted his chin. "What about?"

"I want to know what happened to you and Mary Katherine."

It was tempting to tell her that it was his business, but he'd learned a long time ago that she was relentless. If she didn't get it out of him, she'd get the other women in the family to join forces.

"I said something—"

She gave him a long-suffering sigh. "You and that big foot you stick in your mouth. Should I go get the salt and pepper shakers?"

But she must have seen something in his face because her expression softened. "You're such a good *bruder*. Such a good man. I thought Mary Katherine knew that. If a woman judges a man only by what he says—"

"Daniel's so smooth," he said and he couldn't hide the bitterness. "Someone let me know that he'd come back into town and was seen holding Mary Katherine's hand."

She grabbed his shirt and pulled him out of the room full of people. He slapped at her hands and finally dislodged them just as Mary Katherine looked up across the room and he saw her try to hide her smile.

Well, to see that smile bloom again . . . it was worth being embarrassed by his sister.

He followed her out onto the porch.

"So you were jealous," she said, putting her hands on her hips.

"I'm a grown man," he said. "I don't need to be scolded like a little *kind*."

"*Nee*. But jealousy is something we shouldn't see in an adult. And especially not in an adult male. Women don't find it attractive."

He sighed. "That I know."

She tapped a finger against her mouth, frowning and thinking hard. "Is it that you were jealous because you thought no one else should have Mary Katherine? Or is it that you're afraid of losing her?"

"The second, of course," he said, affronted. "I'm surprised that you would even think that I'd be like that guy in the next town who was obsessed with his ex-girlfriend."

She shivered. "I know. But there are some men who don't take rejection well." She studied him. "There are men who have smooth tongues, who can charm a woman and manipulate them like that man. Then there are men who choose to let their actions speak what kind of man they are. You're not the first. Will you be the second?"

"You really think I have something to offer her?"

"Oh my," she whispered, staring at him.

"What?" He wondered if he had something on his face she stared at him so.

"I never thought that you might be insecure. How did I miss that?"

"Shh!" he hissed and looked around to see if anyone walking in and out of the house had heard her.

She gave him an impulsive hug. "You have so much to offer a woman. And it's wrong to think otherwise. Besides, remember, she must have thought so if the two of you grew so close. It was you that caused the problem with insecurity and jealousy."

With that she left him.

⌒⌒

The day was rainy and gray. Few ventured out in the wet. Anna sighed happily as she sat, knitting, before a fire crackling in the fireplace. Naomi sat in a nearby chair stitching on a quilt, and their grandmother dressed the little faceless dolls she had made for the shop, a fond smile on her lips.

She glanced up at Mary Katherine sitting before her loom. "I remember making these dolls for all three of you."

"I still have mine in my room."

"I know. I've seen it."

"It's probably a little childish to have her sitting on my dresser."

Leah swept a fond glance over them. "Not at all. I'm pleased you loved her enough to keep her."

"She reminds me of my childhood."

Anna grinned. "I still have mine. She's wrapped up in her own little quilt in a box in my closet, waiting to be given to my own daughter when I have one."

"I gave mine to one of our little cousins when she was spending the night," Naomi confided. "She woke from a nightmare and it comforted her. But the next day she didn't want to give it back, so I let her keep it. I'm afraid that the doll was well-loved and isn't in any shape to pass on to a daughter."

"A doll should be loved like that," Leah said, tucking stuffing into a doll's cheek. "I'll make you another."

Leah glanced over at Mary Katherine. "You're being awfully quiet."

Mary Katherine poked her finger at the last few rows she'd woven. "Something's wrong with this."

Anna rose and came to stand behind her. "Looks fine to me."

She shook her head. "There, don't you see the flaw?"

"*Nee.* Naomi, you come look."

Naomi tucked her needle safely in her quilt, stood up, and walked over to study the pattern. "I don't see anything, either. Sorry, Mary Katherine." She walked over and resumed her seat.

Something was off about Naomi. Mary Katherine couldn't help wondering if she was having a problem with John, just as she was with Jacob.

She pulled out a row, then another and another, until she'd pulled out a half-foot and her breath was coming hard. Tears burned behind her eyelids.

"*Kumm*," her grandmother urged, taking her by her shoulders and helping her rise. "Let's go into the back room and talk."

She jerked her head up and found Anna and Naomi regarding her with sympathy.

"Lock the door and turn the sign to "Closed,'" Leah told Anna.

"No, no, if a customer comes out in the rain I don't want her to go away disappointed."

"We haven't had a customer in two hours," Leah said. "I don't think we have to worry about that."

"I'll watch the shop," Anna volunteered. "If we get a herd of customers, I'll yell for you."

So Mary Katherine followed Leah and Naomi into the back room and watched as Naomi made tea. She rubbed her forehead. It always seemed to be hurting lately. Crying herself to sleep some nights probably didn't help. Lying awake others didn't either.

"I remember telling you once that a cup of tea didn't cure everything," she said, looking at her grandmother. "You said that it's the talking that does that."

Leah nodded. "And it's time you did some talking. To Jacob. You've avoided him long enough. You hurt. Tell him so. Either the two of you will fix it or you'll walk away from each other. Pray, talk, and then know it's in God's hands."

Such simple words. Such a huge task. She didn't think she was up to it. "I'm afraid," she whispered.

Her grandmother reached for her hands and held them. "*Ach*, I know. But it's not fair to blame Jacob for too much hurt, is it?"

"But he was the one who hurt me."

Leah shook her head. "You've been carrying around a lot of hurt for a long time."

"My father."

Nodding, Leah patted her hand. "It's made you afraid to love. Afraid to trust."

"You have to give him another chance," Naomi said quietly. "He's tried to say he's sorry."

"And that's supposed to be enough?" Mary Katherine asked. "What if he just keeps hurting me and expecting another chance?"

"You won't know until you give him a second chance," Naomi told her. "Then you can decide if you go forward . . ." She paused. "Or not."

Mary Katherine stood and walked to the door. "Anna, could you come in here for a minute?"

She appeared a moment later, holding a bolt of fabric in her arms. "What is it?"

Holding out her arms, Mary Katherine gestured for them to step into her embrace. "I love you all. I wouldn't know what to do without you."

"Don't even try," Anna warned, her breath coming out in a squeak. "I'm getting squished here!"

Mary Katherine laughed and stepped back, letting her arms fall to her side.

"So you'll talk to Jacob?"

"Yes."

"When?" Anna wanted to know.

"Soon."

"After church tomorrow would be a good time," Leah said, bringing the tea to the table. She sat and smiled. "Don't you think?"

Mary Katherine bit back a smile as she shook her head and rolled her eyes. She picked up her tea and drank it. "Soon."

～～

Funny thing, Mary Katherine thought. She'd been sitting in church every other Sunday for more than a year now—well, not in a church building but in different homes that held church services—and she'd never really heard God speaking to her until she and Jenny had talked that one recent Sunday.

And today.

Well, it wasn't God, exactly. It was Ike, one of the lay ministers, a bookish young man who worked in an RV assembly plant during the day and helped on his family's farm on the weekends.

Looking over the wire-rimmed glasses he wore, he stroked his beard and talked about a passage in Exodus about honoring parents.

Mary Katherine felt some resistance for just a moment, remembering how she and her father had fought that day when he talked of the same thing. Ike spoke of God's love for His children—and His children's love for their children. Generations of love, he said, but sometimes the generations didn't get along because they didn't speak the same language. Their words and their actions weren't what the other used or expected, and so there was distance and misunderstanding. Even anger.

But when we looked beyond these differences in words and actions, he said, used empathy and understanding and forgiveness, we could know a greater love: God's visible love in all areas of our lives.

Mary Katherine found herself thinking about Ike's words long after he had finished. When she realized people were milling around, getting ready to leave, she looked for her grandmother.

"Have you seen *Mamm* and *Dat*?" Mary Katherine asked her when she found her in the kitchen.

"I spoke with your mother yesterday, and she said your *dat* had wrenched his knee planting. She wasn't sure they'd be here today."

"Oh." She looked around.

"I believe Jacob just walked outside."

"I don't want to—"

"Remember how Jacob was worried Daniel might steal you away?"

"Well, I don't think those were his exact words but—"

"I saw Becky Raber follow him outside."

With a swish of skirts, Leah turned and headed toward the kitchen door.

Mary Katherine considered that for a moment. Becky was a sweet girl but a big flirt. Mary Katherine might think she had time to talk to Jacob, but Becky moved fast . . .

<hr />

Jacob exchanged a greeting with Matthew Bontrager and Chris Matlock as he went to get his buggy.

"How's planting going?" Matthew asked.

"*Gut*. Yours?"

"*Gut*. God had a wonderful plan when he put a brother-in-law on the farm next to me. Chris has been helping me."

"And Matthew's been helping me," Chris responded.

Jacob had known Matthew all his life since they had grown up here together. But Chris had been *Englisch*, like Matthew's wife, Jenny, and studied to join the Amish church when he married Matthew's sister, Hannah.

Amish life was so different from what the *Englisch* thought that Jacob knew some were surprised at how well Jenny and then Chris had acclimated.

"Can I hitch up your buggy for you, Jacob?"

He smiled at Joshua, Matthew's son and Jenny's stepson who'd grown up to be a horse-loving preteen who'd live in a barn if he could.

"*Schur,*" he said. "*Danki.*"

Jacob chatted about the weather—a favorite topic of farmers—until Joshua led his horse and buggy to him.

"Are you going for a picnic, Jacob?" Joshua jerked his head at the picnic basket in the back of the buggy.

Surprised, Jacob stepped forward to look. He'd never seen it before.

"Jacob!"

He spun around. "Mary Katherine! *Guder mariye.*"

The others faded away as he stepped toward her. "It's so *gut* to see you."

"You, too." She stood there, watching him with her hands clasped in front of her.

If he didn't know her so well, he wouldn't have seen how she did that with her hands to still their nervous movements. She was nervous. Not angry. Maybe he had a chance . . .

She looked past him and her eyebrows went up in surprise. "What's my grandmother's picnic basket doing in your buggy?"

"I don't know, Little Red Riding Hood. Did you put it there?"

Laughing, she shook her head. "*Nee.*"

"Well, I think we should put it to good use, don't you?"

Glancing back, she saw her grandmother, Anna, and Naomi standing on the porch, looking expectantly toward them.

"*Ya,* we shouldn't disappoint them."

They hadn't gone a block when Mary Katherine shook her head and waved her hands. "Stop! Stop!"

Jacob pulled over, off the road. "What's the matter? Are you feeling sick?"

She stared out her window. "I'm sorry. I can't do this."

"Do—what?"

"I can't go on some picnic with you and have you say 'I'm sorry' and everything's okay!"

He blinked. "Wow."

"Yeah, wow," she muttered.

She jerked back when he took her hands, and tried to pull them away. But he wouldn't let her.

"I tried to apologize—"

"I trusted you to not hurt me!" She looked down at their joined hands and felt him jerk when a tear dripped down her cheek and plopped on them.

"I was so caught up in my own pain I didn't think what it would do to you," he admitted, rubbing the fragile, sensitive skin on her wrists. "I thought I'd lost you to Daniel."

"I've had enough years of living with a man who never thought of my feelings. I can't do that again. I won't do that again. It's not good for either of us."

"I know. I know." He leaned his forehead against hers. "I'm sorry. I can't explain about jealousy."

"It's misplaced. I've never given you reason to think he meant anything to me."

"Jealousy isn't reasonable. Or logical."

"I know." She laughed self-deprecatingly. "Well, I didn't before today. Then my grandmother pointed out to me that she'd seen you go outside and Becky Raber follow you."

He stared at her with dawning understanding. "You were jealous?"

"Cautious," she said, lifting her chin. "Not willing to let someone else move in—"

"Jealous!" he accused, grinning.

She hesitated, and then she nodded, smiling reluctantly.

His laugh was delighted. "So you can understand about jealousy?"

"Don't you dare try to make this the same as what you did!"

His grin faded. "No, you're right. I'm sorry. I'm sorry," he said again. "I'll say it again and again until you believe me. Until it's enough."

"You've said it enough for this time. But what about next time?"

"Next time? There's not going to be a next time."

"You can't promise you won't hurt me again."

A car horn honked, startling Jacob's horse. He spent the next few moments getting him under control.

He turned to her. "Let's go to that little park down the road."

She nodded.

He took them to a small park that bordered a pond. After a long, cold winter, it was a pleasure to spread out a quilt and sit on it. The sun felt warm on her face. Daffodils danced as a gentle breeze drifted through them.

Mary Katherine smiled as she watched a mother duck lead her little ducklings to the water.

Jacob reached over and ran a fingertip across her lips, his eyes dark with desire. "I've missed that smile. I've missed you."

"Me, too." His touch was sending shivers through her. Her cheeks heated, and she found her breath started coming faster.

His hand moved to cup her cheek and he moved closer, bending to kiss her.

An *Englisch* couple walked past and looked at them curiously.

"We could go someplace where we can be more private."

"Is that a good idea?" she asked, licking her suddenly dry lips.

"No. You're right."

"I don't want to be right." Disappointed, she opened the top lid of the picnic basket, then shut it again.

He sighed heavily. "I just planted my fields."

She crossed her arms over her chest. "Well, I'm sorry, but I don't really care about that right now." She could hear the slight note of petulance in her voice, but she didn't care.

"You hate farming that much?"

"No," she said at last. "I'll love it because I love you." She blushed when she realized what she'd blurted out.

"*Danki.* For saying it first. I didn't think I'd hear those words." He took a deep breath. "I didn't think I deserved them."

Turning back, she studied him. "Why wouldn't you deserve them?"

"I'm not smooth talking like Daniel. Or as wealthy."

"Oh, so now I'm shallow and acquisitive." She glared at him.

"No. According to my sister, Rebecca, I didn't think I had anything to offer you."

"You have yourself, Jacob Miller. What more would I want?"

"And we just planted," he said again, his voice heavy with regret.

"There are those fields again. You're obsessed—"

He leaned forward and kissed her, hard. "There's something you're forgetting."

She touched her fingers to her tingling lips. "I'll never forget that."

"We can't get married until the fall harvest."

"Oh," she said.

He laughed. "Yeah. Oh."

His humor faded. He took her hand, and his clasp was so warm, so reassuring. "I'm sorry I let my feelings about hearing you'd been with Daniel ruin your news about joining the church that day."

"It's okay."

"It's not okay."

"No," she said. "But as long as it doesn't happen again." She looked him in the eye. "I won't be my mother. I won't become a quiet little mouse about things."

"From what I saw today, I don't think that'll happen."

"And I won't let you be like my father."

"That's *never* going to happen," he said firmly.

She took a deep breath. "I'm scared."

"Scared? Of what?"

"You," she said, and watched the expression of shock spread across his handsome face.

<hr />

She was afraid of him?

Jacob felt numb. He loved her. How could she think he'd hurt her? He'd never do that.

Then a horrible thought struck him.

"Mary Katherine, did your father hurt you?"

"Oh, my, not the way you're thinking!" she cried. "You can't think that of him!"

"He never beat you?"

She shook her head violently.

"Or . . . touched you?"

Her face turned white. "No!"

"Then tell me," he said. "Help me understand."

"You don't have to do the things you mentioned to hurt someone," she said slowly. "Sometimes words are enough."

He let out the breath he didn't realize he'd been holding. "I know." He sighed. "I can't promise never to hurt you with words—"

"I know—"

"Let me finish." He took her hands in his and was relieved when she let him touch her. "I'm a man who sometimes opens his mouth without thinking. My sisters and *Mamm* will tell you that. I've been working on that. But I promise that I'll work even harder to think before I talk, and I promise that there'll be so many more words of love that you'll hear."

"Words of love?"

"*Ya.*" He saw he had her attention. "Like, 'I love you,'" he said, moving closer again. "Like, 'Be my beloved *fraa.*'" He bent his head until their lips were a breath apart. "Like, 'I hope we have many *kinner* and live to dangle many grandchildren on our knees.' And like, 'A hundred years with you won't be enough.'" Tears welled up in her eyes and ran down her cheeks. He pulled a snowy handkerchief from his pocket and wiped them away.

"And you thought some other man could speak better words than you?" she whispered. "Be my love, Jacob. Be my *mann*, and I won't fear any words from you."

She leaned forward to kiss him, and he met her lips with passion. Her head spun with dreams of this with him for years to come.

And then a thought intruded, and laughter bubbled up inside her, like a fountain of joy.

"What's so funny?" he demanded as she drew back from him.

She pressed her fingers against her mouth and her eyes danced. "I've watched too many movies with Jamie. I was thinking that you'll only hurt me if I ask you to make love to me one night and you say, 'Not tonight, dear.'"

Laughing, he shook his head and gathered her closer. "I promise you, those words are never going to leave my lips."

Jacob's Macaroni and Cheese

Preheat oven to 350 degrees

¼ cup butter or margarine (reserve 1 tablespoon)
¼ cup flour
1 cup milk
8 ounces (½ pound) Velveeta cut in small cubes
2 cups cooked elbow macaroni (or any shape macaroni)
½ cup shredded cheddar cheese (any kind—sharp, mild, etc.)
Optional: 6 buttery crackers (Ritz), crushed

Melt 3 tablespoons butter in a pan on low heat, add flour, stir, cook for about two minutes. Add milk, stir, bring to a boil without burning. Gradually add the Velveeta, stir until melted. Add macaroni. Pour into baking dish that has been sprayed with cooking spray or greased with some butter or margarine. Sprinkle with the cheddar. Mix remaining tablespoon butter or margarine with crumbled crackers, then sprinkle over the casserole.

Set timer for 20 minutes (this is very important). Bake casserole until heated through and top cracker crust is browned.

Amish Coffee Cake

Preheat oven to 400 degrees

¼ pound butter, softened
1 cup sugar
2 large eggs
2 cups flour
¼ teaspoon salt
1 teaspoon baking powder
1 teaspoon baking soda
1 cup sour cream
1 teaspoon vanilla or almond extract

Topping
½ cup light brown sugar
1 teaspoon cinnamon

Cream butter, sugar, and eggs. Add salt, baking powder, and soda together, then add sour cream and vanilla. Pour into baking pan. Mix topping ingredients, and sprinkle over the batter. Bake for 30 minutes or until done.

Amish Zucchini Bread

Preheat oven to 350 degrees

3 cups flour
1 cup sugar
4 ½ teaspoons baking powder
1 teaspoon salt
4 ounces chopped nuts (walnuts or pecans)
4 ounces raisins
3 eggs
2/3 cup oil
2 cups shredded zucchini

Mix ingredients (don't over-mix) and pour into 2 loaf pans. Bake for 1 hour or until done. Cool for at least 15 minutes before taking out of pans, and then cool completely on wire racks.

Glossary

ab im koff—crazy
ach—Oh
aenti—aunt
allrecht—all right
boppli—baby
bruder—brother
daed—dad
Danki—thank you
dat—father
dawdi haus—grandparent apartment at back of home
Der Hochmut kummt vor dem Fall.—Pride goeth before the
fall.
Dumbkoff—dummy, stupid person
Englischer—what the Amish call us
fraa—wife
grossmudder—grandmother
Guder mariye—Good morning
gut—good
Gut-n-owed—Good evening
haus—house
hochmut—pride

kaffe—coffee

kapp—prayer covering or cap worn by girls and women

kich—kitchen

kind, kinner—child, children

kumm—come

liebschen—dearest or dear one

maedel—young woman

mamm—mother

mann—husband

nee—no

onkel—uncle

Ordnung—The rules of the Amish, both written and unwritten. Certain behavior has been expected within the Amish community for many, many years. These rules vary from community to community, but the most common are to not have electricity in the home, to not own or drive an automobile, and to dress a certain way.

Pennsylvania Deitsch—Pennsylvania German

rotrieb—red beet

rumschpringe—time period when teenagers are allowed to experience the *Englisch* world while deciding if they should join the church. The time period ranges in different communities but usually starts around sixteen and ends in the mid-twenties.

schul—school

schur—sure

schweschder—sister

scholars—students

sohn—son

verdraue—trust

Wie geht's—How goes it? How is it going?

Wilkumm—welcome

wunderbaar—wonderful

ya—yes

Discussion Questions

Please don't read before completing the book, as the questions contain spoilers!

1. Mary Katherine is restless. Have you ever had a time when you were restless? Were you aware of the reason for your restlessness, or did you only find out later why you felt that way?

2. Jacob seems the opposite of Mary Katherine. But there's something missing in his life. What is it?

3. The Amish believe in traditional roles for men and women. Is that true for your family?

4. Do you craft or have a hobby? What is it? Why were you drawn to it? What do you get from it emotionally? What craft would you most like to learn to do?

5. Mary Katherine is an only child, but her cousins are like sisters to her. Do you have siblings? Is there anyone in your extended family you're closer to than a sibling?

6. Have you ever worked with family as Mary Katherine does? What was the experience like?

7. Mary Katherine thinks her restlessness means she might be happier in the *Englisch* world. Did you ever have a time when you thought "the grass is greener on the other side"?

8. What part of Amish life appeals to you most? Could you bring that to your everyday life?

9. Jacob has a challenging time learning to cook. What was the biggest challenge you had learning to cook?

10. Mary Katherine's decision to join the church feels long and arduous to her. Who do you think influences her the most and why?

11. Do you think God listens to you? When did you feel He didn't? What did you do?

12. Have you committed to a particular religion or church? Why or why not?

Stitches in Time is a very special shop run by three cousins and their grandmother. Each young woman is devoted to her Amish faith and lifestyle, each talented in a traditional Amish craft and in new ways of doing business—and yet each is unsure of her path in life and love. It will take a loving, insightful grandmother to gently guide them to see that they can weave together their traditions and their desire to create, and forge loving marriages and families of their own.

And now for a sneak peek into the first chapter of *Journey of the Heart*, Book 2 of **Stitches in Time**, Naomi's story.

1

She should be the happiest young woman in Paradise.

But Naomi dreaded being asked about her upcoming wedding. She feared she'd scream if one more person asked her about it.

Marriage in her Amish community was more traditional than an *Englisch* marriage, to be sure. But she'd never thought she'd have to change so much to please the man she was to marry soon.

Sighing, she set her quilting aside, got up, and walked over to look out the front window. Business had been brisk that morning at Stitches in Time, the shop she worked at with her grandmother and two cousins.

Stitches in time . . . and place: she and her two cousins were working together as they had played and studied together all their lives. Their wise grandmother, Leah, had bought this place and they'd all fixed it up and now they created items for sale. Mary Katherine was a master weaver, Anna knitted, Naomi quilted, and their grandmother created little Amish dolls and other crafts. They were two generations of Amish women who were bound by strong threads to each other as well as to their creativity and their community.

Here in this shop crowded with colorful quilts and hand-knitted items, with fabrics galore and every single thing you could ever need to quilt or knit or sew . . . well, she should feel she was in heaven working on a quilt and helping customers of this very successful shop with family members who loved her.

Instead, she felt more and more false, covering up how she felt, wearing a mask each day.

"Looking for someone?" her grandmother asked, smiling as she looked up from tallying the day's receipts. "Is John coming to pick you up after work?"

Everyone thought it was a sign of his attachment, his devotion to her, that he came for her nearly every day after work. In fact, it was a way of keeping track of her, of making certain that she didn't make other plans.

She'd become so cynical. It was enough to make her sigh, but she noticed her grandmother was still watching her.

"*Ya*," she said, pasting a smile on her face.

She walked back to sit and begin stitching on her quilt. Its bright, cheerful pattern should have propped up her sagging mood with its pattern of watermelon slices and little black ants marching across it. Anna had already asked to use it when it was finished for the summer window display, along with some props to make it look like it would be perfect for a picnic.

Off she'd gone to plan what she'd knit for the display, then she badgered Mary Katherine and her grandmother for what they'd make.

Naomi glanced over at Mary Katherine when she heard quiet humming. "What are you making?"

"Some fabric for big floor pillows," she said, looking up. "You don't think this looks too . . . rough or nubby, do you?"

"I think it looks really sturdy for a kid's room. The pillows'll fly out of the shop."

Nodding, Mary Katherine went back to weaving and humming, weaving and humming.

That was what a woman who was happily married and soon to celebrate her first anniversary looked like, Naomi thought. Happy, content. Dreamy. She and Jacob were a good match. They'd been friends since they were scholars in the same school, and when he'd thought he'd lose her to Daniel, a charming Amish Mennonite man from exotic-sounding Florida, well, Jacob had woken up and shown her he was the *mann* for her.

And soon, Naomi would be marrying John. Two cousins married in two years.

Anna was still looking for the right man and enjoying flirting with several young men. The three of them—Naomi, Mary Katherine, and Anna—were cousins who looked much alike with their oval faces and brown hair. Well, Mary Katherine was taller and her hair was more auburn, but they looked more like sisters than cousins.

But their personalities were so different, Naomi mused. She'd often wished she were as outgoing and assertive as Anna or as creative as Mary Katherine, who'd even been invited to speak about her skill of weaving at the local college of arts and design.

A shadow fell over her as her grandmother carried some bolts of fabric to the storage room. She heard her talking with Anna, and then her cousin emerged, following Leah as she walked back to the cash register. Leah handed her a slip of paper and then opened the cash register and withdrew some money. Anna slipped out the shop door.

Then Leah went to stand at the shop window, and she stood there for so long, staring out with an unreadable expression, that Naomi got up and walked over to her.

"Is anything wrong?"

"No, I just sent Anna to get pizza for lunch. My treat."

"And you're watching to make sure she gets there?" Naomi asked, smiling indulgently.

"No," Leah said, shaking her head and laughing. "Although Anna *has* been known to dilly-dally."

Turning, Leah sighed. "I'm just feeling a little restless, maybe a little moody, that's all. I have to confess, I'm not usually pessimistic, but I'm not looking forward to another winter here in Lancaster."

"That's a ways off, *Grossmudder*."

"I know. Just ignore me. Like I said, I'm a little restless and moody. This probably started it." She held up a postcard of a scene in Florida. "Daniel's mother's trying to get me to come down there to Pinecraft for a visit."

"Well, maybe you should this time. It'd do you some good. All you do is work here and at home."

For the first time she noticed that her grandmother—just in her late fifties—looked tired. Older.

Anna bustled in, carrying a pizza box that smelled of pepperoni. "Come on, everybody, let's eat it before it gets cold."

"Or before you eat it all," Mary Katherine teased as she got up from her loom. "I'm starved. I'm so hungry all the time lately." She stopped as she realized the three women were staring at her. "What?"

"All the time?" Leah asked, a hopeful note in her voice.

"I've been working a lot lately. It's not easy juggling a job here and being a farm wife, you know. Sometimes I forget to eat."

Anna shoved the pizza box at Naomi, who fumbled to catch it and winced as one of her wrists complained.

Walking over to Mary Katherine, Anna counted on the fingers of one hand. "You could be . . ." she trailed off meaningfully.

"Could be what?"

Anna patted her cheek. "Think about it," she said. "You're a bright girl."

Mary Katherine followed her into the back room. "Oh, honestly, you all want me to have a *boppli* so badly that you started making comments a month after I was married."

"It can happen that fast," Naomi told her.

"Yes, and we know it can happen even before marriage, no matter what community people live in."

Mary Katherine goggled at Anna's words. "You're not suggesting Jacob and I . . . anticipated our vows, are you?"

"No, dear, although some of those looks the two of you exchanged when you thought no one was looking were quite sizzling." Anna waved her hand as if she were overheated. "I wondered if flames would erupt."

She took the pizza from Naomi and sailed toward the kitchen.

"Well, she's certainly not moping around, feeling moody, is she?" Naomi remarked.

"She never is, especially this particular month," Leah noted, jerking her head toward the calendar. "I don't want to see her depressed, but there's such a thing as covering up your feelings and that can be harmful. I feel like she goes around with a cheerful mask on."

Frowning, she walked toward the back room, and Naomi followed and helped get out plates and soft drinks.

She and Anna knew all about cheerful masks, Naomi thought as she nibbled on her own piece of pizza and found it tasteless.

"Is something wrong with it?" Mary Katherine asked.

"I'm just not very hungry today." She pushed the box closer to her cousin, who took a third piece.

They chatted about the weather—it was the time of year between the too-brief Pennsylvania spring and the always-long summer that drew customers. They'd be returning after they enjoyed a big Amish lunch.

Mercifully, her wedding plans weren't a topic of conversation today. She managed to force down a few bites of pizza, then covered what was left on her plate with her crumpled paper napkin. She rose and walked to the sink to wash her plate and place it in the drying rack.

"Done already?" Leah asked.

"I'm full," she lied. "I'm going to get back to the quilt. I promised it to a customer by next week."

She sat by herself and sewed the wedding ring quilt, trying not to think of how one day she and other women would gather around the big quilting frame and stitch hers.

Someone knocked on the window and she jumped. She looked up and saw John staring at her through the glass. But instead of gesturing for her to open the door they'd locked so they could eat lunch, he waved casually and walked on.

"Who was that?" Leah asked as she walked over to sit in a chair next to Naomi.

"John."

Surprised, Leah stared at her. "He didn't want to come in?"

Naomi shook her head. "He was just making sure I was here."

"Where else would you be this time of day?" Leah pulled her chair up to the quilting frame and threaded a needle.

"He likes to make sure I'm where I said I'd be." Her voice sounded flat.

Leah's hands, which had been busily threading her needle, stilled. Her eyes searched Naomi's face. "There's something wrong, isn't there? It's not my imagination."

Naomi started to say it was nothing, but her grandmother placed her hand over hers.

"Tell me," she said quietly. "Tell me."

That's all it took. The floodgates opened.

"John's turned into—into someone I don't know," she said, reaching into her pocket for a tissue. "He tells me what to do and where to be and checks on me all the time. Like just now."

She dabbed at her cheeks. "I want to be obedient and learn to be a good *fraa*," she said. "But he—he scared me the other night."

"How?" Leah asked, her voice almost a whisper. "How did he scare you?"

Naomi couldn't look her in the eye.

"Tell me, how did he scare you?"

"I went to walk away from him, and he grabbed my wrist and hurt me."

Leah reached over and unerringly chose the very wrist John had grabbed. Naomi winced. Her grandmother didn't release it, but pushed the sleeve of Naomi's dress back, exposing the bruise.

"I thought you were favoring it," she said, frowning. She looked up at Naomi.

"It only hurts a little," she said, wiping at her cheeks again with her tissue.

"It only hurts a little there, but a lot in your heart." Leah's eyes were damp and filled with sympathy.

"He said he was sorry."

Leah pulled down the sleeve. "And how many other times has he said he's sorry?"

Sobs rose up in her chest. "Too—too many," she admitted.

There was a knock on the door. Naomi jumped.

"You go wash your face," Leah said. "Then let's go in the back room and talk."

"We don't have time. We have to work."

Leah stood. "We'll make time."

True to her word, after Leah opened the door and took care of the customer, she got Anna and Mary Katherine to run the shop while she and Naomi talked.

"You have to break it off with him."

"Maybe counseling—"

"Counseling is a good idea. For you."

"Me? I'm not the problem."

"But how you respond to John's treatment worries me. I want you to think about it." She hesitated, then forged ahead. "I know that some people who act like John can be helped, but I wouldn't count on it. And it's a terrible way to start out in a marriage. I don't want to be harsh or seem unforgiving. But it's too big a risk to take."

Naomi nodded. "I know."

"Next time it could be a bigger injury."

"I know! Don't you think I know?" she burst out. "That's why I kept it to myself."

"Which is what he counted on—so he could exert more control." Leah sighed. "And it's so important to make a good match. There's no divorce. You'd be with him until one of you dies."

Naomi shuddered and got up to take some aspirin for the headache that was pounding behind her eyes. She turned to her grandmother. "I don't think I love him anymore."

"Yes, you do," Leah disagreed gently. "Otherwise you would have spoken up by now."

The door opened, and Anna poked her head inside. "Everything okay? We heard Naomi raise her voice." She glanced at her cousin and saw the tears. "What's wrong?"

Naomi started to say it was nothing but then realized that was how all of it had started. "I'm having problems with John."

She watched one emotion after another chase across Anna's face. "I thought something was wrong, but I could never get you to talk."

"I didn't want to burden anyone."

"You thought I wouldn't understand, didn't you?" Anna asked her. "Happy, carefree Anna hasn't got the depth to understand, right?"

Shocked, Naomi stared at her. "No, I didn't think that at all. But you've had enough sadness."

"You have no idea what I've experienced," Anna said. "Maybe I haven't wanted to face it myself."

With that, she spun on her heel and went out, shutting the door firmly behind her.

"I need to go after her."

Naomi stood, but Leah put her hand on her arm, stopping her.

"Let me. I think I know what's wrong. And I've let her get away with it for too long."

Leah hurried after her, and Naomi followed, watching helplessly as her grandmother opened the front door of the shop, stepped out, and slipped and fell.

Want to learn more about author
Barbara Cameron and check out other great
fiction from Abingdon Press?

Sign up for our fiction newsletter at
www.AbingdonPress.com
to read interviews with your favorite authors, find tips
for starting a reading group, and stay posted on what
new titles are on the horizon. It's a place to connect
with other fiction readers or post a
comment about this book.

Be sure to visit Barbara Cameron online!

www.BarbaraCameron.com
www.AmishHearts.com
www.AmishLiving.com

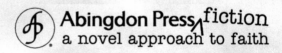
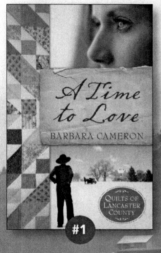
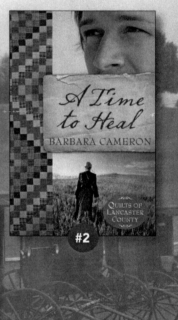